H 50
RB

Praise for Roy Johansen's

THE ANSWER MAN

"A tale of power and manipulation, of avarice and violence, with an array of interesting characters trying to stay alive. A thriller all lovers of the genre can sink their teeth into." —*Booklist*

"This is a gripping debut thriller, brimming with dangerous seduction and unrelenting suspense."
—*Buffalo News*

"Johansen's portrait of a man facing temptation and his darker side rings true."
—*Tulsa World*

"Johansen ... comes up with aces. He plots like a string of firecrackers ... not a moment's rest."
—*Kirkus Reviews*

"Races cleanly through a maze of techno clues and multiple suspects, pulling readers along for a quirky ride with likable companions."
—*Publishers Weekly*

BEYOND BELIEF

ALSO BY ROY JOHANSEN

The Answer Man

Beyond Belief

DEADLY VISIONS

ROY JOHANSEN

BANTAM BOOKS

DEADLY VISIONS
A Bantam Book / July 2003

Published by
Bantam Dell
A Division of Random House, Inc.
New York, New York

ISBN 0-553-58426-X

Manufactured in the United States of America
Published simultaneously in Canada

OPM   10   9   8   7   6   5   4   3   2   1

For Dad,

who is everything a father should be.

1

Joe Bailey handed the bald man a crumpled fifty-dollar bill. "This will change my life, right?"

The man smiled and pocketed the fifty. "Only you can do that, my friend. But I can help show the way."

Joe nodded. He and Steve Muren stood in a packed coffeehouse in the Sandy Springs neighborhood of Atlanta. It was a few minutes past nine on a Thursday night, and the place reeked of incense, cigarettes, and burnt coffee. Most of the clientele were under twenty-five, Joe noticed. He was thirty-nine, but he liked to think that he didn't look too out of place among the college students and young artsy types who made it such a popular gathering place.

"Why here?" Joe asked.

Muren shrugged. "Manager's a friend of mine. Are you ready?"

"Sure."

Muren led Joe down a dark hallway past the pay phone and bathrooms until they reached a purple door. Muren pushed it open, and Joe walked inside to see five people sitting around a large round table.

"How is everyone tonight?" Muren said.

Everyone mumbled their "good"s and "fine"s while Joe sat down.

Muren jammed his hands into his pockets and paced around the room. His dark, penetrating eyes flicked to each person at the table. "I see that about half of you are return visitors. Good. I like that. It shows commitment and passion. If you don't have those two things, you're wasting your time here."

Joe glanced at his tablemates. Three men and two women. Muren had their complete attention.

"Each of us is born with a gift. My gift is helping others discover the power within themselves. It takes concentration and practice, but before you leave here tonight, you'll be amazed with what you're capable of. And, in the weeks to come, I'll help you refine and develop your gift."

Muren tossed a book of matches to a skinny woman with close-cropped hair. "Think you're ready?"

She bit her lip. "I'm . . . not sure."

"Not certain enough. Tell me yes. Even better, tell me *hell* yes!"

"*Hell* yes."

"Good." He sat down in the one remaining seat. "Tear out one of the matches and put it in the palm of your hand."

She did as she was instructed, then stared blankly at Muren.

"Don't look at me, look at the match. The key is to visualize your tool. Those who have been here before know what I'm talking about. Everyone has a different mental tool that works for him. One person might imagine a lever prying it from the palm of your hand. Another might visualize a powerful vacuum cleaner sucking it upward. Very often, only one thing will work for each person."

The woman wrinkled her nose. "Why?"

"I have absolutely no idea, but it works. Go ahead and try it."

She stared at the match, but nothing happened.

"Don't get discouraged," he said. "It may take a while to discover the right tool, but when you do, a new world will open up for you."

Again, she stared at her palm. The match wiggled. The woman gasped and held her hand out toward Muren.

"I see it," he whispered. "Work with it some more. Whatever you just did, do it again."

Joe watched her intently as she drew her hand closer. She concentrated on the match, and the end slowly rose into the air until it reached a forty-five-degree angle. The woman squealed nervously, "I'm doing it. Look, I'm doing it!"

"Maintain your focus," Muren said. "Remember what you're doing now, it'll help you next time."

Her hands shook, but the match end still levitated. The woman frowned as it began to droop. "What's wrong?"

"Nothing's wrong," Muren replied. "Just get your focus back."

The match finally came to rest on her palm. The woman gave Muren a disappointed pout.

"Don't worry. Your power is like a muscle that

needs to be exercised. "We'll work on it a little more each week. Before too long, you'll be able to do this and more even without me around." Muren tore out another match and tossed it on the table in front of Joe. "Would you like to try?"

Joe nodded. "Sure. Can I leave it on the table?"

"Whatever you want. There are no rules here. If there's anything I want you all to take away from this, it's that you create your own reality."

Joe glanced at the match and it immediately jumped.

The others laughed in surprise and Muren clasped his hands together. "Excellent! You're a natural."

Joe smiled sheepishly. The match scooted a few inches, then stopped. He picked it up, examined it from every angle, and placed it into his left palm. The end of the match bobbed up and down. He placed his right hand over and around it, but that had no effect on its movement.

"You are exceptionally gifted," Muren said. "It would be my honor to help you nurture your talents."

Joe reached into his jacket pocket. "Uh-huh. For fifty bucks a pop?"

"We can work out an arrangement."

Joe yanked his hand from his pocket and flung hundreds of BBs across the tabletop. The others reacted in surprise as the round metal pellets shot in every direction, rolling toward the ends of the table.

"What the hell—?" Muren yelled.

Joe stood and surveyed the table. In front of each person except Muren, the BBs were clustered in tight circles.

"What was *that* for?" The spike-haired young woman brushed BBs off her clothing.

"My apologies," Joe said. He held up his police badge and pointed at Muren. "Atlanta PD. Move away from the table."

"Aw, man . . ."

"Now."

Muren stood up. "I wasn't hurting anybody."

Joe turned toward the others. "I need your help. Please pull your chairs away and turn the table over for me."

Muren sighed. "Look, I'll give everybody their money back. Is that what you want?"

"Be quiet." Joe watched as the others turned the table upside down to reveal a crude network of wires connecting five round metal plates with an array of lantern batteries and a single control dial.

"What the hell is that?" one of the other men asked.

Joe put away his badge. "It's how he was able to cheat you out of your money. Muren used that dial to apply current to those metal plates and they became magnetically charged."

"Magnets?" another young woman said. "The matches were made from cardboard and, in case you didn't notice, they were moving *away* from the table."

Joe picked up the book of matches and opened it. "You can buy these matchbooks in packs of a dozen from all the mail-order magic retailers. They're cardboard, all right, but the heads are coated with a magnetic compound. Do you know what happens when you try to push two magnets together? They repel each other." Joe held up the open matchbook and tore out a match. "These are made for street magicians. They strap magnets to their arms, under their jacket sleeves, then hold a match in their open hand and pass it over the magnet." Joe turned the power knob and held his upturned palm over one of the metal plates. As his hand neared the plate, the match head rose. He glanced up. "You've been had."

A woman with a tongue stud turned toward Muren and lisped, "You goddamn bastard, I've given you over four hundred dollars."

Muren feigned a look of total innocence. "Are you really going to listen to this cop? He doesn't believe in the psychic powers within you, but I do. After I get this cleared up, we can start over. Have faith in yourselves, everyone, just visualize—" He suddenly grabbed a chair and threw it at Joe.

The chair back struck Joe's knees, and spasms of pain shot through his lower body.

Shit. Muren hadn't seemed like a runner.

By the time Joe steadied himself against the wall, Muren was out the door.

Set aside the pain. Get this bastard.

Joe leapt over the overturned chair and ran through the doorway into the coffeehouse. Muren was pushing through the crowd, elbowing his way to the exit. Joe held up his badge. "Police! Move! Move! Move!"

His command barely made a ripple in the crowded coffeehouse. Jesus. Still holding up the badge, Joe shoved through the crowd. "Muren, you're under arrest!" Police Procedures 101. Can't bust a guy for resisting arrest unless he knows for sure that he's being arrested.

Muren pulled over a tall table, knocking it into Joe's path. Hot lattes spilled onto the laps of nearby customers as he barreled out the door. Joe jumped over the table and came within inches of grabbing him by his nylon jacket.

Outside, Muren ran smack into a woman with short red hair. She gripped him by the back of his neck and shoved him facedown on the sidewalk.

Muren groaned and tried to wriggle free, but the woman was too strong.

Joe pocketed his badge as he pushed past a group of bystanders. Jesus, all he needed was for some well-meaning vigilante to beat the hell out of his suspect. "That's not necessary, ma'am. Step away, please."

The woman turned and glanced up, flashing him a crooked smile. "Hiya, Joe. Is that any way to talk to a Good Samaritan?"

Joe smiled as he recognized Detective Carla Fisk, his helper, who was one of the most popular officers on the force. She was one of the most homely—and most beautiful—women he knew. Despite her plain physical appearance, her warmth and sense of humor captivated almost everyone who crossed her path. He'd heard that she had rejected half a dozen marriage proposals in the past few years.

Carla stood up and planted her foot on the back of Muren's neck. "Something tells me this guy wasn't just skipping out on his check. Of course, the coffee *is* waaaaay overpriced here."

Joe cuffed the man's hands behind his back. "What

brings you here, Carla? This doesn't seem like your kind of place."

"And what do you think *is* my kind of place?" she drawled. "Shirtless guys beating the hell out of each other while NASCAR races play on the TV and Travis Tritt songs play in the background?"

Joe shook his head. "Nah. Guys drinking shots out of your navel while the B-52's play in the background."

"You got me pegged, Spirit Basher."

The man on the ground moaned. "Spirit Basher? Aw, shit. Of all the people in this city."

Carla's face lit up. "Hey, you're famous, Bailey. This guy knows you."

Joe shrugged. The Spirit Basher nickname had been given to him by a local newspaper a few years before, after he'd busted several phony spiritualists in midtown. The paranormal fraud cases were only part of his duties in the Atlanta PD bunco squad, but they always attracted the most attention. Everyone was looking for a little magic in their lives.

Carla glanced around. "Where's your backup?"

"There's a patrol car behind this place. They thought he might go for the back door." Joe pulled a small radio from his pocket. "Miller, I got the perp on the front sidewalk, you copy?"

Officer Miller's nasal voice blasted from the radio, "Copy that, Bailey. I'm coming around."

Joe read the man his rights and put him in the back of the patrol car. He and Carla watched it disappear around the corner. "Good collar," Carla said. "Unleash the psychic power within, huh?"

Joe gave her a curious look. "How did you know?"

"Kurtz told me down at the station. I didn't just happen to be here. I was waiting for you."

"Why?"

"I'm on the Spotlight Killings. Have you been keeping tabs on that?"

"Yeah, who hasn't?" Six well-known citizens had been murdered in the past two months—an athlete, an attorney, a college president, a newspaper columnist, a PR firm owner, a former deputy mayor, and the only apparent link between the victims was their local prominence, hence the name Spotlight Killings. The department was taking major heat for its inability to find even a single suspect. "Having fun?"

"Oh, yeah. It's been a hoot. Between the media, the chief, and everyone else in town, I'm about to go out of my mind."

"I can imagine."

"A city councilman, Edward Talman, has been leaning on the chief to accept some outside help in the investigation."

"The FBI?"

"I wish. No, he thinks we should allow a psychic to join the investigation."

"You're kidding."

Carla shook her head. "Nope. Of course, these psychic detectives have been coming out of the woodwork, like they do on all the high-profile cases."

"I'm sure."

"Except this time one of them happens to be Monica Gaines."

Joe lifted his eyebrows in surprise. Monica Gaines was among the world's best-known psychics, due to her frequent talk show appearances, 1–900 psychic chat line commercials, and best-selling books. In the space of four years, she had built an amateur website into a multimillion-dollar media corporation. Gaines's syndicated talk show, *Monica Gaines's Psychic World,* was a ratings phenomenon, and her distinctive rectangular glasses and clipped speech patterns made her a frequent target for *Saturday Night Live* send-ups.

Carla sighed. "This councilman has been jumping up and down, yelling that we should take help anywhere we can get it, especially from the great Monica Gaines. I don't need to tell you that these people are usually a humongous waste of time. I worked on the Virginia-Highland killings a few years ago, and psychics came from all over. I had to chase down dozens of leads that went absolutely nowhere."

"That's the usual outcome," Joe said.

"Well, that didn't stop the chief from knuckling under. Gaines flew into town today, and me and my partner have been assigned to take her around and hold her hand."

Joe didn't need psychic powers to see where this was heading. "Just the two of you?"

Carla grinned. "The captain wants you to tag along. You know, to keep an eye on her and make sure she doesn't pull any funny business. After all, you're the Spirit Basher. You know all the tricks."

"FYI, Carla, I'm not too crazy about that nickname."

"Yeah, but when this kind of thing comes up, you're the guy. You used to be a magician, right? There's nobody more qualified than you to spot the phonies."

"But these psychic detectives don't deal in sleight-of-hand tricks. They conjure up feelings and impressions. There's not much I can expose there."

"We're taking her out to the most recent crime scene in Conyers tonight. You can catch a ride with me."

"Tonight?"

"Two-thirty in the morning, actually."

"*What?*"

"She feels it's best to be there at the approximate time of death. In the case of Ernest Franklin, that's two-thirty. If you'll check your voice mail, you'll find a message from the captain. I'm afraid that it's more than a request."

Joe looked away. This was getting worse by the minute. "Listen, I have to go down to the station and write up the arrest I just made."

"Perfect. After you finish that, I can go over the case files with you before we drive out to Conyers."

"You're too good to me."

Joe stared out the passenger-side window of Carla's Chevy Nova as they drove into the town of Conyers, twenty-five miles southeast of Atlanta. God, he didn't want to be there. He had an eleven-year-old kid at home, for Christ's sake. It was tough enough for her to have a cop as a father, but the unpredictable hours made it even harder.

He'd called Nikki and explained that he wouldn't be home before she went to sleep. Fine, she said. No problem. She was having fun with her baby-sitter for the evening, Sam Tyson. Sam was the eighty-one-year-old owner of his own downtown magic shop, and he enjoyed trying out his new illusions on Nikki during his frequent visits. Sam had been a mentor to Joe and half the professional magicians in the city.

It didn't seem so long ago that Joe had aspired to be one of that tiny handful of magic superstars, but he soon came to realize that the style of magic he admired—the smart, edgy illusions of Houdini, Keller, and Thurston—had given way to slick, packaged Vegas-style productions with cheesy music and garish lighting effects. His father had been on the force for forty years, and many of Joe's childhood friends were second- and third-generation cops, so the transition had seemed to be a logical one. Who would have guessed that he'd become known as a paranormal investigator, hoping against hope that he'd someday encounter phenomena that he *couldn't* explain? It hadn't happened yet.

Well, maybe once.

"We're almost there," Carla said, peering though the windshield at a dense patch of fog. "Any last questions?"

"I don't think so. You covered it well." Carla had gone over the files for each of the spotlight murders, showing Joe the crime scene photos and discussing the statements they'd taken. Unlike most serial killings, there was no strong pattern to the murder methods, and there was little similarity among the victims besides their social stature and high visibility. Milton Vinnis, the criminal attorney, had been strangled with the chain from his mountain bike; Thomas Coyle, whose PR firm represented many of the largest corporations in the Southeast, was tied to the rear bumper of his Rolls-Royce and dragged two miles down a gravel road; Derek Hall, the president of Anderson College, had been electrocuted when he touched the booby-trapped door of his garage; journalist Connie Stevenson, author of the widely read "Hotlanta" newspaper column, was drowned in her kitchen sink; former deputy mayor John Danforth had fallen—or been pushed—from the top floor of his four-story office building; and the most recent victim, Atlanta Hawks basketball star Ernest Franklin, had his throat torn out half a mile from his home in Conyers.

The investigators may not have made a connection between the killings had it not been for two bizarre common elements—the voices and the skin markings. Strange voices, described as "threatening," "unreal," and "ghostly" to friends and family members were heard by each of the victims in the last days of their lives. None of the individuals had previously exhibited psychotic or delusional behavior, but they'd been at a loss to explain the voices that no one else heard. Equally perplexing to the investigators was a symbol they found on the chest of each victim—a hazy, ill-defined circle with two intersecting bars. The symbol appeared with varying degrees of intensity, but it spanned roughly two inches in each instance. While the voices were common knowledge in the news media, the symbols were, for the moment, a secret.

Carla turned onto a dark, narrow road and pulled to a stop behind a parked car. She smiled. "When you woke up this morning, did you ever imagine your day would end up here?"

Joe climbed out of the car. "I'm still having trouble imagining it."

The October night was damp and sticky, and a nearby swamp belched foul-smelling gases. A man and a woman climbed out of the other car and walked toward them. Joe recognized them immediately, Monica Gaines and Detective Mark Howe. Gaines was more attractive in person, Joe thought. Her pronounced cheekbones and curly brown hair were striking, and she walked with confidence and determination.

Howe grinned at Joe. "You look tired, Bailey."

"Thanks to you. Together again, huh?"

"You know it."

Eight months earlier he and Howe had partnered on a bizarre homicide case in which a local parapsychology professor appeared to have been killed by the telekinetic dreams of an eight-year-old test subject. It was the only time that Joe's psychic debunking specialty had been applied to a murder case, and he and Howe had formed an uneasy though successful alliance.

Howe nodded. "Welcome to my nightmare, Bailey."

"So I'm a nightmare," Monica asked dryly.

Howe turned toward her. "I didn't mean—"

"Sure you did." She extended her hand to Joe. "I'm Monica Gaines."

"Detective Joe Bailey."

Monica studied Joe. "I sense disbelief. Skepticism. Doubt. Very strong."

"Did your psychic abilities tell you that?"

"They didn't have to. It's all over your face and body language. You're pissed, Joe. You think I'm here for a chapter in my next book. You think I'll come here, throw out some lame generalities, and take all the credit when you guys eventually catch the sick son of a bitch who did this."

"You got all that from my body language?"

Howe chuckled. "Either that or she's picking up *my* thought waves loud and clear."

"The faces change, but the attitudes never will, guys." She clicked her tongue. "Let's get on with this so you can get home to your wives and girlfriends and tell them how you wasted your night tagging along with a fruitcake."

Joe motioned toward the large sketch pad she held under her right arm. "Are you going to play some psychic Pictionary tonight?"

"You never know."

Monica's haunting, expressionist sketches were one of her trademarks. Often, as she quizzed guests about lost loved ones or incidents from their past, she scribbled furiously on a large pad and easel. Almost invariably, the guests found something in her drawings that connected with their situations.

"So tell me, why is it so important that we be here at the time of death?" Joe asked.

"If I'm to sense the victim's thoughts and impressions, it's best that I attempt it as close to the actual place and time of his death as possible." She glanced around the eerie surroundings. "I'm already feeling some strong, powerful emotions. There was great fear here."

"Can you see the killer's face?" Carla asked.

"Perhaps. Take me to the exact place where the victim died."

Carla motioned toward a cluster of mimosa trees. "This way."

They silently walked toward the crime scene. Joe tried to reconcile the dark, shadowy setting with the lush, beautifully sunlit area in the police photos he had examined. Ernest Franklin's body had been found here, less than half a mile from his sprawling estate, with his throat split open. It almost appeared as if an animal had attacked him, but there were no footprints, no hair, and no physical evidence to support any such conclusion.

"Horrible . . . just horrible," Monica whispered.

"What?" Howe asked.

"He knew he was going to die. He knew it, and he was helpless to do anything to stop it."

"Stop who?" Carla asked.

"I can't tell yet. I don't think he knew the person. He was confused; he didn't know why this was happening to him. He sometimes went by the name Bobo, am I right?"

Joe glanced at Howe and Carla. They each responded with a vague shrug. Joe pulled out his notepad and jotted down the name.

"His last moments were filled with fear . . . and regret."

"Regret?" Joe asked.

"Unfinished business. He knew his life was over."

"Okay, we're going to need a little more than this," Howe said. "Can you tell us something, *anything*, that gives us a hint as to who the killer was?"

Monica smiled sardonically. "Something other than lame generalities?" She uncapped a Sharpie pen and drew on her pad. "It's bizarre. . . . I'm having a tough time sensing another physical presence here."

"We seriously doubt he tore out his own throat," Carla murmered.

"No, I'm not saying that. I just feel—" She stiffened. Her eyes sprung open.

Joe cocked an eyebrow. "Get something?"

Monica dropped to her knees and took several sharp breaths. She glanced upward, her eyes glittering in the moonlight. "Two attackers."

"Two?" Howe repeated.

"Yes. I'm sure of it."

"Describe them," Carla said.

"I—I can't."

"Why not?" Howe asked.

She didn't reply as she drew furiously, although Joe couldn't see how she could sketch anything in the dim light.

"You drawing us a picture of 'em?" Howe asked.

"It won't be much use to you," she said, still squinting at her pad. "There are no faces."

"What's that supposed to mean?" Carla asked.

Monica glanced away. "You're going to think I'm crazy, but I believe his attackers were . . ." Her voice trailed off as she suddenly tensed.

"What?" Carla said.

"We have to get out of here."

Joe studied Monica's face. Her forehead was pinched, and her lips were trembling. "What's wrong?" he asked.

"No!" Monica ran back toward the car.

They sprinted after her. "Ms. Gaines?" Joe said.

"Oh, God," she cried out. "Please, God, *no*." She slipped on the wet grass and fell to the ground.

Joe crouched next to her. "Are you okay?"

She wiped her perspiring face with the sleeve of her jacket. "The killers weren't . . . human. At least, one of them wasn't."

"Then, what were they?"

Monica glanced back toward the murder scene. "You're going to think I'm out of my mind."

"Try us," Carla said.

"They . . . were spirits."

The three detectives stared at her in silence.

"I know. Sounds weird as hell to me too." She tried to smile. "If you want to have me fitted for a strait-jacket, a size six should do the job."

"Spirits," Joe repeated.

She nodded. "Ghosts, maybe, although I'm not sure they ever really lived. Their souls are many thousands of years old."

Howe chuckled. "Okay. And in what language do we read them their Miranda rights?"

"Lay off, Howe." Joe could see the woman was absolutely terrified. Her hands shook, her breathing was ragged, and tears ran down her face.

"I can't tell you any more," she whispered. "Can we leave now?"

"That's it?" Howe said. "You drag us out here in the dead of night and tell us that a pair of *ghosts* did this? Is this some kind of sick joke?"

"No joke." She nervously glanced around the site. "Can we please leave?"

Joe took her hands and gently pulled her to her

feet. "How many other times have you sensed anything like this?"

"Never. Check my record. I wasn't even sure that I believed in ghosts."

"But you do now."

"Yes," she whispered. "Oh God, yes. I do."

Joe picked up the sketch pad. There, in Monica's distinctive style, was a drawing of a man being attacked by wispy, cloaked figures floating over him.

"Shit," Howe whispered.

"Is there anything else you can tell us?" Carla asked. "Anything that might help us to—"

"A circle with two intersecting lines," she said.

Joe tensed.

Monica caught their shocked looks. "It was on him someplace, wasn't it?"

"Can you tell us what it means?" Carla asked.

"I don't know. It may have been a signature . . . or a warning."

"A warning about what?" Joe said.

"I can't be sure." She looked down at her sketch pad. "But I have a feeling we're about to find out."

After dropping Monica off at her hotel, Joe, Carla, and Howe stood on the sidewalk along Courtland Street to compare notes. For a long while they didn't say anything. Joe watched a homeless man gathering cans nearby, trying to stay ahead of the approaching street-sweeper.

"Ghosts," Howe finally said with disgust. "If we didn't already look like asses for listening to a psychic, we sure will now."

"She had the symbol pegged though," Carla said. She turned to Joe. "Any idea how she did that?"

Joe shrugged. "The same way most psychics do it. There are dozens of people in our department and the coroner's office who knew about that symbol on his chest. She or an advance person could have posed as a reporter and bribed someone for the information. She may have even approached an employee at the funeral home."

Howe grimaced. "Really?"

"It's been known to happen. If you wave a hundred-dollar bill in an embalmer's face, chances are good that he'll talk to you."

"Good to know," Howe said. "When I go, I'll make sure my kids just put me out with the garbage."

Carla chuckled. "So what's next?"

"Now she wants to visit the other crime scenes." Howe sighed. "She thinks it might help give her a stronger impression as to what happened. Are you up for it, Spirit Basher?"

"Only if you promise to stop calling me that."

The soft rays of dawn began to appear as Joe parked in front of the three-story apartment building that had once been the Robert E. Lee Elementary School. Joe had attended fourth and fifth grades there, but the reconfigured corridors and converted lofts bore little resemblance to the place where he had once been so mesmerized by Ms. Eversole's fluorescent eye shadows and terrified by Mrs. Lydecker's cruel taunts. He'd moved there with his wife, Angela, during his days as a professional magician, and the large, high-ceilinged loft had allowed him the space to construct and rehearse his stage illusions. Now, almost eight years after he'd abandoned his performing career, he couldn't imagine living anywhere else. He hadn't particularly enjoyed his elementary-school days, but he did love the life that he and Angela had made for themselves there.

Angela. It had been almost three years since she'd died of ovarian cancer. Three years since she had let out that long last breath that he could still hear sometimes in the dark dreams that crept into his head every week or so. Throughout the twenty-two months of doctors, hospitals, and lab tests, he'd tried to prepare himself and his eight-year-old daughter, Nikki, for that moment, but it was impossible. Hell, he *still* didn't know how to deal with it. It had been too easy to worry about his daughter and not dwell on the fact that he had just lost the love of his life. But now, with Nikki growing older and maturing into an intelligent, well-adjusted adolescent, it was harder than ever to escape the feelings of loss.

He unlocked the door to his apartment and walked into the spacious living area. The streetlights cast a pale glow over the wood floor, broken by crisscrossing grids of shadows from the wire-reinforced windows.

Sam Tyson sat upright on the sofa, sound asleep, as an infomercial for teeth-whitening strips flickered on the television in front of him.

"Hi, Daddy," Nikki whispered. She stood in the doorway on the other side of the room, wearing her glasses and the oversized Stars on Ice T-shirt that she slept in.

"What are you doing up?"

"I heard you come in. I wanted to make sure you weren't some thief who was going to hurt Sam."

"Yeah, good thing he came over for you to baby-sit him, huh?"

Nikki picked up a cotton throw blanket and gently pulled it over Sam. "That's okay. He told me stories about what a good magician you were."

"Again? Sorry about that."

"He thinks you should quit being a cop and go back to doing that."

"Is that what you think too?"

"Nah. Mommy told me that you were hardly ever home back then."

He smiled. "That's right. And I gotta tell you, these days a magician is even lower than a mime on the show-business food chain."

Nikki made a face. "*Nothing's* lower than a mime on the show-business food chain."

"You may have a point."

"So what's Monica Gaines like?"

Joe glanced at Sam, but he was still sound asleep. "She's interesting. A little more intense than she is on the 1-900 commercials."

"Does she know who did it?"

Joe thought about telling Nikki about Monica's reading of the crime scene. Probably not a good idea. "I'm afraid she doesn't. I think she's going to check out some of the other ones though."

"Good."

"Why is that good?"

Nikki sat on a chair arm. "After you told me you

were going to meet her, I checked out her website. She's helped solve over a hundred cases."

"Don't believe everything you read, okay? The way these people work, they throw out dozens of impressions in every investigation, and if one or two of them happen to hit, they claim that as a success."

"But she has quotes from police detectives."

"Often even the officers involved in the cases tend to forget about all the false clues and focus just on the hits. Almost anytime that anyone has recorded the psychics and logged all of their impressions and compared those with things that turn out to be really worthwhile, they end up looking a lot less miraculous."

"Did you record Monica Gaines tonight?"

Joe smiled and pulled a micro cassette recorder from his jacket pocket. "You bet."

Monica Gaines knelt before the hotel minibar, trying to decide whether or not to grab a second bottle of rum.

What the hell.

She twisted off the cap and poured it into her half-empty can of diet Coke. If only she could maintain her buzz for the rest of time she was there. She'd flown in the previous afternoon, and she already wished she were back home, asleep in her own bed or curled up on her sofa and reading prep notes for the next batch of shows.

After hundreds of investigations, it was easy to size up the cops she encountered. That night, Carla was the only faintly open-minded one. Howe was too busy playing the part of a smart-ass, and Joe Bailey would probably never believe in her. She'd heard of the Spirit Basher, but Bailey was younger and more personable than she'd imagined. She was relieved he hadn't displayed the cynical, nasty streak that most die-hard skeptics had. Despite his obvious disbelief in her abilities, he seemed to be a reasonable man.

A knock at the door.

Before Monica could answer it, she heard a sharp click, and the door swung open.

A pale, plump man in his mid-forties stepped into the room. Derek Haddenfield. "Hello, Monica."

"I knew I shouldn't have given you a key."

Haddenfield chuckled. "Did you have a productive evening?"

"I don't know yet."

"When *will* you know?"

"When I can tell them who the killer is. You know how this works."

Haddenfield nodded. "My team gets into town early tomorrow. I thought it would be a good idea for you and me to get together and coordinate."

She took a sip of her drink. "Couldn't this have waited until later?"

He smiled. "I know you can never sleep after going out for a reading." He glanced at the two empty rum bottles. "At least not until you drink enough to pass out."

She turned away. "That's none of your business."

"Sure it is. Everything you do is my business. We're partners."

"I'm starting to have regrets."

"It's too late for that, Monica." Haddenfield sat on the edge of the bed. "Get some rest. You've just begun the most important seventy-two hours of your life."

2

Joe stared at Captain Sheila Henderson. "You're kidding, right?"

"Afraid not, Bailey. We want you to stick with Monica Gaines for a while." Henderson, a forty-seven-year-old woman whose hair was pulled back so tight that it threatened to tear off her face, sat on the corner of her battered maple desk. She had only recently been promoted, which ignited another round of innuendo that plagued all fast-tracking female cops; i.e., they slept their way to the top or were lesbians who benefited from a mysterious "gay network." As far as Joe could tell, however, Henderson had risen through the ranks only because she was a damn good cop.

He'd been summoned to Henderson's office only minutes after arriving at headquarters. Although he'd tried to catch a few hours' sleep, he was still groggy.

"Look, I was useless out there. Gaines said the murders were committed by evil spirits. They're just words. There's no way I can debunk that."

"I know. But if she does decide to put something over on our guys, I need you there to explain it. What do you have going on now?"

"Well, I'm gathering evidence on the Northlake insurance fraud ring. This afternoon they're going to be in the parking lot of an abandoned shopping center, practicing choreography for auto accident setups. I'm planning to camp out in one of the storefronts and videotape them."

"Put Garrison or Saunders on it. We need you on this."

Joe gave her a puzzled look. "With all due respect, why not just send Monica Gaines on her way and tell her you'll be on the lookout for any homicidal spirits?"

"I'd like nothing better, but I can't do that. We initially refused her offer to help, just as we refuse the assistance of all psychics. But she began talking about the cases on her television show, and suddenly everyone is wondering why we don't take all the help we can get. Then Councilman Talman started breathing down the chief's neck."

"Since when does the chief of police answer to a city councilman?"

"Since he found out that Talman has been quietly gathering support for a run at the mayor's office next year."

Joe grimaced. "That explains a lot."

"I don't have to tell you that most people have at least some belief in the paranormal. Even if they're on the fence, they believe we should try anything we can to catch this killer. I know it's probably a waste of your time, but if this Gaines woman puts any crap over on us, we could come out of this looking worse than we probably already do. Even if she doesn't go in for the sleight-of-hand stuff, you're up on the methods these people use, aren't you?"

"To give the appearance that they have psychic powers? Sure."

"Then I need you in there to keep an eye on her. Work with Carla Fisk and Mark Howe on this. Misery loves company, right?"

"If you say so."

Henderson reached for a faxed document on her desk and handed it to Joe. "Councilman Talman is hosting a reception for Gaines on his dinner-cruise boat this afternoon. He's invited the officers involved in the case to attend. Be there."

Derek Haddenfield closed his eyes and felt the late-morning sun on his face. Nice to be outdoors, away from the buzzing, flickering fluorescent lights where he'd spent the previous several months. If only there wasn't so much work to do.

He motioned toward the Foster Window Treatments van parked on the dirt road. The rear doors flew open and his three team members jumped out, carrying cameras, surveying equipment, and trifield meters. They weren't the experts he would have chosen for this kind of fieldwork, but there wasn't time to send for anyone else. Dammit.

They were at the scene of Ernest Franklin's murder, where, less than nine hours before, Monica Gaines had gathered her first psychic impressions related to the spotlight murders. Haddenfield wished he had gotten there earlier, but he'd needed time to brief the team.

"The checklist is in the van," he said. "Make sure we get everything."

They moved quickly and efficiently, measuring the area and using a compass and surveyor's scope to pinpoint the precise geographic coordinates where Franklin's body had been found.

Haddenfield turned to Gary, a bearded young man holding a custom-built 3-D digital video camera with two large lenses. "Okay, circle the perimeter with that thing and keep tightening the circles as you go around. When you finish, I want you to end up at the target zone, got it?"

Gary smiled, his beard almost covering his bottom row of teeth. "Got it."

"And, Gary, tell me the 3-D glasses that work with that thing won't make me cross-eyed."

"No can do, boss."

"Terrific."

Haddenfield glanced around to make sure no one else was watching. All clear. The last thing he needed was for the police to come nosing around, asking what the hell they were doing there. He had phony press credentials in the van, and although he was sure he could convince the cops they were a camera crew working for a tabloid TV news show, it could make things difficult for him to carry out the job he had to do in the days ahead.

Nothing must stand in the way of that.

*   *   *

Joe rode with Howe and Carla to the Lake Lanier dock where the *Carlotta* was moored. Easily the largest craft on the lake, the *Carlotta* was a popular destination for tourists and well-heeled locals. Joe had once taken Nikki there for a birthday lunch, but he had no idea that Edward Talman owned it until Henderson had told him that morning.

"The boat must come in handy for fund-raising dinners, huh?" Howe said as they neared the *Carlotta*. "If I owned that thing, *I* could be city councilman."

"Now, that's a scary thought," Carla said.

They pulled alongside the boarding ramp, where an army of valet parking attendants was waiting to whisk the guests' cars away. Howe surrendered his vehicle, and he, Joe, and Carla stepped onto the boat. It was a 120-foot craft with two main decks, each filled with tables covered with white tablecloths, flowers, expensive china, and gleaming crystal. The lower deck was enclosed, dark, and luxurious, with a rich cherry wood covering the walls and ceiling. The upper deck, which Joe preferred, was light, open, and spacious.

The place was packed. In the first ten seconds after he boarded, Joe spotted a United States senator, a CNN anchorwoman, and the manager of the Braves baseball team.

"What the hell are we doing here?" Carla muttered, shifting uncomfortably.

As if in response, a strong voice called out, "Detectives, glad you could make it!"

Joe, Howe, and Carla turned to see Edward Talman walking toward them. Talman was shorter than Joe imagined, about five foot five, but otherwise just as he appeared on television, with close-cropped gray hair, trademark western string tie, and eyes that always appeared to be squinting. Joe figured he must be in his mid-fifties.

Talman shook hands with each of them. "I can tell a cop from a mile away."

Joe smiled. "What gave us away? The ill-fitting blazers, the bad haircuts, or the sour disposition?"

"Don't sell yourselves short," Talman said. "It was your sense of authority. Plus, our guest of honor just pointed you out." Talman motioned toward Monica, who walked toward them.

"Hello, Detectives," she said. "Get a good night's sleep?"

Howe rolled his eyes. "Ha. Good one."

Talman stared at Joe. "I was surprised to see your name on the guest list this morning. You're not a homicide detective. Why would you be investigating the Spotlight Killings?"

"I'm not."

"Then, why—?"

Monica put her hand on Talman's. "He's investigating *me*."

"You?"

She smiled. "The Spirit Basher is on the case to keep me honest."

Talman turned back to Joe. "We have a crisis in this city, Detective, and Ms. Gaines has been kind enough to try to help us. I don't know what you're trying to prove, but in the absence of any real progress by your department on this case—"

Joe cut in. "Did she tell you about her reading of Ernest Franklin's murder scene?"

Talman glanced at Monica. "Yes. It was inconclusive, correct?"

Monica didn't respond. She just stared at Joe.

"Inconclusive?" Joe's gaze didn't leave hers. "I guess you could say that."

Talman's eyes narrowed as they moved between Monica and Joe. "Is there something I should know?"

Joe stared at Monica a moment longer before finally replying, "It's an ongoing murder investigation, Councilman. I'm afraid I can't discuss the details."

Talman was obviously miffed to be out of the loop, but he managed a faint smile. "Remember that she's our guest in the city. Please show her the respect she deserves." He took Monica by the arm. "If you'll come with me, I have some people you should meet."

Howe leaned close to Joe as Talman escorted her away. "Ten'll get you twenty she's telling him to pressure the chief to have you taken off the case."

"I don't think so," Joe said. "She thinks she can handle me."

"Can she?"

"No."

While Carla and Howe went to the bar to place their drink orders, Joe climbed to the upper deck and watched the tall pines along the lakeside swaying in the wind. The air rushed through the millions of pine needles, sounding like distant waves crashing.

"It's beautiful."

He looked over his shoulder to see Monica strolling toward him. He smiled. "Yes, it is."

"Thank you," she said.

"For what?"

"Not telling Talman about my reading last night."

"You don't stand behind it?"

"I do, but I'm not entirely sure what it means. And until I am sure, I'd rather not discuss it. I know how ridiculous it sounds."

"I don't think you do."

"Sure I do. If I was going to make something up, don't you think I'd come up with something a lot less crazy-sounding than that? This is my reputation on the line."

"It's the Atlanta PD's reputation too."

"I know that. I just have a lot I need to sort through. That's why I want to visit the other murder scenes."

"You will, and we'll be right there with you."

"Good." She leaned against the railing. "Hey, would you consider appearing on my show sometime?"

He smiled. "You want me on *Monica Gaines's Psychic World*?"

"Sure. We could fly you up to Vancouver, or we could do a satellite uplink with you in one of the studios here in town."

Joe shook his head. "I don't think so."

"Too bad."

"I thought you had only believers on your show."

"Oh, I have all kinds of guests. You'd be great. You're not like most skeptics I've met."

"Is that good or bad?"

"Very good. A lot of people are hostile when they meet me. Vicious. They don't even try to understand what I'm doing."

"After last night, I'm not sure *I* understand."

"That makes two of us. But at least you were trying. So many people are afraid to admit even the possibility of psychic abilities, but I don't think you're one of them."

Joe gazed at the choppy water. "I used to be. I didn't want to believe that any of this stuff was possible, because I was afraid it would color my objectivity. I've seen a lot of so-called paranormal investigators spend months deluding themselves into believing they've found the genuine article, when it takes me only ten minutes to pull apart the whole thing. It's not because these people are stupid, but their will to believe is so strong that they don't want to see the truth. I didn't want to fall into the same trap."

"You feel different now?"

"A little."

"What changed your mind?"

Joe studied Monica. Was she following the pattern of most con artists, mentally compiling a profile of the mark to formulate her strategy? Possibly. He finally replied, "I met someone who showed me some things I couldn't explain. I discovered that I actually liked the feeling."

"You're speaking in the past tense. You eventually found an explanation?"

"No, not yet. I guess it's still a work in progress." He shrugged. "I think I'm a better detective now. I'm a little more open, and I think that I give people more of a chance to try to prove themselves. The only difference now is that I get disappointed every time I do my job well. I think there's something in all of us that makes us want to believe in magic. That's why you're a millionaire."

Monica moved closer. "Do you think I'm going to disappoint you, Joe?"

He looked away. Her offbeat charm was as effective in person as it was over the airwaves. He actually liked her. "Yes, I think you will disappoint me."

"I won't. I promise."

After lunch, Talman summoned everyone to the upper deck for self-serving speeches and toasts to the guest of honor. Predictably, there was an outcry from the guests for Monica to give them an impromptu demonstration of her abilities.

Talman waved them off. "Please, Ms. Gaines is our guest here today. Let's not ask her—"

"It's all right." Monica smiled and stepped forward. "I've met a lot of you today, but there are many I haven't met. I'm trying to reach out to those of you I haven't had the chance to speak with. I just ask that you try to be open with me, okay?"

Standing at the back of the crowd, Joe, Howe, and Carla watched as Monica closed her eyes. Howe leaned toward Joe. "If I feel her rummaging around in *my* head, I'm jumping overboard."

"There's someone here who had a birthday not long ago," Monica said. "A lot of attention was paid to it, more than usual. I'm getting the initials L.K. Does that mean anything to anyone?"

There was an "Oh my God" in the crowd, then a slender woman with dark wavy hair raised her hand. "Me! Me!"

Monica gestured for the woman to step forward. "What's your name, honey?"

"Laurie Klempner. I turned forty last week."

The crowd was obviously impressed by the revelation as Joe pushed his way forward. Time for him to get to work too. He bumped into an older man, quietly apologized, and kept moving.

Monica stared at the woman. "Laurie, we've never met, have we?"

"No."

"Okay, I can feel that you have a good sense of humor and that you're a very loving person. I'm not sure if you're in a relationship right now, but I can tell you that you have a lot of love for animals, one in particular. Am I right?"

The woman nodded.

"A small dog, maybe a Scottish terrier?"

The woman gasped. "Yes!"

"You work in a large building, very large. You're sometimes frustrated that people there don't communicate with each other as well as they should."

The woman nodded. "Yes. And just so you know, you're freaking me out."

The guests applauded as Joe stepped to the front of the crowd. Talman caught Joe's eye and smiled triumphantly. "There's no way you can explain that away, Detective."

Joe shrugged.

Talman's eyes narrowed. "You think you can?"

"Maybe."

"Be my guest."

Joe turned toward the crowd. "I'm getting the initials T.R. A man born in mid-June, I believe. A man who loves his three grandchildren very much."

An elderly man raised his hand and stepped forward. "That would be me. My name's Tracy Ray."

"Nice to see you, sir. Three grandchildren, is that right?"

He nodded. "And another one on the way."

"Congratulations. How's the Stingray driving?"

The man stared at Joe, stunned.

"It's a yellow Corvette Stingray, right?"

"Yes, but I didn't drive it today."

"Of course not, mostly weekends. Did you restore it yourself?"

"Yes."

"I can tell that you put a lot of yourself into it."

Talman walked toward Joe. "What the hell are you doing?"

"Exactly what you asked me to do."

Joe could see that Talman wanted to rip him apart, but the guests would obviously keep him on his best behavior.

"Apparently you know this man," Talman said.

"No, we've never met. Have we, sir?"

"Nope."

Joe glanced back at Monica. If anything, she seemed amused by the demonstration. She sipped her champagne.

"Then, how did you do it?" Talman asked.

Joe held up a brown billfold. "Simple. I lifted his wallet."

The man frantically patted his pockets while the guests laughed.

Joe handed the billfold back to him. "I had only a few seconds to look it over, but I saw his driver's license, which gave me his name and birth date. There was also a picture of him and a lady I assumed to be his wife with three young children, and two pictures of him posing proudly next to a yellow 1964 Corvette Stingray."

A vein was standing out on Talman's forehead. "You think Monica Gaines stole this woman's wallet?"

"Of course not, but I think it's entirely possible that she saw it." Joe turned toward the slender woman. "Ma'am, was your wallet on your table at any time since you boarded, or maybe during lunch?"

She looked away. "Uh, maybe. I'm not sure."

"All it would take is a few seconds," Joe said. "If she happened to come by your table, moved your wallet so that it fell open to show your driver's license and business card, she could have gotten most of the information she needed. Your name, the fact that you just turned forty, and that you work in a large building. If your business card has a high floor number, that would tell her."

"What about the other things?" Talman asked. "How she felt about the communication within her company?"

"How many people who work in a large company don't sometimes feel that there's a communications problem? For psychics, that's a standard reading whenever it's determined that the subject works in a big corporation."

The woman shook her head. "But what about my dog? There's nothing in my purse that would tell her that."

"Not in your purse. Step forward, please."

She moved toward Joe and he turned her around to face the crowd. He kneeled next to her and pointed toward several short dark hairs on her brown slacks. "Look. And none of the hairs are higher than your shins. It's a small dog with short dark hairs. A Scottish terrier is the most popular dog fitting that description, so she may have guessed." Joe stood up. "I'm not saying this is how she did it. I can't prove that. But I do think it's important for people to know that there are possible explanations other than psychic ability."

The guests were silent. Talman still looked mad as hell. Carla and Carla stood at the rear of the crowd, lips pursed, and shifting uncomfortably. The only one who didn't look uncomfortable was Monica. She raised her champagne glass to Joe and downed the rest of her drink.

Glen Murphy adjusted his headphones and listened to the percussion track again. It was almost four in the morning, and he'd been at the mixing console since noon the day before. He was already four months late in delivering his new R&B album, *Night Riot,* to the label, and they were pressuring him to finish it by the end of the week. Whenever he thought it was done, there was another background vocal to be tweaked or guitar riff to be rerecorded.

He'd practically been living at the Peachtree Summit Studios, the facility where he'd produced all of his albums for the past nine years. His most recent work, *Street Meat,* had won him Grammy nominations in the R&B vocal and producing categories, and he knew that a lot of people were waiting to judge his follow-up.

Not until it was ready, dammit.

He yanked off the headphones and tossed them onto the console. The percussion track still didn't sound right, and he didn't know how to fix it. Shit.

Murphy stood and shuffled out of the sound booth. Things would be clearer after a few hours' sleep. Maybe. He hadn't slept well lately, with those whispering voices he thought he heard every night. Probably from all the speed he'd been popping.

He looked at the glass-paneled vending machine in the lobby, but all the good stuff was gone. He'd cleaned it out of Kit Kat bars, Hostess cupcakes, and Lay's Sour Cream & Onion potato chips.

"Glen Murphy . . ."

The voice again. It was coming from directly in front of him.

"Glen Murphy . . ."

He went still.

The voice again. The same whispering voice he'd been hearing for days. He backed away from the vending machine. "Who is it? Where are you?"

"Come with us. . . ."

He glanced around, but he was alone in the studio lobby.

"Come with us, Glen Murphy. . . ." The voice now came from behind him.

Gotta get the hell out of here.

Murphy ran for the door. Locked. He fumbled for his keys.

"Glen Murphy . . . join us now."

He found the key, shoved it into the lock, and turned. He pushed the door open and ran into the studio's rear parking lot. The voices stopped.

Thank God. He ran through the narrow parking lot toward his Jaguar, parked alongside the rear of the studio. He scratched his chest. He'd developed a bizarre-looking rash there, and it was itching like crazy.

Keep going, man. Don't let the voices catch up.

Another sound. A low metallic roar at the parking lot entrance, at the top of a long slope that rose to the street.

Definitely time to lay off the pills.

Another clanging sound, then a soft rumble from the top of the slope. He glanced up. In the shadows of the parking lot, it appeared that a large wall had suddenly been erected at the entranceway.

It began to move toward him.

Jesus. The wall, or whatever the hell it was, almost spanned the width of the narrow lot. It moved faster, its groans and sharp, high-pitched squeaks echoing off the building.

Murphy leapt for the car door, fumbling for the key-chain remote. Where in hell was that unlock button? He pressed them all. The trunk popped open and the panic alarm sounded. The siren blared in his ears as he finally pulled open the door.

The roar behind him grew louder.

Shit.

Blinding light suddenly lit up the entire back of the building. He jumped for the driver's seat. This couldn't be happening. There's no way that he—

Murphy never finished his thought. The cold steel ground into his torso and abdomen as the car door slammed through him.

3

P retty, huh?" Howe stood in the rear parking lot of Peachtree Summit Studios, revealing Glen Murphy's twisted, bloody body with the same casualness as if he were showing off a new lawn mower.

Joe grimaced at the sight. Murphy's eyes were open, staring upward. Joe wanted to close the corpse's eyes, but he knew better. It was seldom as easy as the palm-down glide-over in the movies. He'd once watched a rookie beat cop spend five horrible minutes trying to close a corpse's uncooperative left eye.

"Where's the symbol?" Joe asked.

Howe pointed to the victim's chest. "There's blood on it, but it's right here. A hazy circle with two intersecting lines. There's another fainter symbol intersecting it, which we saw on a couple of the other victims."

Joe squinted at the mark on Murphy's dark skin. He looked back at Howe. "Okay, so what the hell happened here?"

Howe pointed to a massive yellow forklift angled away from Murphy's pulverized Jaguar. "This forklift belongs at a construction site a couple doors over. Near as we can figure it, someone waited for him to come out, then steered it down."

"Physical evidence?"

"Doesn't look promising. The forklift's been dusted for prints, and there are no footprints to be seen on the street. Whoever's doing this is good at covering his ass."

Captain Henderson strode out of the studio's rear exit. "Bailey, what are you doing here?"

"I was told that Monica Gaines would be here."

Howe motioned toward the street. "She's with Carla in the alley. She wants to come down here as soon as possible."

Henderson nodded. "Only after the scene's broken down. And try to keep the journalists away while she's here, got it?"

Howe nodded. "Sure."

Henderson turned toward Joe. "I heard about your performance on Talman's boat yesterday."

"I thought you might have."

"Your job is not to make Monica Gaines look like a fool, Bailey. You're here to watch her investigate these murders and point out any possibly deceptive behaviors as they relate to this investigation. Anything else she does is her business, not yours. Got it?"

"Sure."

"This is not a time for the Atlanta PD to be pissing people off." She glanced down at Murphy's body. "Jesus. Throw a blanket over him, will you?"

Howe nodded. "Yes, ma'am."

Henderson stepped back into the studio.

Joe made his way up the sloping parking lot to the street. He spotted Carla and Monica standing on the sidewalk, sipping coffee from Dunkin' Donuts cups.

"Glad you could make it," Carla called out to him.

Joe approached them. "And why didn't you see this coming, Ms. Gaines?"

"Please call me Monica. I generally can't see the future, but I did have terrible dreams last night. I dreamed that the beasts who killed Franklin knew that I sensed them, and it made them angry."

Carla half smiled. "Angry enough to kill again?"

"It was probably just a dream." Monica turned toward Joe. "Or do you have an explanation for that too?"

"I meant no offense to you yesterday."

"Is that an apology?"

"No. Are you expecting one?"

"Of course not."

Carla pointed to the parking lot entrance, where a uniformed officer took down the yellow crime scene tape. "Looks like they're breaking down the scene. Ready?"

Joe and Monica followed Carla to the lot and walked down to Murphy's body, which was now covered by a white plastic tarp. Monica tightly crossed her arms in front of her. She had the attention of everyone on the scene, including Howe, four uniformed cops, and the medical examiner.

"Ms. Gaines?" Howe said.

"Please, not now," she said. "I need a moment." She stood still, staring down at the pavement.

Everyone was silent as Monica took a few long,

deep breaths. She closed her eyes. "Nothing . . . nothing but the stars," she whispered.

"What?" Joe asked.

"Nothing but the stars."

Carla moved closer to her. "What does that mean?"

She didn't answer. She was motionless, head thrown back, facing the gray sky. "It mattered to him," she finally said. "It mattered to this man."

"What mattered?" Howe asked.

"Nothing but the stars." She looked at them and shook her head. "Whatever it means."

"Okay," Howe said. "What about his death? Can you tell us anything?"

She stared at the plastic tarp. "Uncover him, please."

Carla put her hand on Monica's arm. "I'm not sure you want to do that."

"It would help me to see him," Monica said. "Please."

Howe bent over and yanked the tarp from Murphy's body. If Howe expected a startled reaction from Monica, he was probably disappointed, Joe thought. She stared at the bloody corpse with clinical detachment.

"Did he hear the voices?" Monica asked.

Howe shook his head. "Don't know yet."

She placed her hands a few inches over Murphy's face. "There was fear. Intense fear." She slowly drew back. "He *was* hearing the voices, but he couldn't understand them."

Captain Henderson reemerged from the studio and watched her. "Did he know his killer?" she asked.

"I don't believe so, no. I get the sense that he

wasn't sure what was happening to him. Almost as if—" She took a sharp breath. "Oh God."

"What?" Henderson asked.

She shuddered. "It's the same feeling as the other night."

"How?" Joe asked.

"I don't think his killers were"—her voice dropped to a whisper—"flesh and blood."

"So we're talking about evil spirits again?" Joe asked.

"Again, I'm not sure. Maybe just one spirit. But I do know this is no ordinary murder."

"Anything else?" Carla asked.

"Yes." The color suddenly drained from her face. "Whoever—or whatever—it is, they can sense me reaching out for them."

"Like in your dream?" Carla asked.

She nodded. "They know I'm trying to find them. I wish I could be more specific, but I can't understand what I'm sensing. It's clear as day in front of me, but I just don't know what it is. Kind of like trying to read a foreign language." Her teeth sank into her lower lip. "I've never . . . experienced anything like this before."

Howe threw the tarp back over Murphy's corpse. "Ms. Gaines, we're looking for a solid, living, three-dimensional murderer. We appreciate your efforts here, but you're not giving us anything to work with."

"I know that. When we get back to the car, I'll see if sketching helps. And maybe it'll be more clear after we visit the other murder scenes."

"We'd planned to take you to see them today," Carla said.

"Good." She shuddered. "The sooner I finish, the better. I don't mind telling you, this is scaring the hell out of me."

Derek Haddenfield focused the electronic binoculars and peered through the van's tinted side window. He and the team had found a hilly section of Red Run Avenue that gave them a distant view of the recording studio's rear parking lot. His sound expert, Paul Doyle, aimed a high-sensitivity parabolic microphone toward Monica Gaines and the cops.

"What are you getting, Paul?"

Paul adjusted his headphones. "Right now, a whole lot of nothing."

"Don't lose her. We need this."

"Then we should be closer. We're four football-field lengths away in the middle of a city in the morning rush hour."

Haddenfield shot him an icy look. "Make it work."

"Remember who you're talking to here. It'll work. But you have to tell me what the hell 'nothing but the stars' means."

"Your job is data collection. Others will handle the analysis."

"Others including you, right?"

"Never mind that. Just make sure you get everything you can."

Haddenfield glanced toward the front of the van, where Gary juggled his still camera with the 3-D digital video camera. Donna sat in the driver's seat, drumming her blue nails on the wheel to the rhythm of a song only she could hear.

Donna's heavily made-up eyes flicked to Hadden-field in the rearview mirror. "You want atmospheric readings?"

"No," he said. "We'll get them later, when it's safe to move closer."

"Gotcha."

"Looks like they're on the move," Gary said, squinting through his long zoom lens. "Are we following Gaines or staying on the site?"

"We're staying here for a bit," Haddenfield said.

"Good," Paul said. "You can entertain us by letting us know what the hell we're doing."

"You know the drill. Strictly need-to-know."

Donna stared at Haddenfield in the rearview mirror. "Does Monica Gaines know about us?"

"Let's just say she's a participant in this project."

Paul shook his head. "Why would we hide our project from the police?"

"You knew that was a condition of this project. In case you've forgotten, you're being very well paid."

Gary leaned back. "*Very* well paid. Don't rock the boat, Paul. I kind of like the cloak-and-dagger stuff."

"I just wish we had a little more information," Paul said.

Haddenfield turned away. "Just know that this is a very sensitive project."

"Sensitive *how*?"

Haddenfield picked up a pair of binoculars and inspected the studio parking lot. "There are people out there who wouldn't hesitate to kill all of us for the answers to your questions. Shall we get going?"

*   *   *

Joe, Howe, and Carla escorted Monica to the five remaining murder scenes, and each time her impressions matched those at the first two locations. She made sketches at each site, and they all featured the same wispy, cloaked spirits. The readings were vague yet disturbing, and Monica still insisted that dark supernatural entities were responsible for the killings.

They broke for an early dinner at Houston's, across from the Lenox Square shopping center.

"I'm sorry I wasn't more help," Monica said after they'd placed their orders. "I've been places where I came up with absolutely nothing, but I've never had an experience like this."

"Neither have we, I assure you," Howe said.

Carla shrugged. "Well, it made things interesting. Good material for your TV show, huh?"

"I'll discuss it, of course." Monica pulled her sweater tightly around her, even though it was warm in the restaurant. "Something's out there that senses me every bit as powerfully as I sense it. I'm not sure if it feels threatened by me, or just . . ." Her voice trailed off.

"What?" Joe asked.

"Amused."

"You think you're being laughed at?"

"I don't know. I suppose that would be better than having it angry at me."

"Listen, I'm curious," Carla said. "You've been working with us for a couple of days now. Did you pick up impressions on any of us?"

"Of course."

"Anything you'd care to share?"

"Other than the fact that you're in a romantic relationship that you're trying to keep secret?"

Carla swallowed hard. "What—what do you mean?"

"You have strong feelings for someone, don't you? But you and this person aren't ready to share it with the world."

Carla's face reddened.

Howe roared with laughter. "It's true, isn't it? Come on, Carla. Tell us about him. If it *is* a him."

"Shut up, Howe."

Howe was enjoying himself. "Is there something you want to tell us about yourself, Carla? Come on, 'fess up."

"No." Carla clasped her hands in front of her. "I don't want to discuss it."

Monica smiled. "Don't worry. Your secret's safe with me." She turned to Howe. "Congratulations, by the way."

"For what?"

"Didn't you recently get engaged?"

Howe coughed for a good ten seconds before taking a drink of water. "No."

She frowned. "Hmmm. I guess we'll have to chalk that one up as a miss."

"Not exactly." Howe turned to Joe and Carla. "I'm planning to propose to Regina this weekend. I haven't told anybody." He faced Monica. "You're freakin' me out, lady."

She smiled. "That's what I do best."

Howe motioned toward Joe. "What about the Spirit Basher here? What kind of vibes do you get from him?"

"Well, I know that his daughter is angry with him."

Joe put on a poker face, trying not to give her the nonverbal cues that encouraged phony psychics to pursue a particular line of guesswork. "What makes you think that?"

"She wanted to go somewhere with her friends, and you wouldn't let her. A concert, I think."

"Go on."

"She thinks that if her mother were still alive, she would have let her go."

Carla nudged him. "Come on, Bailey, is she right or not?"

"I'll tell you when she's finished." He glanced at Monica. "Anything else?"

"Only that a disaster has been averted for you in the last couple of weeks. You could have had a serious traffic accident, but you changed your course somehow. Did you get a new car, or change something about the vehicle you drive?"

Joe stared at her, expressionless.

She smiled. "Fine, don't tell me. You . . . you *repaired* your car. That's what you did, and I think you may have saved your life."

"Is that all?"

"For now."

Joe nodded. "Well, I did have words with my daughter. She wants to see some band with her friends in Midtown this weekend, and I told her no way. I know she's still upset about it. And I did have new brake shoes put on my 4-Runner a couple weeks ago."

Monica used her napkin to wipe the corners of her mouth. "Of course, you still don't believe I have any special abilities. You think I'm spying on you, or maybe bugging your house?"

Joe shrugged. "Maybe."

"Do you have any proof of that?"

"No, and I probably won't, since I'm not doing a full-fledged investigation of you. Our focus is on the murders."

Howe was still dazed. "Jesus, I didn't tell *anybody* I was going to propose to Regina." He cocked an eye at Monica. "I don't suppose you can tell me if she's gonna accept, can you?"

"I hope you impressed them, Monica."

Monica turned from the sidewalk newsstand and glared at Derek Haddenfield. The bastard. She'd left her hotel room to avoid another visit from him, but he'd found her anyway. There was no getting away from this guy; it was now a quarter past nine and, for all she knew, he'd been watching her all day.

"They were plenty impressed, Haddenfield. Are you doubting me now?"

"Of course not. I have the utmost faith in you and your abilities."

"Then why are you here?"

"Just checking in on you, making sure that you haven't lost sight of the objective."

"I haven't lost sight of anything. You don't need to worry about me."

"I *am* worried. I thought you'd be on a plane back to Vancouver by now."

"I'm not ready yet. You can't rush psychic abilities, you know."

He sighed. "Oh Lord."

"If you don't like it, just leave. I'll take care of things here."

"No, I understand. You must follow your instincts. As long as you remember why we're here." He cocked his head toward the hotel behind her. "You can invite me up, you know."

"I'll pass on that." She turned and walked toward the hotel's main entrance. "Lay off on the unannounced visits to my room. If you want to talk to me, my telephone works just fine."

"It's not as secure."

"Good night, Haddenfield."

Monica felt his eyes on her as she entered her hotel and walked across the spacious lobby. Damn him. And damn her for agreeing to this crazy scheme.

He'd practically begged her to come to Atlanta and let his team study her in the field. It would be good for everyone, he promised—him, her, and their entire cause.

Their cause. He'd said it like it was some kind of goddamned crusade, like it was her duty to convert the world to their way of thinking.

What the hell was she doing here?

She took the elevator up, entered her room, and headed straight for the minibar. They'd restocked the rum. Good. She needed it.

She ran a hot bath as she called in for her messages. Just the usual crap. Guests needing to be rescheduled, requests for charity dinners, and a stack of audition tapes waiting for her perusal back in her office. The syndicator wanted a hip young "special correspondent" to host remote segments, so they were on the lookout for some young stud to appeal to the eighteen-to-forty-nine-year-old women whom advertisers coveted so much.

She tossed her cell phone onto the bathroom counter. Screw them all. She peeled off her clothes and lowered herself into the bathwater, trying to imagine all of her tensions floating from her body. It usually worked, but tonight she couldn't stop thinking about—

"*Monica . . .*"

She froze. A sharp, eerie whisper from the other side of the bathroom. Surely she had only imagined it.

"*Monica . . .*"

She stood, clutching the plastic shower curtain across her torso.

"*We've come for you, Monica.*"

She glanced around but saw no one.

"*Your time has come.*" The voice appeared to emanate from the bathroom counter.

She huddled against the wall. The tiles were cold against her back. "What the hell do you want?"

There was a pause, then a long-drawn-out whisper, "*We've come for you.*"

Her tears fell hot against her cheeks. What in the hell was going on?

Still gripping the shower curtain, she stepped from the tub. One foot, then the other. Her heart was trying to jump out of her chest.

She didn't breathe as she stepped across the bathroom, bracing herself for that awful, slithering whisper. She moved past the washbasin, almost afraid to look toward the mirror. She glanced up in spite of herself.

She gasped. This couldn't be happening.

There, on her chest, was the circle-intersecting-bars symbol that had marked the murder victims.

She rubbed it with her fingertips, but it wouldn't go away.

Oh, Jesus. Get out, she told herself. Just get the hell out of there.

She hurried from the bathroom, reached into the closet, and pulled out her robe. She yanked it on.

"Die, Monica . . ."

She screamed and jumped for the door. She turned the knob and pulled.

The chain. The goddamned security chain. She fumbled with it as the whispers grew louder and more intense.

"Monica . . . Die with us, Monica. . . ."

She pulled the chain free and yanked the door open wide. She stumbled into the hallway. "Leave me alone! Leave me the hell alone!"

"We're coming for you, Monica."

"No!"

Her screams drew other hotel guests from their rooms behind her, but she couldn't stop. Not while that . . . *thing* was after her.

The glass elevators loomed ahead, but she couldn't stop and wait for the car. Must keep moving. She reached the stairwell door and reached for the handle.

In the next instant, there was a sickening roar and flames erupted over her entire body.

"Die with us, Monica. . . ."

Fire everywhere. Not everywhere, she realized. Just on her. White-hot flames attacking her, rolling over her legs and chest, licking at her neck and hair.

Pain. Agony.

It was as if the fires of hell had come for her.

4

Joe stepped off the musty elevator and paced down the hallway toward Grady Memorial Hospital's intensive care unit. Carla and Howe were waiting at the nurses' station.

"What the hell happened?" Joe asked.

Howe shrugged. "We're about to find out. All we know is that Monica Gaines made like a human torch in front of about half a dozen witnesses at her hotel."

"I got that much from the precinct," Joe said. "Any idea how it happened?"

Carla shook her head. "I just talked to a uniformed cop on the scene, and according to the witnesses, she was running down the hall, screaming. Then, a few seconds later, she just ignited. It was like spontaneous combustion."

Before Joe could respond, a doctor with silver hair and round-shaped eyeglasses strode through a doorway. Howe was on him immediately. "How is she?"

The doctor took off his spectacles and wiped

them on his green scrub shirt. "It's very serious. She has first- and second-degree burns over twenty-five to thirty percent of her body. She was in shock from fluid loss when they brought her in. We have her stabilized right now, but she still may not survive."

"I guess talking to her is out of the question," Carla said.

"Actually, she wants to talk to you."

"She's conscious?" Carla asked.

"Heavily medicated, but awake."

"Isn't that a good sign?"

"Not necessarily. Her real problems could begin in a few days, when infection sets in. Her body may not be able to fight it, and if that happens, her organs will shut down."

"And there's nothing you can do to help fight the infection?" Joe asked.

"To *help* fight, yes. But that's all."

Joe nodded. "Take us to her."

The doctor led them through the double doors to the intensive care unit. As they walked through the wide hallways, the hospital smells almost made Joe sick to his stomach. They reminded him of Angela's awful final weeks.

Let it go. At least for now.

They followed the doctor into a dim, single-bed ICU. Monica's face was red and swollen, and her delicate features were puffed beyond all recognition. Her arms and midsection were heavily bandaged.

Joe clenched his jaw. Only hours before, she'd been so full of life. Shit.

She whispered something. Joe leaned closer to hear. "What is it?"

She whispered again. "Pretty, ain't I?"

Joe managed a smile. "How did this happen, Monica?"

She stared at the ceiling. "They—they came for me."

"Who did?" Carla asked softly.

"The spirits. The ones who killed the others."

"You saw them?" Joe asked.

"I heard them. Voices in my room, terrible voices. I ran, but they caught me." Joe could see tears welling in the thin slits of her eyes. "They burned me."

"How did the fire start?" Joe asked.

"I don't know. It happened all at once, all over me. I couldn't stop it. I couldn't—" She sobbed, and an alarm went off from the pulse-oxygen monitor.

The doctor stepped forward and reset the alarm. "Relax, Monica. Just relax." He stared at the monitor until he was satisfied that the readings had stabilized. He turned toward the detectives. "Sorry, but I have to cut this short. You can come back later."

"Poof, just like that. She lit up like a Roman candle." Jerry Tillinger shook his head. He and his wife, Emily, stood in the hallway outside their room, staring at the spot where Monica had caught fire. They were well into their eighties, and they seemed to be competing with each other to tell Joe, Howe, and Carla their version of the event.

"Did you see a spark or anything that precipitated the fire?" Joe asked.

"Not at all," Jerry said. He wore thick black-framed eyeglasses and a white goatee that reminded Joe of

Colonel Sanders. "We had no warning. One second she was yelling and carrying on, the next she was burning up."

"Everybody was just standing around, doing a fat lot of nothing." Emily turned proudly toward her husband. "But not Jerry here. He whipped off his coat, threw it around the woman, and tackled her. He probably saved Miss Gaines's life."

"I'm sure he did," Carla said.

Jerry smiled modestly. "I was on an aircraft carrier in the navy. I saw how the fire crew worked."

Joe retraced the steps from Monica's room to the place in front of the stairwell. The carpet was singed from the blaze. "Did you see anyone else around here?"

Jerry shook his head. "Nope, just the people who'd come out of their rooms to see what the ruckus was about. I'd say there was nobody within twenty feet of her."

The elevator chime sounded and the doors slid open. A portly, thirtyish man with a thick mustache stepped through the door. "Atlanta PD?" he asked.

Joe flashed his badge. "You got it. And you are?"

The man flashed his own ID. "Ed Bonafas, director of hotel security. I'm an ex-cop."

"Where?" Howe asked.

"In Charleston. I'm just doing this until something opens up around here."

"Something will open up, don't worry," Howe said. "Catch me on the right day, and I'll give you my job."

Joe cocked his head toward a ceiling-mount security camera aimed in the direction of the elevators. "Please tell me that thing was working."

"That thing was working," Bonafas assured him. "That's why I'm up here. Wanna see a show?"

Joe, Howe, and Carla followed him to the plush first-floor security offices, where a monitor rested at the end of a long conference table. Bonafas pressed the remote, and a black-and-white image flickered on the monitor.

"Jeez," Howe said. "You guys spend a fortune on this office but can't kick in a few extra bucks for color cameras with decent resolution?"

"Priorities," Bonafas muttered. "Do me a favor and repeat what you just said to the hotel manager, will you?" He pointed to the screen. "Look."

The camera offered a clear view of the elevators and stairwell doors. Monica ran toward the camera, and although there was no audio, it was obvious that she was screaming. As she reached for the door handle, a flame suddenly ignited on her sleeve and midsection. She stumbled backward, writhing and twisting until Jerry threw his overcoat around her and pulled her to the ground.

"Jesus," Carla said. She turned to Joe. "Do you believe in spontaneous combustion?"

"No."

"What are you talking about?" Howe said. "There are all kinds of documented cases of people burning up and their clothes aren't even singed."

Joe shook his head. "Many of those victims happened to be smokers in poor health. It's probable they suffered a stroke or heart attack while holding a cigar or cigarette, which began a slow ignition of their bodies that took place over a period of several hours. The bodies would be consumed, while the clothing may only burn slightly. A few years ago, there was a study done with pig carcasses that bore this out."

Howe grinned. "Your explanations for some of this stuff are freakier than if they were the real thing."

Carla pointed toward the monitor. "This took only a few seconds."

"And her clothes were burned too." Joe took the remote control from Bonafas and scanned the picture back. He replayed the ignition one frame at a time. "Amazing. It looks like the fire erupted everywhere between one frame and the next, in just one-thirtieth of a second."

"If that's not spontaneous, I don't know what is," Bonafas said.

Joe put down the remote. "Do you know anything about the voices she said she heard?"

Bonafas shrugged. "Only that she was running from them."

"Did anybody else hear them?"

"Not that I know of."

"Has the room been disturbed since this happened?"

"No. I did a walk-through to make sure nobody was in there, but I didn't touch anything."

"Good."

Howe lifted his eyebrows. "Time for the spirit kit?"

Joe nodded. "You got it."

Ten minutes later, Joe strode into Monica Gaines's hotel room, carrying the worn black leather case that

he kept in his car trunk. Containing an odd assort-
ment of high-tech test instruments, evidence-
gathering tools, and ordinary household objects, his
"spirit kit" came in handy whenever he investigated
the scene of a séance or other paranormal activity.
Someone at the station had once affixed a *Ghost-
busters* "no ghosts" insignia on its side, and when the
decal wore off, had even replaced it with another. Joe
had no idea who the joker was, but he left on the
sticker for his fellow officers' amusement.

He placed the kit on the bed, opened it, and pulled
out a pair of electronic goggles as Bonafas walked
into the room.

Joe switched on the goggles and put them on. "Are
Howe and Carla talking to the other witnesses?"

Bonafas nodded, staring curiously at Joe's eyewear.
"Yeah . . . I got 'em in the conference room downstairs. They all have pretty much the same story
though."

Joe glanced around the room until his eyes fixed
on the far wall. He pointed. "I suppose there's a TV
right about there in the room next door."

Bonafas took a moment to orient himself, then
nodded. "Yeah. Every room on this floor flip-flops the
layout of the one next to it, like a mirror image. That'd
put the TV about there. Are those some kind of X-ray
glasses?"

"Infrared. It lets me view heat waves. I can see a
slight bit of heat buildup on that wall, concentrated
in a small area about four feet from the floor."

Bonafas whistled. "Wow. Those things aren't standard issue in Charleston."

"Here neither, at least not in the Fraud Unit. I

picked these up secondhand from an army surplus wholesaler."

"You bought 'em yourself?"

"I do some freelance debunking work for a university parapsychology program, and that helps pay for some of this stuff." Joe glanced around the room. "These glasses are amazingly handy during nighttime séances."

"What are you looking for now?"

"If someone was in here, waiting for her awhile, it's possible though not likely there might still be some heat residue. Also, if there's some kind of electronic mechanism in place that transmitted the voice, this may find it."

Bonafas watched as Joe surveyed the room with his glasses. "See anything?"

Joe turned toward the bathroom and stopped. "Wait. There's something in there."

Bonafas drew a snub-nosed .38 from his shoulder holster.

Joe shook his head. "That's not necessary." He pulled on a pair of plastic evidence gloves and walked into the bathroom, where he immediately saw that the heat source was the tub of now-lukewarm water. He turned toward the washbasin. Nothing unusual.

Bonafas holstered his .38. "Does she have fillings?"

"I don't know," Joe said. "Why do you ask?"

"They say some people can pick up radio broadcasts with dental fillings. It sounds crazy, but maybe someone was transmitting to her."

Joe took off the goggles. "There are anecdotal reports of that happening, but no one's been able to bring that about in any kind of controlled circumstances." He paused at Monica's closet, where there was a stack of sketches on the upper shelf. He picked up the drawings and looked at them.

"What are those?" Bonafas asked.

"Sketches that Monica made. They're a lot like the ones she drew at the crime scenes, but these—" Joe studied them. "These are different."

"Different?"

"These look more polished, and yet the backgrounds are all wrong. It's almost as if—"

"What?"

"Hmmm. I'll have to take these with me." Joe put them on the bed. He picked up a pair of black plastic headphones, flipped a power switch, and adjusted the gain control.

Bonafas smiled broadly. "I used to wear a set of 'phones like that when I was a kid, stayin' up all night listening to Deep Purple."

"Not like this. This detects high-frequency sounds like radio waves and RF control signals and converts them to sounds I can hear." Joe put on the headphones.

"What could that tell you?"

Joe adjusted the gain control. "It tells me that you're wearing a digital watch."

Bonafas lifted his sleeve to reveal an inexpensive LCD wristwatch. "You can actually hear it?"

"Your watch, the refrigeration unit on the minibar, and the bathroom lightbulbs." Joe cocked his head. "But nothing else, I'm afraid." He took off the headphones. "I'll go over the room with some of my other equipment later, but I want the fingerprint guys to pass through first."

"Got it. Until you tell me otherwise, no one gets in here without a badge."

"This Bailey guy has some pretty cool gear. He might be able to teach *us* a thing or two." Paul adjusted his parabolic microphone and glanced back at Haddenfield, Gary, and Donna. They were on the fourth level of the Flesher Pharmaceuticals parking structure, directly across the street from Monica Gaines's hotel room. Paul leaned out the van with his microphone, recording the details of Joe Bailey's initial sweep of the room. The audio had been channeled to a small speaker for the others to hear.

Haddenfield nodded. "Bailey's a sharp guy. We should monitor him. He could make our jobs a little easier."

"Our jobs?" Donna asked. "Aren't they pretty much over?"

"What are you talking about?"

"Gaines is out of commission. A toasted Ry-Krisp. She's not going to be doing much of anything for a while, except maybe shuffling off this mortal coil to a place I have no intention of going for a long, long time."

Haddenfield's face was taut. "There are still questions to be answered."

Gary frowned. "Answered by *us*? This is a little different than the assignment I was given. Whatever happened to Monica Gaines tonight, we're moving into foreign territory. None of us have any experience dealing with this."

"Nobody has, Gary. Which is why it's so important." Haddenfield spotted a uniformed security officer steering a white golf cart on the other side of the garage. "Okay, everybody, let's move to the other location. We got everything we need here."

Joe picked up Nikki from Wanda Patterson's apartment, where he'd hastily left her when the call about Monica Gaines came in. Wanda was a successful sculptor who lived down the hall, and Nikki occasionally earned extra money walking her dog. Nikki was silent as they walked back to their apartment.

"You're usually talking a mile a minute when you leave Wanda's place," Joe said. "Is everything okay?"

"You had to go because of Monica Gaines, didn't you?"

"Yes."

"We heard what happened to her. It was on the news. Is she going to die?"

"I don't know, honey."

They entered their apartment, and Nikki walked quickly toward her room.

"Hold on," Joe said.

"I'm tired." She strode into her room and closed the door behind her.

Joe pushed her door open. "Not so fast. Are you still mad that I wouldn't let you go to the concert?"

"No. Janey's and Giselle's moms wouldn't let them go either."

"Then what's wrong?"

She plopped down on her bed. "What happened to Monica Gaines?"

"I don't know, honey. We're trying to figure that out. She was burned pretty badly."

"Why can't someone else figure it out?"

"Maybe someone else will. But the detectives need my help, and I think I should do what I can to find out what happened to her."

"It's not really evil spirits, is it?"

"Where did you hear that?"

"It was on the news. They were interviewing her TV producer in Canada, and she said that Monica thought maybe bad spirits killed the other people here."

Joe sighed. Christ, the media would go nuts over this one. "Sweetie, even if you believe in spirits, there has never been a documented case of one hurting anybody."

"Well, you don't believe there's been a documented case of a spirit *period*."

"It doesn't mean I wouldn't love to be the first to find one."

"Maybe you should call Suzanne. She's good at this kind of stuff."

Joe nodded. He knew that Nikki missed Suzanne. Hell, *he* missed Suzanne. They'd dated earlier in the year, but things had gotten complicated. After the way he'd bailed on their relationship, he wasn't sure she'd ever want to see him again.

Nikki wrinkled her nose. "Just call her."

Joe suddenly glanced away. "I'll think about it."

She studied him. "I just did it again, didn't I?"

"What?"

"I did something that reminded you of Mommy."

He smiled. "I'm beginning to think *you're* a psychic. How did you know?"

"You always get the same look. Kind of happy and sad at the same time. What did I do?"

He hesitated before replying. "You twisted your nose in a way that your mother used to. I've never seen you do that before. As you get older, you're more and more like her."

Nikki sighed. "I miss her."

"Me too, honey." He kissed her forehead. God, if only Angela were here. More than anything in the world, she'd wanted to watch Nikki grow up. As the cancer ate at her system, Angela's ever-retreating bargains with the almighty centered on her wishes to see Nikki finish college, then high school, then her sixteenth birthday. Nikki was eight when her mother finally slipped away, still angry and confused at being taken from her family so soon. There was no peace, no nobility in her death, just tragic, devastating loss.

"Did Mommy worry about your police work?"

"Sometimes, but she thought what I was doing was important."

"I think it's important too."

"I'm glad. Then you understand why I have to do this?"

Nikki nodded. "Yeah. You have to find who tried to kill Monica Gaines. If you don't, they could hurt someone else."

"That's right." He stared at her. She was trying so hard to be brave, but he could see she was worried. With good reason. During his only other homicide investigation, she'd watched a man die only a few feet from her. She was probably thinking of him now.

"It'll be okay, honey." He leaned down and kissed her on the end of her nose. He whispered, "I promise."

Shawn Dylan strode past the intensive care unit nurses' station, letting his white lab coat billow behind him like a long cape. He'd adopted the arrogant swagger of an "I-am-your-God" medical doctor, and no one seemed to be paying him any attention.

Perfect. Monica Gaines had been there only a few hours, and the nurses on duty had no reason to suspect that he didn't belong there. By tomorrow, there would be systems in place that would make such a visit difficult—an established routine, an assigned medical team, a private guard, or even a police officer nearby. As it was, the only police presence was corralling the television news reporters outside the main entrance downstairs.

Dylan had heard about Monica's accident just as almost everyone else had—from the television news. How had things gotten so hopelessly fucked up? He should have stayed closer. No, he couldn't blame himself.

He stepped into her room in the ICU. Most of Monica's torso and half of her face was covered in white bandages. He studied the pulse-ox monitor in the manner of a real doctor, then leaned over her.

"Monica," he whispered.

No response. Probably on some major meds.

"Monica?"

Her eyes opened, and her monitored pulse rate quickened.

"I've been worried." He checked to make sure no one was watching from the corridor. "I never would have wanted this to happen, Monica. We have to get you away from here."

"Hurts . . . hurts so much," she whispered.

"I have something I need to finish here first. It may take a few days. In the meantime, you are to say nothing about our purpose here. Do you understand?"

No reaction.

He leaned closer. "There will be people talking to you, Monica. Your judgment may be clouded by the medication, but you must not discuss why we're here. Am I making myself clear?"

No reaction.

He gripped her hand harder. "I could end this right now, Monica. I could kill you, leave here, and no one would ever know. I'm giving you the benefit of the doubt, but if I hear you're saying too much, I'll have no choice but to come back. I don't want to do it, but I will. No matter how confused you get, how disoriented you are, you must not tell. Do you understand?"

A single tear ran from her left eye.

He released her hand. "I'll take that as a yes."

Morning, Bailey." Carla took a huge bite from her onion bagel as the other cops in the conference room turned toward Joe. Detectives with any involvement with the Spotlight Killings were gathered for a meeting to discuss the Monica Gaines incident. Carla smiled. "You impressed the hell out of that hotel security guy with your spirit kit last night. Did you bring it with you?"

Joe threw his jacket over the back of a chair. "I don't need my spirit kit today unless you guys suddenly get weirder and creepier than you already are." He showed Carla and Howe the sketches he'd found in Monica's hotel room. "Do you see anything strange about these?"

Howe flipped through the drawings and nodded. "It looks like she spent a lot more time on these. Not the rush jobs she did for us. Maybe she wanted prettier versions for her website."

"That's what I thought at first," Joe said. "But the

backgrounds are different. It's like she wasn't familiar with the locales when she drew these."

Carla stared at a picture of the first murder scene they visited, with its floating spirits, shadowy tree branches, and full moon. "You think maybe these are first drafts, drawn before she even got here?"

Joe nodded. "Exactly. I may ask her about it later. Any idea how she's doing today?"

Howe shrugged. "She slept through the night, but her condition's still critical. I don't know if she's conscious or not."

Captain Henderson entered the room with half a dozen well-dressed men and women. Howe whispered to Joe, "Mayor's office flunkies. I just met some of them in the hall. This meeting is for their benefit."

Although Howe and Carla were visibly annoyed by having to endure what was probably their twentieth meeting on the killings, Joe appreciated the discussion and slide show that followed. Aside from his crash course from Carla the other night, he had little direct exposure to the case, and he was glad to hear directly from the officers who worked the various crime scenes. At the end of the officers' presentations, Henderson introduced a slick young man named Alex Spengler, the department's media relations director.

"Gentlemen, while you work this case, please be mindful of the fact that this has now become an international media event," Spengler said. "Monica Gaines's books are published in over thirty languages, her television show is seen in something like twenty countries, and her website receives several hundred thousand hits a day. She's not just a normal celebrity. Her fans see her as a savior, and they're already lining up in front of the hospital. We've already received reports that they're flying in to stand vigil. They may try to go to the places she's been. Her producer is continuing production of her show with guest hosts."

"Guest hosts?" Carla asked. "A different psychic every night?"

Spengler shrugged. "They'll be doing daily reports from here. Watch what you say. You may think you're shooing away some nut with a camcorder, but that footage of you could be beamed all over the world by nightfall."

"Got it," Howe said sarcastically. "Priority one is for us not to look bad on camera."

"No one's saying that," Henderson said, "but you're more than cops on this case. You're representatives of this city. Be nice."

The room filled with cops' grumbling as if they'd been asked to make a monumental sacrifice.

Henderson motioned toward Joe. "Detective Bailey will be assisting us. If you have questions about any purported psychic phenomena, talk to him."

Someone in back whistled the *Twilight Zone* theme.

After the meeting adjourned, Joe accompanied Howe and Carla to the Peachtree Summit Studios, where Glen Murphy's coproducer, Chris O'Connor, was finishing up work on the singer's final album. O'Connor had bleached-blond hair, a cheerful red face, and a boisterous Irish accent that somehow made everything sound like the punch line to a joke.

"Murphy was going daft, if you ask me," O'Connor said. "Which, of course, you didn't, but when has that ever stopped me, eh?"

"Why did you think he was . . . daft?" Howe asked.

O'Connor leaned back in his chair at the mixing console. "Why, he was hearing things. That's not good for a music producer when he's mixing an album. The hearing's everything."

Joe nodded. "So what was he hearing?"

"Voices, mostly. Scared the hell out of him, I must say."

"Where was he when he heard these voices?"

O'Connor gestured around the studio. "Around here, mostly."

"Did anybody else hear them?"

"Not at the time. That's why I thought he was daft. Not daft, maybe, but exhausted. He was practically living here. The album was late, and the label wanted it something awful. But something strange happened when I came in here to try and wrap things up. That's what made me call you fellas last night."

"What happened?"

"I was cataloguing some of the tracks he'd laid down for this song, and I heard something I couldn't explain." O'Connor's fingers glided over his console. "Listen for yourself. This was a percussion track that Murphy recorded sometime in the last week of his life."

O'Connor pushed a button and moved up a slider until they heard a slow, rhythmic drumbeat through the sound booth's speaker system. Chris suddenly pointed at the speakers. There was a faint whispering sound.

"Hear that?" he said.

"What was it?" Carla asked.

O'Connor grinned. "I couldn't tell at first either. I thought maybe Glen was trying to lay in a subliminal message or something." He pushed a red button. "So I filtered out the drum and took a closer listen. Here's what I came up with."

He pushed another slider, and a low voice whispered from the speakers, *"Come with us, Murphy. . . . Die with us, Murphy. . . ."*

Carla stepped away from the speaker as if the voice might reach out and grab her. "Holy shit."

"Leave your world behind you, Murphy. . . . The time has come. . . ."

The whispers had a bizarre, ethereal quality unlike anything he'd heard, Joe thought. "Is this what Murphy claimed to be hearing?"

O'Connor nodded. "Near as I can tell. He was wearing headphones playing the other tracks while he recorded this, so he might not have known he actually got the voice on tape. But he described it to us, and this sounds like it." O'Connor rewound the recording and played the whispers back.

"Die with us, Murphy. . . ."

Howe pointed through the booth's glass window. "Are you telling me that this voice somehow came from that room?"

O'Connor nodded. "That's where the microphones are."

Carla nervously moistened her lips. "This is incredible. Most of those victims claimed to hear voices, but this is our first evidence that they actually existed."

"Can you make us a copy of this?" Joe asked.

O'Connor picked up a CD and handed it to him. "Already done, my friend. I hope it helps. You know, I think I may leave it in the song. Couldn't hurt sales, you know. I think this is going to be the album's breakout single."

"What's it called?" Carla asked.

" 'Nothing but the Stars.' A real catchy tune."

Sam Tyson stared at the boom box in the cluttered back room of his downtown magic store. "Jeez, kind of chills you to the bone, doesn't it?"

Joe pushed the stop switch. He'd made a cassette copy of Murphy's percussion track before turning the CD over to the police crime lab. The techs already knew that the song's title, "Nothing but the Stars," had been "read" by Monica at Murphy's crime scene, and they pestered him for an explanation. All in good time, he'd told them. "The voice doesn't sound real, does it?" Joe said.

"Neither does the music, for that matter. How do people listen to that crap?" Sam picked up an armload of packing straw and shoved it into a wood crate. He was packing up a custom-built illusion he called Ice of Atlantis to send to a Las Vegas magician who had become rich performing Sam's spectacular tricks.

Joe smiled. "Let's forget for a moment that you hate any music past Rudy Vallee's time."

"I'm not that old, kid."

"Crosby and Sinatra's time."

"Now you're talking."

"Most of the spotlight murder victims heard strange voices in the last days of their lives. This is the only recording we have. Do you know anybody who specializes in audio tricks?"

"Like ventriloquism?"

"Not exactly. There was no one else around in most of these cases."

"I'll have to think about that one." Sam leaned against the crate. "I bought a new TV last year, and it has a setting that gives the illusion that the sound is coming from behind you."

"Surround sound?"

"Yeah, but there aren't any speakers behind you. The circuitry plays with the sound in such a way that it fools the ear into believing that part of it is radiating from behind."

Joe nodded. "A lot of newer televisions do that."

"Well, I know a ventriloquist who can do it without a lot of fancy electronics. Whatever that TV is doing to the sound, he must be able to do by sheer instinct. You'd swear his voice was coming from behind you."

"Like I said, there was no one else present at these places. And as bitter as I'd be if I had to make my living as a professional ventriloquist, I don't think it's bad enough to turn one into a serial killer."

"Well, being a professional magician was bad enough to turn you into a cop."

"Good point."

"All I'm saying is that there are all kinds of ways to

fool the human senses. We know how easy it is to fool the eye, kid. I'll try to put you in touch with some people who can fool the ear."

"Just what I was hoping you'd say. Thanks, Sam."

"Anytime. Give me a hand with the lid, will you?"

Joe helped Sam lift the heavy wooden lid and position it squarely atop the packing crate. Joe smiled as he caught sight of Sam stealing one last look at his hand-crafted illusion before sealing it for the long cross-country journey. It obviously pained him to release each new illusion, like an artist being forced to part with a favorite work of art.

Sam met Joe's eyes and nodded at the understanding he saw there. "This is a good one, Joe. It's gonna make a lot of people happy."

In a suburban neighborhood off Peachtree-Dunwoody Road, Haddenfield pulled to a stop and climbed out of his car. Shawn Dylan was already there, waiting in the shadows of a large sycamore tree.

"You're late." Dylan spoke matter-of-factly, without a trace of anger in his voice. The way he always sounded, Haddenfield thought, until his cooler-than-cool demeanor suddenly erupted.

"I was busy," Haddenfield said. "We're setting up a new base across the street from Monica Gaines's hospital. There were some details to hammer out."

"You know my feelings on the matter."

"You're not the least bit curious about what happened to her?"

"Of course I am. But there are matters that require

our more immediate attention, and I still think Monica Gaines is a liability."

"She's an integral part of our work."

"She *was* an integral part. Now she could destroy everything."

"I don't feel that way."

"My superiors agree with you. Otherwise . . ." Dylan glanced away.

"Otherwise what?" Haddenfield stared at him. "You would have killed her already? Is that what you're saying?"

Dylan was silent.

Christ, Haddenfield thought. "Your superiors recognize this as an opportunity, Dylan. I haven't lost sight of our objective. You'll get your prize, and I'll get mine."

"Until we leave, I'll be staying close to Monica. There may be other interested parties, you know."

"I know."

"And just so you know, there's a limit to my superiors' indulgence. Believe me, you don't want to be around when their patience is at an end."

Joe stepped inside Monica Gaines's room.

"Yes, Detective. I'm still here." Monica's face was still red and swollen, but she looked more alert than when he'd last visited.

Joe smiled. "Hi, Monica. How do you feel?"

"Like I've been set on fire." Her voice was thin and weak.

"Did they give you something for the pain?"

"Only a little. They wanted to dope me into oblivion, but I didn't let them."

"Why?"

"If I'm going to die, I don't want to spend my last days in a fog."

"Nobody says you're going to die."

She glanced through the floor-to-ceiling windows toward the nurses' station. "The plump nurse with the red hair thinks I won't make it past Friday."

Joe turned and spotted the nurse, who was at the desk, filling out paperwork. "How do you know?"

Monica managed a smile even though the effort was obviously painful. "I'm psychic, remember? She's been leaking information to a tabloid newspaper."

"Are you sure?"

"Positive. She even promised to snap some pictures of my body after they wheel me down to the morgue."

Joe stared at Monica in shock.

Monica nodded. "She wants ten thousand dollars, but they're willing to pay only five. Poor thing."

"If you're sure about this, I'll talk to her supervisor on the way out."

"Don't. At least not yet. She has a call in to one of the paper's competitors, and I'd like to see if they meet her price." Monica closed her eyes, obviously fighting a wave of pain. After a moment, she glanced back at Joe. "You're dying to find out how I know this, aren't you? I have no telephone, and no one else has come to see me today."

"Look, I didn't come here to debunk you."

"But you do want to ask me about the sketches you found in my hotel room."

Joe raised the large manila envelope he was holding. "Very good. Do you know what I want to ask?"

"I'm not in peak form. Fill me in on that one."

Joe pulled out the sketches and showed them to her. "Did you draw these before you actually visited the crime scenes?"

"Of course not. You were there when I gathered my impressions."

"It looks like these were drawn without any knowledge of the actual area."

"I display my drawings on my website and in my books. When I'm in the field, my sketches are often rushed. Sometimes I like to refine my drawings. If the settings look a bit different, chalk it up to artistic license." She gritted her teeth and suddenly turned away.

"Do you want me to get someone?"

Monica turned back. "No."

Almost anyone else would have gladly taken a morphine drip, Joe thought. The lady was a fighter. He put away the drawings. "Okay. I'm also here to ask you who might have done this."

"How could I possibly know that?"

"Well, given the fact that you're a world-famous psychic—"

"Are you actually giving some tiny shred of credence to my abilities?"

Joe pursed his lips. "You're a very intelligent and intuitive person. I'd be remiss if I didn't get your impressions."

She settled back and stared at the ceiling. "I have no idea. I haven't been able to sense anything since this happened. Whatever it is, I still don't think it's human."

"So you're standing by that."

"Of course."

"Listen to me. Whoever is committing these murders may be afraid of you. They may have somehow engineered this attack to keep you from discovering them."

"I've thought of that."

"I know your show and website are making a lot of noise about this 'spirit killer' angle, but it may be obscuring the real issue here. There may be a flesh-and-blood murderer out there who wants you dead."

"I appreciate your concern."

The plump nurse walked into the room carrying a clipboard. "Don't mind me, keep talking." She studied the instrument readings.

Monica raised her head. "There's a disposable camera in your locker, isn't there, honey?"

The nurse suddenly wore a startled expression. "Uh—yes, ma'am."

Monica nodded. "I can see it. Tell me, dear, why would you want a camera in a place like this?"

The nurse turned red. "Well, there's a—a party later."

"A party? Hmmm. I'm getting a slightly different reading. I can't quite put my finger on it. I see the camera, its flash going off—"

"I'm sorry, I have to run." The nurse bolted from the room.

Joe chuckled. "I still think I should talk to her supervisor."

Monica closed her eyes again, but this time she

wore a faint smile. "Only if I don't make it. In the meantime, I'll enjoy torturing that poor girl."

What a bunch of clowns, Shawn Dylan thought.

Sitting at a window table of a tiny coffee shop, he watched Derek Haddenfield and his woefully inexperienced team scouting the area around the Grady Memorial Hospital. They were obviously looking for sites to set up surveillance on Monica Gaines's room. This wasn't their specialty, and they were using technology that was at least two years out of date. What the hell did they hope to gain from this?

Dylan paid his tab and walked toward the hospital. It was dark enough that Haddenfield and company wouldn't spot him, though he doubted they would recognize him anyway. They were always so wrapped up in their insular little world.

He passed a group of Monica Gaines's fans standing vigil with signs and candles. A teenage girl sat cross-legged on the sidewalk, rocking back and forth, chanting, "I love you, Monica, I love you, Monica. . . ."

Dylan shook his head. Wow. Gaines's fans were nuttier than he thought.

What utter bullshit, he thought. Not the prospect of Monica Gaines's psychic abilities, but the mere fact that an operative with his training and experience would be mixed up in this. Another town, another assumed name, another set of disguises. There was a time when Mother Russia led the world in psychic research, and other countries sent agents to spy on *it*. But that time was long past, and here he was, scrounging around for goddamned table scraps. He'd heard of the old guard's experiments in grooming psychic spies; interesting stuff, he thought, but he'd never seen any proof that the attempts succeeded.

This could change all that. In this new era, such a force could be more important to his people than ever. Not merely to obtain state secrets, but high-tech innovations that could replace trillions in research and development. If this panned out, it could be huge: the information-age equivalent of the atomic bomb. This engine could bring an entire economy back from the dead and restore his government to its rightful place in world power.

He stared at Haddenfield. It was incredible that such an awesome power could rest in this foolish man's hands. He appeared to have discovered the Holy Grail of psychic research. Yes, it was worth the time to come here and confirm the project's results.

Soon the secret might be his, Dylan thought. When that happened, Derek Haddenfield would be totally expendable.

Nikki scooped up the Risk game pieces and dropped them into the box. "You just got lucky, Dad. Next time I'll slaughter you."

"I have no doubt." He'd beaten Nikki tonight, but just barely. He didn't dare lose intentionally; she could spot any attempt to throw a game from a mile away. Whether she won or lost, she was a good sport. She enjoyed her wins and carefully analyzed each loss to keep from making the same mistakes again.

She hugged him. "Good night, Dad. I love you."

"I love you too, honey."

She pulled away and bounced to her room. "Next week, you're annihilated, Mister!" She closed her door behind her.

He smiled. It was all part of their regular Wednesday game night. After Angela's death, it seemed important to maintain a sense of order in the household, with regular meals and set times to spend together. Although work had recently intruded more than he liked, game night was off limits to anyone—or anything—but Nikki. They always ordered a pizza and took turns deciding which music would be played. Nikki preferred classical pieces, while Joe chose '70s or '80s rock.

He turned off Nikki's Ahn Trio CD and plopped into a chair. How many more years would their game nights continue? Nikki insisted they'd continue via computer modem long after she moved away and had a family of her own, but he knew that probably wouldn't happen. Life tended to get in the way of such nice, cozy plans.

He settled back into the couch. How long had it been since he'd talked to *his* father? It was ten-fifteen. Dad would be sitting in the projection booth at his Celluloid Palace movie theater in Savannah, catching up on his reading or just listening for audience laughter if a good comedy was playing. Dad beamed whenever the crowd cracked up at a Laurel and Hardy routine or Billy Wilder flick, as if he'd just performed it himself.

As Joe decided whether or not to call him, Nikki's bedroom door flew open. She ran across the room and threw her arms around him. My God, she was crying. . . .

"Honey?"

"Daddy, I heard her."

"Who?"

Nikki trembled. "Mommy. I heard Mommy. She just talked to me."

6

Joe moved across Nikki's bedroom and checked the windows. Locked. "Where did you think the voice came from, honey?"

Nikki sat on the bed, her cheeks still red from crying. "I don't know. Kind of all over the place."

He glanced around. It was a small room, ten by twelve feet, with windows on two adjoining walls. Thick padded carpet covered the floor, and posters of Nikki's classical music heroes shared wall space with the latest *Teen Beat* heartthrobs.

Joe sat next to her. "You're sure it sounded like Mommy?"

"It was her. I know it."

"Tell me exactly what happened, okay?"

She pulled a pillow into her lap and held it close. "I was asleep, but something woke me up. I think it was the whispering. Mommy's whispering."

"What made you think it was her?"

"I remember how she sounded, the way she talked

when she tucked me in." Nikki laid her head on his chest. "She was here, Daddy."

"What did the voice say?"

"When I woke up, she kept saying, 'Time to toddle, time to toddle.' "

Joe stiffened. "Time to toddle" had been Angela's way of telling Nikki it was bedtime, always spoken in the same singsong voice.

Nikki sat up to face him. "And she called me Monkeyhead."

Another Angela-ism. He looked away. Just hearing Nikki say those words brought back a tidal wave of memories.

God, he missed her.

He stroked Nikki's hair back from her temple. "Sweetheart, do you think you might have been dreaming?"

She shook her head. "It was so real."

"I know, honey, but think about it. You've been following the Monica Gaines case very closely, and you know about the voice she said she heard the other night. Plus, you yourself said you'd been sleeping. Don't you think it's possible that you may have dreamed it?"

"It didn't feel like a dream."

"That's the way it is sometimes." Joe pulled the covers up. "Lay back down, honey."

Her eyes opened wide. "You're not leaving, are you?"

"No. I'll stay here as long as you need me."

"Good." Nikki lay back and pulled the covers around her chin. "You think I'm crazy, don't you?"

"Of course not. When Mommy passed away, I talked to her all the time."

"I thought you didn't believe in spirits."

Joe scooted to the foot of her bed. "Well, I imagined what Mommy would say back to me. It made me feel better. After you and I would see a movie, I'd pretend to talk to her about it. We'd almost always disagree. Your mother and I had a lot of things in common, but we didn't have the same taste in films."

"I guess that explains all the Judd Nelson videos."

"Yes, that and the Vanilla Ice movie. But we always agreed that you were really great. The point is, we all imagine what it would be like to talk to people who are gone. There's nothing wrong with that. Maybe you were sort of doing the same thing."

"She sounded so real. Especially when she said—" Nikki let the thought hang.

"Said what?"

"What does it matter if it's only a dream?"

He shrugged. "I'm curious."

"Mommy wants you to be careful. She thinks you may be in danger."

"Only you, Bailey, could find someone who sets himself on fire for a living."

Joe and Howe stepped over the cables snaking over and around the Smyrna filming location of *Blood Avenue,* a straight-to-video action movie. The thirty-five crew members were preparing to film a car roll on a suburban street. It was a few minutes past eleven A.M., and Joe had done almost nothing but worry about Nikki in the previous twelve hours.

She seemed fine on their morning drive to school, but it was so hard to tell; she was good at hiding her feelings, especially when she knew he was worried.

What had brought on this imaginary visit from her mother? Maybe a father who wasn't around as much as he should have been?

As if he didn't feel guilty enough.

Joe turned to Howe. "This guy actually *extinguishes* fires for a living. He's a fireman in Douglas County. Stunt work is just his part-time gig."

"How did you find him?"

"A friend of mine did security for another movie this company made. They grind out six films a year, all straight-to-video. Lots of bare breasts and stuff blowing up."

Howe grinned. "My kind of flick."

"This stunt guy's specialty is fire gags. I figure he might be able to help us figure out what happened to Monica Gaines."

"Have you heard anything from the fire inspector?"

"Nah. I heard he visited the scene, but he's just as clueless as—"

"—as you are?" Howe finished for him.

"I was going to say as *anybody*, but yes, if you want to put it that way."

An assistant director's whistle cut the air, and a strong voice shouted, "Quiet, please! We're rolling!"

Fifteen yards away, a gorgeous blond woman in tight black jeans and a ripped T-shirt held up an automatic handgun and aimed it down the street.

"Hey," Howe whispered, "I think I saw her in *Playboy* a few months ago."

A Jeep rounded the corner and sped toward her. She raised the gun and opened fire, grimacing as each blank shell flew. The car abruptly veered to the left and rolled twice. It ignited, and the driver stumbled out onto the pavement, screaming as flames covered him.

A camera operator moved in for a close-up. After a few moments, the driver held his hands over his head, obviously a signal to the two firemen waiting just off camera with large chrome extinguishers. They were on him in an instant, covering him head-to-toe with white foam.

"Cut!" the director shouted.

There was halfhearted applause from the crew members, but it was apparent that they filmed scenes like this all the time. Just another day at the office. The firemen pulled the charred clothing from the stuntman, leaving him with a form-fitting black body-suit.

"Yes!" The stuntman smiled broadly, obviously stoked by adrenaline. His blond hair was soaked with extinguisher foam, and his sunburned face glowed. "You sure you don't want another take, guys?"

The director shook his head. "We got the shot. Guess you'll have to do something else for your beer money this week."

"Aw, hell, I'd do it again for free."

"Sorry, Pete. We're moving on."

As the crew prepared for their next camera setup, Joe and Howe walked toward the stuntman.

Joe smiled at him. "Pete Treadwell?"

Pete winced as he spotted the badge clipped to Howe's belt. "Aw, shit. Cops. Look, guys, the director just came up with that bullshit car roll in the past couple of days. We didn't have time to get permits, but if you wanna talk to the production manager—"

"Relax," Joe said. "We're not here to bust your chops about filming permits. I'm Detective Joe Bailey, this is Mark Howe. Nice work out there."

Pete still wore a guarded expression. "Thanks."

Joe lowered his voice. "Pete, have you heard about what happened to Monica Gaines?"

"You mean the human torch?"

Joe nodded.

"Sure. Me and the guys were taking bets on whether she set it herself for the publicity."

"Not likely," Joe said. "Even if you think she's a fraud, she has no experience with this kind of thing. Plus, we have it on video. If she engineered it herself, she put on one hell of a show."

Pete lifted his eyebrows. "Video?"

Joe held up a brown padded envelope. "Security camera caught the whole thing. Anywhere we can show you this?"

Pete led them to a dilapidated Winnebago recreational vehicle that served as the production's onsite office. The lime-green interior was littered with production reports, storyboards, and hundreds of cigarette butts.

"Classy," Howe said.

"Hey, this isn't exactly big-budget stuff we're doing here." Pete pointed to a VCR/TV combo unit resting on a small card table. "Go ahead and show me your tape."

Joe inserted the cassette and played the Monica Gaines fire footage.

"Awesome!" Pete shook his head in disbelief. "Can I see it again?"

They watched it four more times, and Joe noticed that Pete seemed to be viewing it more as a piece of action-packed entertainment than as a tragic occurrence.

Joe finally ejected the tape. "Show's over. Any ideas?"

Pete scratched his head. "Well, you need to find the trigger. The ignition mechanism had to be somewhere on her."

"She was wearing only a robe," Joe said. "She slipped it on less than thirty seconds before this happened."

"That's too bizarre. If I were to try to rig something like this, I'd cover her with a flammable compound, then strap a remote-controlled igniter under her clothes somewhere."

"Remote controlled?" Howe asked.

"Yep. I push a button on my keypad, and as long as she's within three hundred feet, it creates a spark, lights the compound, and up she goes. Poof."

Joe shook his head. "She said she'd just stepped out of a bathtub, and there was no ignition mechanism. The paramedics would have seen it."

"I'm telling you, there had to be one somewhere. Did you check her clothes, her hair, everything? It could be as small as a hairpin or a button. This stuff has gotten really tiny."

"We'll take another look," Joe said. "What was left of her robe is in evidence. If there's anything there that strikes us as odd, we might ask you to come in and give us your thoughts. Okay?"

"Sure." His glance went back to the monitor. "Think maybe you can show me that again?"

Joe ejected the cassette, remembering the vulture nurse waiting to snap pictures of Monica's corpse. Sickos. "Sorry, Pete. We have to get going."

Joe and Howe walked into the squad room, to find Carla on the telephone, holding up her freckly index finger as an indication that this call was somehow significant to them.

"Got it," she said into the phone. "We'll see you in a few minutes." She hung up.

"What is it?" Howe brushed aside the candy wrappers on his desk, looking for any message slips that may have been left for him. "Is the fajita truck outside already? Pedro's early today."

Carla stood and pulled on her jacket. "Sorry to disappoint you, but this is a little more official than that."

"The doughnut van?"

"Nope. That was the security chief at Monica Gaines's hotel. They apprehended a woman who'd broken into an office there."

Joe and Howe traded puzzled stares.

Carla motioned for them to follow. "She's Monica Gaines's TV producer."

"Either arrest me or let me the hell out of here!" Tess Wayland stood in the small office as Joe, Howe, and Carla entered. Tess was a short, slender bundle of energy with a strong chin, spiked brown hair, and glasses that were slightly too large for her face. She cocked her head toward Bonafas. "Dick Tracy here figured he was going to impress you guys, is that it? Tell me, are you impressed with his crime-fighting skills? 'Cause I sure as hell am not."

Bonafas sighed. "She's been like this ever since we caught her. It's been a real joy, let me tell you."

"What's the story?" Carla asked.

Tess let out a rueful cackle. "The story? I'll tell you what the st—"

Carla held up a hand to silence her. "I was talking to him. You'll get your turn."

Bonafas gestured toward a closed door. "One of the guys caught her in the room next to the monitor bank. It looked like she was about to cart away our security tapes."

Howe turned toward her. "Something in there you don't want everybody to see?"

"Don't be stupid," she hissed. "I know you guys would have already taken copies of the security tapes you needed."

"Then enlighten us," Carla said. "Because right now I'm inclined to treat you as a suspect in an attempted murder."

"Oh Lord," she moaned. "In two minutes I can have a team of lawyers on the phone who can tear you guys to tiny bite-size chunks."

"Bring 'em on," Carla said. "In the meantime, why don't we talk about why you broke into this place?"

"I'm here on behalf of Monica Gaines."

Joe stepped forward. "You're trying to tell us that she sent you here?"

"Not exactly. I produce her television show, a little

thing called *Monica Gaines's Psychic World*. Perhaps you've heard of it."

Howe grimaced. "Aw, Christ."

Joe shared Howe's disgust. "You wanted Monica's fire footage to use on the show?"

"Damned right. It's only a matter of time before somebody gets it. Why not us?"

"For one thing, it's evidence in what may become a murder investigation," Carla said.

"We're doing our own investigation on the show every night," Tess said. "We have the leading psychic authorities appearing on live television and offering their—"

Howe interrupted. "So you thought this footage would spice things up?"

"It's hard to engage in any meaningful discussion without knowing exactly what we're talking about."

"Well, isn't that sort of what your show does every night?" Carla said.

Tess checked her watch. "Look, guys, I have a show to produce. If you're gonna arrest me, I'd appreciate it if you could get it over with. The sooner you book me, the sooner my lawyer will be all over your asses, and the sooner I'll be back with my crew."

Joe glanced at Carla and Howe. They obviously agreed that it wasn't worth incurring the wrath of Tess Wayland's attorneys. He turned back to Tess. "Tone down the attitude, and we might be able to work something out."

Tess hesitated, and then nodded. "Finally, a reasonable man."

Joe sat next to her. "How well do you know Ms. Gaines?"

"I've produced her show for the past two years."

"That doesn't answer my question."

"I guess I know her better than most people. She's a pretty private person."

"Does she have any enemies?"

"Besides the entire editorial staff of *Skeptical Inquirer*? Not really. There's the occasional nut whose feelings may be hurt because she doesn't accept his marriage proposal, but that's pretty standard for any media star at her level."

"Any professional rivals?"

"None that would benefit from her death. Psychics who are as popular as Monica give credibility to everyone else in her profession."

Joe nodded. It was true. Whenever a spiritualist or psychic suddenly gained widespread popularity, there was an upswing in the number of successful charlatans emulating their techniques.

"Has there been anything unusual about Monica's life lately or the people she's been associating with?" Carla asked.

Tess considered the question. "Like I said, she's a private person. To tell you the truth, I don't think she has much of a personal life. She's all about work. But there has been something unusual in the past few months. Between each production cycle, Monica has disappeared."

Howe grinned. "You don't mean literally, as in thin air, right?"

"No," Tess said. "At least, I don't think so. Monica goes away for weeks at a time and no one can reach her. She doesn't post updates to her website and we don't have a clue where she goes."

"Well, we know she has three residences," Howe said.

"We know that too," Tess snapped. "We once needed her to meet with a station group president to close a syndication deal and we sent people to each of her homes. She wasn't at any of them. Even her immediate family had no idea how to contact her."

"Has she ever given you any idea what she's doing?" Carla asked. "Health spa? Plastic surgery? Maybe a married lover?"

Tess smiled. "I know her, and I don't think she'd be especially discreet about any of those things."

"I'll talk to her about this," Joe said. "In the meantime, can you give us the exact dates when she was unaccounted for?"

"Sure. My organizer is out in my rental car. Do I take it that you're not arresting me?"

Howe turned toward Bonafas. "Does the hotel management have any special desire to press charges?"

Bonafas shook his head. "I think they'd like to avoid any more publicity right now."

Tess frowned. "I guess getting a copy of that security tape for tonight's show is out of the question, huh?"

Joe shook his head. Unbelievable.

"Take a look at this, will you?"

In the observation center they had set up in the building across the street from Monica Gaines's hospital room, Paul and Donna joined Gary at his video monitor. It offered a view of an open window in the hospital.

"What's this?" Paul asked, staring at the monitor.

Gary adjusted the brightness. "Monica Gaines's room blinds are closed, so I've been shooting the room next door. This one has glass walls to the corridor, and I've been seeing a lot of people coming and going down the hallway. One guy has been going back and forth all day, but he's been wearing two different disguises."

Paul shook his head. "Dude, you've been looking at this thing too long."

"I'm serious. Look." Gary pushed a button on his console and displayed a still-frame image of a tall man wearing a lab coat and a thick beard. "Okay, this guy walked past Monica's room nine times in the space of two hours."

"Yeah, him and about a hundred other guys," Donna said.

Gary pushed another button and turned a dial. "Okay, look at this one." Another image appeared on the screen, this time a man in a green scrub suit and a matching cap. There was no beard; just high cheekbones and a strong jaw.

The group stared blankly at the screen.

"Can't you see?" Gary said. "It's the same guy."

Donna shook her head. "There's a similarity there, but I think you're reaching. Why don't you take a break?"

Gary glanced between the team members. "I'm telling you, this is the same guy. He's scoping out Monica's room for some reason."

"And he likes to adopt funny disguises and pace hospital corridors." Paul chuckled. "I just don't buy it."

Gary opened a leatherette case and produced an official-looking ID badge attached to a thin chain. He picked up a thin watch battery and placed it into a black receptacle behind the badge.

"Is that what I think it is?" Paul asked.

"It's a wireless video camera." Gary flipped another switch on the console and aimed the badge at Paul, whose face suddenly filled the monitor. Gary put the chain over his neck and squarely positioned the badge. "I'm going in."

Donna shook her head. "No. Wait for Haddenfield to get back."

"I'm tired of waiting."

"If a cop or security officer catches you, it could bring down our entire operation," Paul said.

Gary picked up his jacket. "Our operation, such as it is, has accumulated zero useful data so far. Maybe we need a closer look."

"With that thing?"

"Sure. If I can get into the room or even the hallway outside, I can pop this camera out and position it toward Monica Gaines's bed. That's what we really want, isn't it?"

"I thought all we wanted was a fat paycheck," Donna said. "You really don't even know what you're sticking your neck out for."

"Sure I do." Gary held up the tiny camera again. "For the chance to use these cool toys. Haddenfield will thank me. This is exactly what we've needed."

Paul jammed a finger into Gary's chest. "Don't get caught. Because if you do—"

"—you'll disavow any knowledge of my existence. Gotcha. Will this room self-destruct in ten seconds?"

"Be careful," Donna said. "I wish you'd wait for Haddenfield. He should be back any minute."

"I'm not waiting."

She sighed. "If there's any chance of getting caught, get your ass back over here."

"Don't worry." Gary tapped the monitor. "You can watch it all on TV."

Dylan stepped into the hospital stairwell and pulled off the itchy fake beard. Surely, in the thousands of years since Sophocles' time, someone could have come up with a stage beard that didn't make him want to scratch his goddamned face off. Time for another disguise.

Dylan reached for the black plastic garbage bag he'd wedged under the metal stairs. He took out a pair of spectacles, a blond toupee, and a brown blazer, then shoved the beard and scrub shirt into the bag and stowed it. He donned the new disguise. He didn't need a mirror to know how it looked; he'd used it a few times before. He pulled open the door and walked down the corridor, adopting a stooped posture. Jesus, how much longer would he have to spin his wheels here?

He passed a curly-haired young man with a thick beard. Was the kid staring at him? The kid looked away. Okay, maybe not.

Dylan walked by Monica Gaines's room, glancing at her through the glass windows that faced the corridor. She was unconscious now, alone in the dim room. A private security guard was standing watch outside, shifting uncomfortably in his cheap polyester suit. The guy was probably a local hire accustomed to watching bowling alley parking lots. If Monica Gaines's people were concerned about her well-being, they'd do well to get a real bodyguard, he thought. Not that anyone could stop him if he decided that Monica was a liability.

The curly-haired kid quickly walked past and paused at the end of the corridor. He turned and held up a sheet of paper as if he were studying it intently.

Curly wasn't looking at that paper, Dylan realized. Curly was looking at him.

Dylan walked past Curly again, quickly scanning him for any clues that would reveal who the hell he was. Ragged tennis shoes, no handgun bulge, generic ID badge, and—

Oh, shit. The badge. It was one of those $799 hidden cameras sold at big-city "spy shops" and mail-order stores, aimed at corporate executives who fancied themselves the next James Bond. This idiot hadn't even bothered to change the stock ID card and logo that surrounded the tiny black lens.

Who the hell was he? Curly was obviously more interested in him than in Monica Gaines or anyone else on the floor. Dylan glanced up at the large circular mirror mounted high in the corner of the corridor, put there to keep orderlies from ramming gurney carts into one another. Curly, still holding the paper, was following him.

*   *   *

"What the hell is Gary doing in there?" Hadden-field stared at the black-and-white monitor image.

Donna shook her head. "We told him not to go. He wants to get a better look at this guy who's been hanging around there. He's also going to try to plant his little camera someplace that will give us a better look at Monica Gaines."

Haddenfield squinted at the screen. "*What* guy hanging around?"

"We'll see him in a second," Paul said. "Gary insists he's been there on and off all day, wearing different disguises."

"Disguises?"

Paul nodded. "That's what he thinks. You might consider replacing Gary. He's losing it." Paul pointed to the screen. "There's the guy."

Haddenfield gasped. It was Dylan. He coughed in an attempt to hide his involuntary reaction.

Donna didn't take her eyes from the monitor. "Maybe this guy is a private security officer, or a reporter."

"We have to get Gary out of there now," Haddenfield said.

Paul studied him. "Why? Do you know this guy?"

Haddenfield shook his head. "It's not that. It's just—a security risk. Is Gary carrying his cell phone?"

Donna shrugged. "Probably."

Haddenfield quickly picked up his phone and punched Gary's number. He listened to the ring tones. "Come on, you prick. Pick up."

Donna pointed to the monitor. "No reaction here. He's still on the other guy's tail."

For a moment Haddenfield thought that Gary had

answered, but it was just his outgoing voice-mail message. Haddenfield cut the connection. "Christ."

Paul frowned. "You know, I think it *is* the same guy. Gary may be right. Who do you think it is?"

Haddenfield backed away. "I'm going in. I need to get his ass out of there."

"Good idea," Donna said. "I don't like the idea of—" She leaned close to the monitor. "Where's he going?"

She was looking at a dark, shadowy set of stairs. Gary had followed the man into a stairwell.

"You goddamned idiot!" Haddenfield shouted at the monitor.

All onscreen movement stopped.

"He's trying to stay quiet," Paul said.

"It won't help. Gary is *so* busted," Donna said. "That dude would have to be blind and deaf not to know he's being followed."

The camera turned toward the stairs leading up, then to those leading down.

They watched as the camera slowly traveled downward, catching the institutional green walls and cracked stairwell lighting fixture. It moved to the landing and began the turn.

The picture jerked violently and went black.

"Hey, I didn't know we'd gone to casual Fridays." Howe grinned at Joe as he sat down behind his desk in the squad room.

Joe was wearing a white terry-cloth robe over his shirt, tie, and slacks. "You're the first person here who has said anything to me about this," Joe said. "I was beginning to wonder about you homicide guys."

"Aaah, they probably thought you were going undercover at a bathhouse. So what's with the robe?"

"I picked it up from housekeeping before I left Monica Gaines's hotel. It's standard issue for all of the guests. Monica was wearing one just like it when she ignited."

"Okay. And exactly how does that require you to prance around the squad room wearing it?"

"I'm trying to get an idea where a trigger mechanism may have been placed. And I really don't think I was prancing."

"Sashaying?"

"Strolling." Joe flipped up the back of the robe. "The thing is, any kind of trigger mechanism would have to completely destroy itself. There was no trace of it at the scene, and the guys down in the lab said it wasn't on what was left of the robe."

Howe considered this. "And we know that no one could have removed it from the scene since there was a security camera trained there."

"Right." His cell phone rang, and he answered it. "Joe Bailey."

"Daddy?" It was Nikki. Her voice quavered. "Daddy, can you come home?"

Joe yanked off the robe, keeping the phone pressed against his ear. "Honey, what's wrong?"

"Mommy was here again today."

7

Less than twenty minutes after Nikki's call, Joe and Howe rushed down the third-floor hallway of Joe's apartment building. Sam was waiting outside the door.

"Where is she?" Joe asked.

Sam gestured inside the apartment. "In there. She's pretty shaken up. This must be someone's idea of a sick joke. I took her out for a frozen yogurt, and when we came back, this is what we found." Sam opened the door wide for Joe and Howe to enter.

Joe stepped inside and froze. "Jesus," he whispered.

Howe couldn't see it. "What's wrong?"

"The furniture. It's been moved."

"So?"

Joe glanced around. The couch was now turned away from the television, facing one of the large windows. The coffee table was now on the other side of the large room, in the middle of three chairs. Even the window blinds were set differently, pulled three quarters of the way up.

He turned back to Howe. "This was exactly how my wife left things when she died."

"Are you serious?"

"Yeah. Nikki thought she heard Angela talking to her last night. I thought she'd dreamed it."

Howe shook his head. "This is no dream, Bailey."

Nikki appeared from her bedroom. Her face was tensed. "Mommy did it, didn't she?"

Joe rushed across the room and kneeled beside her. "No, honey. Someone's playing a trick. A mean trick."

"She *did* talk to me last night. She knew you didn't believe it. Maybe this was her way of letting you know it was real."

Howe strode to the telephone. "I'm calling for a forensics team."

Sam glanced around the room. "It was the screwiest thing. We couldn't have been gone fifteen minutes. I locked the place up tight, but when we came back, it was like this."

Joe looked toward the kitchen. The spice jars were now arranged in a pyramid, just the way Angela used to stack them. They would fall whenever Joe slammed the front door too hard.

Nikki pointed to the dinette table. "Look."

Joe leaned over to see that a word had been scratched into the table's glass surface: RAKKAN. It was carved deep, leaving glass splinters scattered across the tabletop.

Sam studied it. "Rakkan? What the hell does that mean?"

Joe pulled Sam and Nikki back. "I don't know, but we shouldn't tamper with it. The evidence team will want a crack at this." He turned toward Nikki. "Your room?"

She took his hand and led him back to her bedroom. The bed was now pushed against the far wall, opposite where it had been only that morning but precisely where Angela had placed it the day they'd moved out the crib and bought Nikki her first real bed. Nikki had decided to move it the year before to keep the early-morning sun from shining on her face.

Nikki pointed to a watercolor print that she'd painted with her mother. "She moved our rainbow too. I had it on the other wall so that I could see it from my bed."

"I'm afraid it wasn't her that did this, honey."

"How do you know?"

She was no longer frightened, he realized. There was something else there.

Hope.

For years he'd refused to believe that Angela's soul could be alive anywhere but in the memories of those who loved her. Nikki was always the believer, the one who insisted that they'd all be together again one day.

He'd seen too many people who felt the same way, who allowed themselves to be duped and conned by the bottom feeders who were all too willing to exploit the survivors' wishful thinking. Only in the past few months had he allowed himself the possibility, however small, that there might be an afterlife.

But it would take more than a few displaced pieces of furniture to convince him.

He gently raised her chin. "Think about it, sweetheart. What's more likely? That a ghost did all this, or that a real live person walked in here and just rearranged things?"

She frowned. "Why would anyone do that?"

"I don't know, honey."

Howe hung up the phone. "A fingerprint kit is on the way. How many people do you know who are familiar with the way this apartment used to look?"

"Not many," Joe said. "Sam, for one."

Sam crossed his arms. "Don't look at me. I'd like to strangle the diseased bastard who did this. I've heard of some sick jokes in my time, but this one's really up there."

Joe shrugged. "A few friends, but no one who'd do anything like this." He glanced at the drink coasters, now neatly placed on the coffee table's four corners. "There are too many little details. I can't imagine how anyone could remember some of these things."

"Photographs?" Howe asked.

"I thought of that. Dad's always been the big photographer in the family, but most of our holidays and special occasions were at his place."

Sam took Nikki's hand. "Come on, sweetheart. You're staying with me tonight. Your father is going to be busy."

"Daddy?" she asked.

"You'd better go with him, honey."

"But I don't *want* to go."

"We have work to do here. I'll come get you as soon as we're finished, okay?"

She didn't speak for a moment. "What if she comes back and I'm not here?"

He felt as if the wind had been kicked out of him. Shit. Who could be so goddamned cruel? He caressed her cheek. "*I'll* be here, okay?"

She nodded, but he could see that the hope was still alive in her eyes.

Damn. If he did his job right, he was going to disappoint the hell out of the one person he loved most in the world.

Haddenfield walked into the stakeout room, his sweat-soaked hair falling onto his forehead. "I looked all over the place. The stairwell is empty, and there's no sign of Gary or the other man." Haddenfield glanced at Donna and Paul. "I guess you guys haven't heard anything."

"No." Panic laced Donna's voice. "Shouldn't we call the police?"

Paul checked his watch. "It's been almost forty-seven minutes. Even if his camera malfunctioned, he should be back by now."

Haddenfield looked away. He'd been trying to call Dylan ever since he left, but there was no answer on his cell phone. Christ, how could this have happened? "Let's not get upset," he said to himself as much as to his team members. "He may still be following this guy. He may have accidentally pulled off his camera badge, or there could have been some massive electrical interference in the area. There are all kinds of equipment in the hospital that could be blocking our reception." He moved to the console. "Let's see the videotape again."

Paul scanned the tape back and found the spot

where Gary's transmission had abruptly broken off. He replayed the action in slow motion.

They watched as the camera moved deliberately down the dim stairwell, panning and tilting in every direction. It stopped on the landing, swung slowly to the right, then suddenly jerked up toward the ceiling. Static filled the screen.

"I don't like it," Donna said. "We need to call the cops."

Haddenfield shook his head. "We're not bringing the police into this. We can take care of this ourselves."

"Like Gary took care of *himself*?" Paul said.

Haddenfield thought for a moment. "We all need to get out there. I'll work the hospital. Donna, you take the four blocks north. Paul, you take the four blocks south. Each of you do long sweeps that extend to four blocks to the east and west." He picked up cell phones and handed them to Donna and Paul. "Whatever you do, don't call anyone but me."

The two forensics experts did their usual efficient work, finishing Joe and Nikki's apartment in a little over an hour. Joe looked at the collection of prints that Sergeant Cindy Potthast had neatly arranged on strips of cellophone in her scuffed black case. "Any prints you can use?" Joe asked.

Potthast nodded. "A few. Can I grab a quick set from you? I can eliminate some of these immediately if we know they're yours."

"Sure." Joe rolled each of his fingers across Potthast's ink pad and laid his prints onto a white card.

Potthast's partner, Todd Evans, gave him a wet tissue to wipe his ink-stained fingers.

Howe stood on the other side of the room, chuckling at a collection of old photographs from Joe's performing days. "Hey, Bailey. Was it absolutely necessary that you wear that tiny Speedo before being chained and thrown into the Chattahoochee River?"

"My manager thought it would give my act some sex appeal. Unfortunately, it was February and the water was freezing. I'm sure I gave every guy there a massive superiority complex."

Evans disappeared into Nikki's room and re-emerged with a drinking glass. "We'll take your daughter's prints from this," he said. "We'll run the prints we lifted through the FBI database. Depending how backed up they are, we may have results as early as tonight."

Joe took another glance around the apartment. "As much attention as they paid to detail, I'm sure they wore gloves."

Potthast shrugged. "You never know. We're dealing with a nut here, aren't we?"

After Howe and the forensics specialists left, Joe called Sam. Nikki was asleep. Better to let her stay that way, he decided. He'd swing by Sam's the next morning with a fresh change of clothes, then take her to school.

Alone for the first time since Nikki's anxious call, he glanced around the apartment. He hadn't realized that the place had changed so much since Angela's death. It had happened so gradually—a piece of furniture here, a picture frame there. He went through, room by room, rearranging the furnishings and erasing all evidence of their visitor. Whoever the hell it was.

He hadn't noticed it before, but a copy of *The Bell Jar* was open on an end table, pages down. Angela had begun reading it but could never bring herself to finish. Too depressing for her at the moment, she'd say. She'd pick it up later. It stayed there, in that very spot, for the last years of her life. Angela herself had finally placed the book back on the shelf before leaving for her final trip to the hospital.

He closed the book and put it on the shelf.

He put the apartment back in shape in less than twenty minutes, then climbed into bed, turned out the light, and stared at the ceiling.

He couldn't blame Nikki for believing. The desire was so damned strong.

What would he say to Angela if she could really come back? Where would he begin?

"Joe . . ."

He sat up. It was a whisper from the other side of the room.

"Hello, old friend. . . ."

His breath left him. The voice was thin and slightly ethereal, but there was no mistaking it.

Angela.

Hello, old friend. Their standard greeting, whether they'd been apart for a few hours or a few days.

"Joe . . ."

He switched on the lamp. He was alone in the room. There was no closet, no place for anyone to hide.

"Hello, old friend. . . ."

It was coming from across the room. At the window, maybe?

Joe leapt from the bed and yanked the cord for the window blinds. The window was closed.

"Be careful, Joe. . . ."

Now it was coming from the other side of the room. Another window. Joe jerked open the blinds.

Nothing. Another closed window.

He backed away toward the center of the room.

Stay cool. Don't let emotions get in the way.

"I love you, Joe. . . ."

Now it seemed to be in the corner, almost floating in space, coming from . . . nowhere.

Jesus.

It sounded so much like her.

He stood perfectly still, waiting to hear that voice again. The voice he'd missed so much.

But that was all. The voice stopped.

He was shaking. His mouth was dry.

Fight it. Keep your grip.

Joe flew into the living room, grabbed his spirit kit, and raced back into his bedroom. Only then did he realize that he had tears in his eyes.

He threw open the kit and picked up a McNaughton sonar pulse reader that he'd liberated from the bomb squad scrap heap. It was constructed to detect areas of mass behind walls, ceilings, and floorboards, but Joe had recently added an army surplus metal detector component that could scan for nine distinct alloys. A "magnetic" setting was particularly useful for finding hidden speakers.

He extended the telescoping sensor and swept it over his walls, ceilings, and windows. No magnetic readings. If there were speakers, it was possible that they were shielded. But where could they possibly be? The room lamp had been on, yet he hadn't seen anything that could have generated the sounds.

He pulled a multiband radio scanner from the kit and powered it up. He plugged in a pair of headphones and listened. Just the usual police frequencies, cordless telephone calls, and what sounded like a baby monitor. The scanner had come in handy a few months earlier, when he'd used it to discover that a faith healer was secretly receiving radioed information about audience members from his team of researchers and professional eavesdroppers.

The scanner was nowhere as useful tonight, however. He pulled off the headphones and left the power on in case he heard the voice again. If it was somehow being transmitted via radio waves, the device could lock in on the frequency within a few seconds.

No use trying to go back to sleep, he thought. At least not for a while. He strode into the other room and stared at the letters scratched onto his tabletop.

RAKKAN.

What did that mean? If it was meant to be another Angela-ism, the reference completely escaped him. It had to be something else.

He walked into Nikki's room and fired up her computer, which was newer and faster than his four-year-old laptop. He eased down onto her small wicker desk chair and entered "Rakkan" into an Internet search engine. Within seconds, a list of results filled the screen. He clicked on the first link, which took him to an Asian folklore website.

He read two paragraphs, then suddenly leaned closer to the screen. "Holy shit," he whispered.

8

Joe stood up in the police headquarters conference room and once again faced the Spotlight Killings task force. He'd phoned Henderson minutes after his discovery on the website, and she immediately called the seven A.M. meeting.

Carla yawned. "You'll have to be mighty entertaining to keep me awake, Joe. I wasn't ready for this."

Henderson shot Carla a cold glance. "We'll talk later about why it took a bunco squad cop to figure out what you're about to hear. Bailey?"

Joe nodded. "Actually, I'm sure that you all would have discovered this in the next day or so. As you may know, someone entered my apartment yesterday and disturbed some of the furnishings. There was a word scratched into my dining table."

"Rakkan," Howe said.

"Right. Well, I looked it up, and it's a somewhat obscure name from Asian mythology." Joe picked up a stack of stapled photocopies and gave them to Howe to pass around. "Rakkan was a spirit who roamed the countryside in search of a worthy man."

"Worthy of what?" Carla asked.

"Worthy of the life that the spirit has been denied. Rakkan was once a panther on earth, but as a spirit he moves from village to village, searching for this truly worthy person. When the people he meets don't measure up, he kills them."

Howe grimaced. "Nice guy."

"In the story as printed in the photocopy you have, the number of victims in the various towns range between two and eight. With each confrontation, Rakkan takes on a different form. He becomes a beggar, a prostitute, an animal, and even a tree. Each time, he ends up killing the people he meets."

Carla thumbed through the pages. "You're saying the Spotlight Killings follow this pattern?"

"Yes. In the last place he visits, a town that was once his home, he seeks out the best and most prominent citizens. They still don't measure up, and he kills them. He's angry this time, and he taunts them before they die, inviting them to their doom."

"The voices," Carla said.

"Exactly. And look at the different ways they die. When he assumes the form of a cloud over the village, he kills one with lightning."

"Just like Derek Hall was electrocuted," Henderson said.

"And when Rakkan takes the form of a horse, he drags his victim for an entire day and night."

"Like Thomas Coyle being dragged behind his car," Carla said.

"Right. You won't find a match in that photocopy

for every murder, but I've found them in other versions of the legend. Whoever this killer was, he was emulating the Rakkan story."

"What about the other towns?" Howe said. "Have you checked to see if—"

"Yes," Henderson cut in. "At least three other cities in the past five years have had murders that somewhat match the Rakkan legend. We've been in contact with the FBI, and they're now running them through the VICAP program."

Howe leaned back in his chair. "No offense, Bailey, by why in hell didn't someone figure this out before?"

Joe shrugged. "Maybe because the legend has Rakkan changing his M.O. in each town. We had nothing to link them together. In most of these cities, there wasn't even anything to link the individual murders to each other."

A tall, long-faced detective spoke from the other side of the room. "We got ourselves a tapestry maker."

Henderson nodded. "That's what it looks like. The killer thinks of each murder as another thread in a grand tapestry that can take years, or even a lifetime, to complete. He thinks of himself as an artist."

Carla wrinkled her brow. "So why was this sicko carving the name into Bailey's dining room table?"

Joe shrugged. "Maybe he got tired of waiting for us to make the connection."

"Maybe it wasn't the killer at all," Carla said. "Maybe it was someone who wanted to tip us off."

"Someone like his late wife?" Howe said sarcastically.

Carla shrugged.

*   *   *

Haddenfield, Donna, and Paul stood in Central City Park, a triangular slab of concrete near the busy Five Points area. It was eight-fifteen A.M., and the park was populated with office workers grabbing their final precious moments of freedom.

Haddenfield wore the same grim expression as he'd had all night. Donna and Paul were getting panicky, and he needed to calm them before they did something stupid. "You know, Gary wasn't happy with the way this assignment has gone. It's possible that he just skipped out."

Donna shook her head. "Not without telling us. Something happened to him."

"It's a no-brainer," Paul said. "It was that guy he was tailing. We never should have let him go."

"Gary knew what he was doing."

"Bullshit!" Donna said. "We should have gone straight to the goddamned police. Instead, we jerked around all night. Give me one reason why I shouldn't take those videotapes and go straight to the cops."

"I'm telling you that you can't. That's all the reason that you need."

"Do better."

"I'll get some people on it, but we can't go to the police," Haddenfield said.

Paul stepped forward. "What people?"

"Extremely qualified people."

"If something happens to me, I certainly hope you'll try harder than this," Donna said.

Haddenfield breathed deeply. He needed to get hold of that bastard Dylan, but so far he'd been as elusive as Gary. In the meantime, he couldn't let these punks push him around. "As of now, Gary is not your problem. We have a job to do. Let's go."

After the task-force meeting adjourned, Joe left the station and walked to the Java Joint for a cup of coffee to go. He took it outside and tried to clear his head.

He couldn't.

Christ. That voice had sounded so much like Angela's.

Can't let it rattle him. Gotta hold it together, not only for himself, but for Nikki.

An antiques store display window caught his eye. There, surrounded by small knickknacks, was a statue he'd been admiring for months. Called "Lillian," it was a beautiful woman with bobbed hair and '20s-era flapper clothing. It had always reminded him of Angela the summer after Nikki was born, when she'd cut her hair short.

Probably the best summer of his life.

He'd considered buying the statue, but it cost a small fortune. And he tried to keep himself from living in the past.

Yeah, sure. Then why in hell had he stopped here for coffee? Maybe a subconscious desire to make contact with Angela again?

What the hell. He wasn't ready to indulge in self-analysis right now.

He turned and headed back to his car.

* * *

Thirty minutes later, Joe climbed the front steps of the narrow two-story home in the Morningside neighborhood, only a few blocks from Piedmont Park. He hesitated before ringing the doorbell. He should have called first, but he probably wouldn't have been welcome in any case. How long had it been? Four, maybe five months?

A succession of locks clicked, and the door swung open. Suzanne Morrison stared at him in surprise.

"I'm sorry," he said. "I know this is kind of crazy, but—"

"I'm busy," she said coolly.

"I can wait."

"You'll be waiting a long time, because I'm just getting started. I have an entire family here. Come back tomorrow, or better yet, call."

She tried to push the door closed, but he held it open with his palm. "Please. You're the only person on earth I can talk to right now."

Maybe it was due to the desperate tone in his voice, but her face slightly softened.

"I can wait in my car until you're finished."

She hesitated, then stepped aside. "You can sit in if you'd like, as long as you promise not to wear your Spirit Basher hat."

"I promise."

"If I see a flashlight or a pair of infrared goggles, you're out of here. These people don't need to be distracted by your routine."

"That's not why I'm here, Suzanne."

"Okay, then."

She opened the door wide and led him up a narrow flight of stairs to a sitting room facing the front bay windows. Three women and two men sat in a circle in the center of the room. There was no table.

"This is Joe Bailey," she said to the group. "He's here just to watch. Does anyone have any objections to him being here?"

They shook their heads. Suzanne picked up a chair from the corner of the room and pulled it into the circle. She and Joe sat down.

Suzanne spoke to a gray-haired woman in her sixties. "Patricia, why don't you tell me something about your daughter?"

Patricia moistened her lips. "I'm hoping to speak to Nadia. She died when she was ten years old. This was over twenty years ago, but I've been thinking about her a lot lately."

As the woman continued, Suzanne nodded compassionately. Joe had seen half a dozen other séances that Suzanne had conducted, and they'd all begun in the same manner. Her M. O. was different from most modern-day mediums, who asked hundreds of questions and constantly refined the line of inquiry to reflect the answers given. This form of cold reading was surprisingly effective, especially for "psychic" television hosts who had the luxury of editing out their numerous wrong guesses.

Suzanne said very little, however, revealing just a few morsels of information before going into the body of her presentation. She closed her eyes. "Okay, I am now going to speak to my friend. She was taken at a very young age too, but she speaks to me and helps me communicate to those who have passed to the other side."

Joe glanced at the others. If they were even slightly skeptical, they hid it well.

Suzanne tilted back her head. "Daphne, I have some nice people here. They miss their daughter, just like your parents miss you. Can you help them?" She cocked her head toward the older woman. "Think about Nadia. Remember her. Feel her. That's the surest way to bring her back here." The guests appeared to be following Suzanne's advice. Some closed their eyes, others just smiled contentedly. Suzanne drew a sharp breath. "She's here."

"Nadia?" the elderly woman asked.

"Yes. Daphne says that Nadia's having trouble remembering what it was like here."

The woman wrinkled her brow. "She's forgotten us?"

"No. But the experience of being human is just a dim memory to her. Since you've last seen her, she's seen wonderful places and done amazing things. But she'd never leave behind her love for you."

One of the men cleared his throat. "Can she see us?"

"No. Anything I can hear, Daphne can hear. She then passes it on to Nadia."

"I understand." A tear fell down the woman's cheek. "Tell Nadia I'm sorry."

"She wants to know for what?"

"I now know that the man who owned our house . . . He did things to her. Like he did to my other daughters."

Joe glanced at the two thirtyish women, obviously Nadia's sisters. Tears ran down their faces.

The floorboards beneath them creaked and groaned even though everyone in the room was still.

Suzanne tensed. "Nadia remembers. Mr. Robertson said he'd hurt you if she ever told anyone."

"That's what he told us all," one of the sisters whispered.

The floor groaned louder. The floor slats were wriggling, Joe realized. Was there someone on the lower level, pushing up on the boards?

One of the slats broke free and the end curled back, inch by inch, until it was almost two feet over the other boards. Joe saw nothing pushing or pulling the wood slat. It then snapped back to the floor as if some unseen force had abruptly let go of the end. The sound startled the séance participants, but they scarcely had a chance to catch their breaths before a dozen other wood slats wriggled and curled upward.

Suzanne spoke over the sound of the other floor panels snapping back. "It's still very emotional for Nadia. It was an unhappy time for her."

Snap. Snap.

Suzanne's eyes were still closed. "She felt so alone."

Joe crossed his legs, swinging his left foot over one of the rising slats. There was nothing over it.

Incredible.

The woman sobbed. "I'm sorry, Nadia. I'm so, so sorry."

"She doesn't blame you," Suzanne said. "And she's the one who's sorry. Sorry that she couldn't be strong for you."

Snap.

"How could she be?" the woman said. "She was only a little girl. . . . Ten years old."

Suzanne's lips tightened. She was obviously hearing something that disturbed her. "Nadia couldn't live in your world anymore."

Patricia shook her head. "It wasn't an accident, was it?"

"No."

"Mother of God," Patricia whispered. "For years, I've thought she stumbled into that quarry pool. There were other kids playing there. But after I found out what she was going through, I was afraid . . ."

Suzanne nodded. "It was too much pain for her."

"Tell her that the bastard went to jail. Tell her that he died a miserable death there."

Joe was startled by a popping sound outside the window. Everyone turned. The top edges of the window screens had broken loose.

"Sweet Jesus," the man said under his breath.

As they watched, the screens' aluminum frames curled outward and twisted over.

Suzanne opened her eyes, but she did not look back at the window. "Your daughter doesn't realize that she's causing these things. It just happens sometimes, especially when we discuss things that affected them emotionally."

Patricia stared in horror at the bending, twisting screen. "I love you, Nadia," she whispered, tears streaming down her face. "I hope you've found peace there, the peace you couldn't have with us."

Suzanne smiled. "She has. She says that you have no idea, Mamacita."

The woman stared at Suzanne in amazement. "She used to call me that. She had a Spanish friend who called her mother Mamacita, and she picked up on it."

The window screens stopped moving.

"She wants you all to remember the past but not to live in it," Suzanne said. "She loves you. That's the one thing that hasn't changed since she was here. She says that will never change."

"I thought you were better than that," Joe said after Suzanne said her good-byes to the family. They had stayed almost a half hour after the séance's end, drinking tea and reminiscing about Nadia.

"What are you talking about?" Suzanne locked the front door.

"Ending with a reassuring message about how they should live their lives? You've never gone in for that kind of thing before."

"It's what that woman's daughter said. I'm sorry if you thought she was being overly sentimental, but maybe you can discuss it with Nadia in fifty or sixty years."

"It just sounded like the second-rate psychics who put up their shingles in Little Five Points."

"I agree. But as much as I don't want to be lumped into that category, I'm not going to sit here and cen-sor a ghost." Suzanne quickly moved up the stairway. "I have to check out the damage. Come on, make yourself useful."

They returned to the second-story sitting room, where Suzanne kicked at a few of the loose floor slats. "This has happened before. A little carpenter's glue and the floor will be fine."

Joe gestured down. "May I?"

"Sure."

He lifted the end of a loose panel, one that he'd seen curling into the air. There was no evidence of tampering, and its dark underside was smooth.

She smiled. "I'll bet you were just dying to bring your spirit kit in here."

Her smile was simply radiant, Joe thought. She wasn't at all nervous about him inspecting the scene, especially impressive since his presence there had been a surprise. He shrugged. "I promised you that I wouldn't be wearing my Spirit Basher hat."

"Yes, you were admirably restrained. Was this the fifth séance of mine you've seen?"

"Sixth. Plus three others that the university 'spook squad' videotaped."

"They prefer to be called parapsychologists."

"I'm sure they do."

Suzanne glanced out the window. "Oh Lord. Help me get those screens inside."

Joe threw open the window and grabbed one of the twisted screens. He ran his hand along the frame, feeling for a piece of wire or anything that may have pulled it down. Nothing. He laid it on the sitting-room floor and retrieved the other one. No signs of tampering there either.

Suzanne tried to straighten the frame, pressing it with the heels of her hands as she spoke. "Okay, Spirit Basher. If you were to duplicate this with trickery, how would you do it?"

Joe shrugged. "I'd brush the aluminum frame with a sodium hydroxide compound to soften it. I'd tie eight feet of heavy-duty clear fishing line to each of the upper corners and let the ends hang down. After your guests were inside, I'd have someone on the street below tie the lines to metal rods. They'd pull the top of the screen away from the window, and the weakened frame would bend and twist pretty much any way they wanted it to."

"Well, if you know where I can get any of that sodium hydroxide compound, I'd sure like to know. Maybe I could use it to bend these things back into shape. I'm going to lose money on this deal."

"You're still charging for your séances?"

"As long as I try to make a living as a classical music composer, I'll probably be charging for this. This takes a lot of time and energy for me."

"Not to mention all the time you spend visiting other spiritualists."

"You know why I do that," she said.

Yes, he knew. Suzanne claimed to be searching for another spiritualist who shared her unique gift. She'd been made to feel like a freak for most of her life, and she wanted to find someone else who could do the amazing things she did. She armed herself with an immense knowledge of paranormal fraud techniques, not to use them herself, she maintained, but to identify those who would try to deceive her.

Suzanne picked up the bent screens and leaned them against the wall. "I'll work on these later. So, why did you come here? Did that family ask you to drop in?"

"No, nothing like that."

"Then, why? I don't hear from you in four months, and you come here now?"

"I'm sorry about that. I should've gotten in touch sooner."

"You were under no obligation."

"Sure I was. We were . . . involved. That meant something to me."

"Funny way of showing it."

"I know. I'm sorry."

She straightened the chairs. "I always knew it was a risk. I'm the only spiritualist you've never been able to debunk, and I think that intrigued you at first. Later it just got frustrating and you couldn't handle it."

"I couldn't handle it, but not for the reason you think."

"Oh, yeah?"

"Yeah. You did change my perspective on things, Suzanne, but I don't want to go into it right now. I'm sorry if I hurt you."

"Hey, don't worry about me. I think you overestimate the power of your charm. I have missed Nikki though."

"She still talks about you."

Suzanne looked away. "Why are you here, Joe? Did you come to apologize?"

"Yes. But I also need your help."

"With what?"

"Have you heard about what happened to Monica Gaines?"

"Everybody has."

"I was assigned to accompany her to the crime scenes when she was in town."

"I'm sure she loved that."

Joe brought Suzanne up to speed on Monica's eerie

impressions, the strange voices, and the fiery attack at her hotel.

Suzanne's eyes narrowed. "Any theories yet?"

"I'm working on the combustion, but I'm especially interested in the voices right now."

Suzanne studied Joe's expression. "You're wound pretty tight. Are you all right?"

He let out a long breath. "I heard a voice last night. It sounded exactly like Angela."

"Are you serious?"

"Yes. Nikki told me she heard it a couple nights ago."

Suzanne considered this. "Amplification?"

"None that I could find. No trace of speakers or magnetic coil."

"Ductwork?"

"One vent, and it was behind me. No way it came from there."

"Jesus. No wonder you're shaken up."

"Yeah, it's kind of knocked me for a loop."

"And Nikki?"

"Very upset. She thinks that Angela is trying to warn me."

"Warn you of what?"

"Of the supposed evil spirits, I guess. And then there's the redecorating."

"What?"

Joe filled her in on the rearrangement of his apartment. As he spoke, it seemed even more inconceivable. Suzanne briefly quizzed him, asking the same questions he'd been asking himself. Who would be so intimately familiar with the apartment's previous layout? Who would have a reason to do something like that? He still didn't have the answers.

"That's just bizarre," she finally said.

"Tell me about it. I was going to go crazy unless I could talk to somebody." He sighed. "Not just somebody. You."

Suzanne was quiet for a moment. "I've never heard of a ghost giving a warning."

"Look, I'm not here for you to play ghost psychologist. I just need your help in figuring out how this could have happened. You're an expert at this kind of fakery."

"So are you."

"I need an objective eye. Where Angela's concerned, it's hard for me to be objective."

"I'd be worried if you *could* be."

"I've talked to Sam about audio tricks, but it's really not his field. You're pretty current on a lot of this stuff. Any ideas?"

"Slow down. I still haven't said I'd help you. I'm not through being pissed."

He nodded. "I don't blame you. I wish I wasn't asking you for help. But it's not just about me, it's Nikki."

"I know. And if someone really is faking this, it's the lowest of the low. It's like the charlatans I see all the time."

"Do you still go to séances every week?"

"The more I see, the better chance I have of finding someone who isn't bullshitting me. Sometimes it takes two or three visits, but I always find out how they do it. Of course, you still probably think I'm doing it to pick up methods for my own use."

"I'm trying to keep an open mind. Whatever your

reasons, it makes you the person I need right now." He paused. "Please."

She bit her lip. "I have an idea. Will you be home tonight?"

Joe caught up with Carla and Howe in the squad room shortly after one P.M. They were studying the medical examiner's report for victim number three, who had been electrocuted by his garage door.

Joe threw his jacket over his chair back. "Does the report tell you anything you didn't already know?"

Carla shook her head. "Just that about twenty thousand volts went through him."

"Hell of a spike," Howe said. "We already figured that whoever did it must have tapped into the power transformer."

"Can the power company back that up?"

Carla shook her head. "They can't even get my bill right. What makes you think they can help us with something like that?"

Howe nodded. "I checked with the company, but if it's not on a meter, they're pretty useless. There are surges all the time."

"Gotcha."

Carla leaned close to Joe. "How are you holding up? It must have shaken you up to come home and find your place like that."

"Yeah." Joe paused.

"Spill it."

"Spill what?"

"Whatever's on your mind. You're among friends here."

Joe smiled. Carla was one of the sweetest and most perceptive people he knew. Another reason why she always got the guys.

Joe took a deep breath and told them about hearing Angela's voice in his room the night before. To his surprise, they didn't look at him as if he were totally crazy.

"Are you sure you weren't dreaming?" Howe asked. "I mean, after what you'd been through, you were already thinking about her."

"You're talking to me the same way I talked to my daughter the other night. It wasn't a dream. I stood up and turned on the light. The voice was still there, and it sounded like Angela's. I'm sure that's what Nikki heard."

Howe frowned. "Each of the victims heard voices in the days before their deaths."

"This is different," Carla said. "Those weren't specific to anyone that they knew. Joe knew this voice." She turned back to face him. "Did you go over the room with your spirit kit?"

"Yeah. I couldn't find anything."

"I don't like this," Carla said. "If you're convinced that it's not your wife—"

Joe interrupted her. "*If* I'm convinced? Surely you don't believe—"

"I don't know what to believe, Joe, but someone could be doing a number on you. It could be the same person who's killing these people, and he was actually in your *home*."

"Believe me, I've thought of that. The fingerprint guys have already been out to my place. There's nothing more anyone can do right now."

Carla pursed her lips. "Have you told Nikki?"

"No, not about hearing Angela's voice. I want to keep this from her as long as I can."

"I don't like this, Bailey. If you notice anything else, let us know right away."

"Don't worry."

Two uniformed officers entered the squad room with a young man with dark shoulder-length hair. "Detectives?"

Howe stepped forward. "What's up?"

"We picked this man up on a trespassing charge. Some neighbors called it in. He was poking around Thomas Coyle's residence."

AKA victim number four, Joe remembered. The man who was dragged behind his car.

"So?" Carla asked. "The crime scene has been broken down. Did he take a swing at you or something?"

"He was unresponsive," the officer said. "He said he'd talk to only one of you."

Joe looked at the man. There was something familiar about him.

"Okay," Howe said. "You have our attention. But first, why don't you give us an idea who the hell you are?"

The man flashed a smile that was unnaturally bright. "Of course. My name is—"

"Barry Roth," Joe finished for him.

Roth looked flattered. "Yes."

"You know this guy?" Carla asked.

Joe nodded. "You would too if you had an eleven-year-old daughter. He's another psychic. He has a call-in show on the music video channel."

"I flew here from New York to help you," Roth

said. "You really should listen to me, Detectives. I've helped several police departments."

Howe nodded. "And I'm sure you have a stack of testimonials from small-town sheriff's deputies, right?"

"Yeah. Small towns like New York, San Francisco, and Chicago. I helped them, and I can help you."

"And help yourself too," Howe said caustically. "Hey, we'd all win."

"That's why you were at Coyle's place?" Carla asked.

Roth nodded. "I've been trying to arrange a more formal meeting with your department, but no one has been interested in returning my calls."

"Look, we're really not interested in seeing this case played out between Snoop Dogg videos," Joe said.

"This isn't for my show," Roth said. "I play to the Clearasil set. They want to know if their boyfriends are going to ask them to the prom or if their parents are going to give them cars for graduation. Trivial things like life and death have little appeal for my audience."

"So why are you here?" Joe said.

Roth pulled a felt-tip pen from his pocket, uncapped it, and wrote something in the palm of his left hand.

"I've had enough," Howe said. "Carla, we have an appointment with the medical examiner to discuss this report. Why don't we just—"

Joe grabbed Howe's arm. "Wait a second."

Roth held up his hand and showed them a circle

with two intersecting lines, much like the ones they had found on Monica and the murder victims.

"Aw, shit," Howe said. "Now we gotta talk to this son of a bitch."

"I'll do it," Joe said. "This is my thing." He motioned to Roth. "Follow me. You just bought yourself a ticket to the Cave."

"What?"

Joe led Roth to Interrogation Room A, known in the squad as the Cave due to its lack of windows and drab pencil-lead color scheme. The hue had been suggested by a high-priced behavioral psychologist, who maintained that it would throw criminals off kilter and elicit faster confessions. As far as Joe could tell, the Cave only threw the cops off kilter.

He pulled Roth's arm across the table, raised his digital camera, and snapped a picture of the circular symbol. He inspected the picture in the camera's LCD screen. "Okay, tell me how you knew about this marking."

"I saw it in a dream. I'm not sure what it means, but I think it's related to these killings."

"You know that this could make you a suspect, right? We've withheld any mention of this to the media."

Roth snorted and placed a fat manila folder in front of Joe. "I guess I was the perp in all of these cases too, huh?"

Joe opened the folder and thumbed through its contents. It was packed with newspaper clippings, magazine articles, and written testimonials from grateful relatives and law enforcement officials. "I'm familiar with some of your cases, Mr. Roth. On the face of it, you've done some amazing work."

"Only on the face of it?"

"For what it's worth, I think you're probably better at your craft than Monica Gaines. Before you started on the music video network, you were associated with some fairly high-profile cases."

Roth shrugged. "I usually donate my services to criminal investigations. Television is where the money's at, I'm afraid."

"Don't apologize. But tell me this, have your gifts ever enabled you to identify a criminal who wasn't already a suspect?"

"Sure."

"By name?"

"By initial."

"Ah. Let's see. . . . His last name begins with S or J. Right?"

Roth stared at him.

"If I look through this file, will I find out that in those cases, the eventual suspect's last-name initial is S or J? Because it's the most common last-name initial in the English language. If it turns out not to be true, it's either forgotten or you can find someone connected to the case whose last name begins with those letters."

"Perhaps I'm talking to the wrong man. Is there someone else—?"

"No. What do you want, Mr. Roth?"

"I want your department's cooperation. I think I have something to offer."

"I'm afraid that our department's cooperation

with the psychic community began and ended with Monica Gaines."

"You're not even willing to listen to me?"

"Sure, I'll listen. Why don't you start by telling me how you found out about that symbol?"

"I told you. I dreamed about it."

"Right. But have your dreams told you anything that we *don't* know? Something we can verify?"

"Not yet."

"Mr. Roth, you don't need our cooperation. Most of the crime scenes have been broken down, and you can go there yourself with permission from the property owners. There's a task force tip line you can call if you get any more insights. I'll make sure the receptionist gives it to you on the way out."

Roth nodded. "I know the drill. But you have to realize that this isn't a normal murder case, Detective. That's why I came all the way here. There are forces at work here that you don't understand. That *I* don't understand."

Joe stiffened. "What do you mean?"

"I wish I knew. Thank you for your time."

Roth reached for his folder, but Joe scooped it up first. "Mr. Roth, would you mind leaving this with me? I'd like to look it over."

"Sure. I'd be honored."

Joe stood and walked him out of the interrogation room.

Forces at work here that you don't understand.

Roth's words probably wouldn't have affected him so much if he hadn't been still reeling from hearing Angela's voice the night before.

Keep it together, man.

*   *   *

"Another glass of wine, Tess?"

Shawn Dylan motioned for the waiter. He and Monica Gaines's producer were comfortably seated in the lounge of the Buckhead Ritz-Carlton. A piano played softly in the lobby nearby.

Tess Wayland leaned back in her chair. "I really shouldn't."

"Why not? You've already taped tonight's show, right?"

"Yes, but there's still tomorrow's show, and the day after."

"You have to learn to relax."

She laughed. "I don't even know why I'm here. I don't usually do this."

"I'll bet you say that to all the guys."

"No, seriously. I don't even know your last name."

He smiled. "Maybe that's because I never told you."

"Maybe I didn't care to know. Maybe I still don't."

"Oh, you care."

She gazed at him. "You're right. What's your last name?"

"After you finish your next glass."

As if on cue, the waiter brought two more glasses of Chardonnay and took away the empties.

Tess smiled.

It was working, Dylan thought. He'd trained for this, and although it had worked for him dozens of times before, he was still amazed it was so effective. A few hours in his hotel room perusing online databases had helped him enormously. An article in *Working Woman* had told him about her background, hobbies, and extensive collection of Murano glass sculptures. He'd waited in her hotel lobby and complimented her on her crystal lapel pin, remarking on its similarity to the *Dark Mystique* sculpture he'd always admired. How could she know that he'd seen the sculpture's full-size replica in the magazine layout of her Vancouver home?

The rest had been all too easy. Just a matter of pushing the right buttons.

"Tell me about the art commodities business, Victor."

His new name. Victor Sbarge.

"My investors trust me to spot paintings and sculptures that will quickly appreciate in value," he said. "I purchase the artwork, then resell when the time is right."

"It's that simple?"

"Pretty much. There are complications here and there, but that's the essence of it. I think your job is far more interesting."

She laughed. "Interesting like a torture chamber."

"Aw, come on."

"Monica Gaines isn't your usual boss."

"Having a boss who reads your mind would be pretty unnerving."

"It's not that. It's that I'm usually the last line of defense, you know? Half the world wants to bring her down and show the other half that she's not what she claims to be."

"And *is* she what she claims to be?"

Tess was quiet for a moment. "Monica Gaines is the most amazing woman I've ever known."

"You didn't answer my question."

"She's the real thing. You can take that to the bank."

"You already have. She was quite an industry."

Tess gave him a sharp glance. "Don't refer to her in the past tense."

"I'm sorry, but she's not expected to live, is she?"

"Monica has made a career of defying expectations. Never count her out."

"I didn't mean any offense. I just know what I've been reading in the papers. I also read that you've been using psychic guest hosts while you're here in town. Are there really that many psychics around here?"

"Oh, they've been coming from all over. With all the media coverage after Monica's attack, every two-bit sideshow performer from Atlantic City to San Jose has poked their noses around here, trying to get their mugs on our show and any news program that will have them."

"Who do you have coming up?"

Tess's eyes narrowed. "Why do you care?"

"Just curious."

"I can't really discuss it."

"Sure you can."

"No, I can't." She shifted in her seat. "Maybe I'd better go."

"No more work talk, I promise."

"It's not that. I just have a lot of work waiting for me in my room."

"I could wait there while you finish."

She smiled. "I wouldn't get much work done, would I?"

"I guarantee that you wouldn't."

"Tempting, but no. It's been a pleasure, Victor." She extended her hand.

Instead of shaking her hand, Dylan lightly caressed it. "I'll see you soon, Tess. Later tonight, maybe?"

She began to draw back her hand but stopped. "That Eastern European accent of yours is going to be the death of me. Tomorrow. Okay?"

"As you wish."

He watched as she walked across the lobby and disappeared into an elevator car.

Tess Wayland was probably a blind alley, he thought. If Monica Gaines had been deceiving him, he doubted that this woman would know anything about it. Still, he had to cover his bases.

The stakes were just too high.

Dusk had fallen by the time Joe returned to his apartment. Nikki was spending the night with a friend, and although he'd been tempted to call her home, he knew he could use the time to check out his and Nikki's rooms. But what more could he do? He'd come up empty the night before. What was he missing?

He inserted his key into the front door and it turned easily. Too easily. Had he forgotten to lock it?

He walked inside. Everything was in order. No ghostly redecorating. "Nikki?" he called out.

No Nikki.

He walked toward his bedroom. Nope.

A crash behind him.

He turned to see a pudgy figure in a long gray overcoat. The man had knocked over a row of dishes on the kitchen counter drying rack. The stranger threw open the front door and bolted into the hallway.

"Stop!" Joe yelled.

He barreled through the doorway. Footsteps pounded in the dark corridor ahead.

Joe rounded another corner, then another after that. One of his neighbors was blasting a stereo, and the thunderous bass thump-thumped through the hallway.

The footsteps stopped.

Dead end, Joe thought. He hugged the wall and slid out his service revolver.

"Hands above your head and against the wall, got it? I'm a cop."

Not a sound.

Joe made his way to the end of the hall.

He listened.

Nothing. Just that heavy bass rattling the windows.

The windows. Shit.

Joe crouched low, hit the floor with his shoulder, and rolled upright with the gun aimed down the other hallway.

Crash. His prey, little more than a shadow in the dark corridor, leapt through the window.

Pieces of glass and wood framing fell as Joe ran to the window and thrust his head outside. Four stories up didn't leave much chance of—

Bammm. A blow from below.

He caught himself before he could be impaled on the daggers of glass protruding from the window frame.

His head throbbed.

His vision blurred.

He finally angled his gun down as he peered out the window. The figure had jumped to the fire escape on the building next door. He kicked in a window, and a shrill burglar alarm sounded.

The alarm obviously startled the man, as he flinched and dropped his knapsack to the street below. He watched it for a moment, then jumped through the broken window and disappeared into the dark building.

Joe stood and pulled out his cell phone.

Shit.

Half an hour later, Howe knocked on the open front door of Joe's apartment. "Jeez, Bailey. You should start leaving out snacks so all of your intruders can have something to munch on."

Joe sat at his dining table, unzipping the knapsack that his visitor had dropped. "Did the patrol cars come up with anything?"

"Nah, the guy's long gone. He got out through a ground-floor window in the building next door. At least you know this one's flesh and blood, right?"

Joe reached into the knapsack and pulled out a silver electronic instrument equipped with a bicycle-grip handle and a foot-long protruding wand.

Howe moved closer. "Is that one of your toys?"

"No. The guy dropped it."

"What is it?"

Joe turned it over in his hands. "It's a trifield meter.

It measures electrical and magnetic energy and records the data in a memory chip."

"You think maybe he ripped it off one of your neighbors?"

"I don't think so." Joe pushed a button and studied the small LCD screen on the unit's upper surface. "There's a time stamp on here. The guy was using it just before I came in."

"In your apartment? Why?"

"These things are often used to detect the presence of paranormal activity."

"You're kidding."

Joe shook his head. "Some people believe that paranormal occurrences are accompanied by surges of electrical energy that linger for hours or even weeks afterward."

"What kind of occurrences?"

"Supposed telekinetic activity, spirit visitations, you name it."

Howe squinted at the device. "And it really works?"

"Well, it does measure energy waves, but you're likely to find variances in any room. Near cell phones or microwave ovens, for instance, or near improperly shielded power lines. But it makes the believers feel more scientific, trying to measure something that can't normally be quantified." Joe put down the tri-field meter and peeled off his gloves.

Howe glanced around the apartment. "Anything missing or disturbed?"

"Nothing. It looks like someone found out about what happened here last night. I hope he came away with more answers than I have."

A sharp knock at the door. Howe answered it, and

Carla strode into the room. She was breathless. "Hi, Joe."

"Hi. Are you okay?"

Carla swallowed. "Has anyone called you yet?"

"About what?"

Carla pointed to the dining table's glass top. "Do you clean that thing often?"

"What?"

"Please. Answer me."

"Uh, sure. With an eleven-year-old in the house? I probably wipe it down a couple times a day."

"That's what I thought. The fingerprint guys got a couple of decent prints from it last night, clean off the surface. They ran them through the FBI database and got a match."

"Anybody we know?"

She hesitated. "Joe, the prints were your wife's."

9

Joe walked quickly down the white-tiled corridor that led to the forensics lab. Word must have gotten out, he thought. The cops downstairs had given him some pretty weird looks. Not that he blamed them.

Carla and Howe were with him. They had offered to drive him to the station, but Joe needed the car time to himself, to absorb what he'd just been told.

Angela's fingerprints on his dining room table. Jesus. Thank goodness Nikki wasn't around tonight, but how long could he keep this from her?

He pushed open the forensics lab doors and walked past the rows of white cubicles that bordered the room. In the back corner, Graham Martin stood at his video telescope.

Martin greeted Joe with a handshake. "I had dinner plans tonight, but I figured you'd want to see this."

"I appreciate that. What do you have?"

Martin pointed to a video screen mounted over

the console. A fingerprint appeared on the left half of the screen, magnified a hundred times its actual size. "Okay, this is the print they lifted from the glass tabletop in your apartment yesterday. The database narrowed it to four possible matches. I honestly didn't even notice the names until I eyeballed them and found the one true match."

"Angela," Joe whispered.

Martin clicked the mouse on his console and brought up another fingerprint. "This is the print of your wife's first digit—her index finger—and, as you can see, it's unmistakable. Tell me, did your wife have a criminal record?"

Joe nodded. "She was arrested sometime during her college years. A protest at an animal testing facility got out of hand, and they took her in. She was probably fingerprinted then."

Martin gestured toward another set of fingerprint slides on his console. "In the past few minutes, I think I've found another set of your wife's prints. Her thumbprint and two fingerprints were on a glass vase."

"Are you serious?"

Martin nodded. "I'm pretty sure it's another match."

Joe stared at the slides. "I really don't think she could have left these prints before she—"

Martin cut in. "These are all fresh. Skin oils are a magnet for dust particles, and there's no way that they're three years, or even three weeks, old. I would guess that they were left just a few hours before they were lifted."

Joe managed a smile. "Someone's trying to screw

with my head. And, I might add, doing a good job of it."

Martin pulled a chair from a nearby cubicle. "Here. Sit down."

Joe couldn't take his eyes from the fingerprints on Martin's screen.

Angela.

He took a deep breath.

Stay cool. Detach.

He finally turned back to Martin. "How could somebody have faked this? How would *you* do it?"

"Well, I'm not sure there's a way to—"

"*Think*. With prosthetics?"

Martin looked doubtfully at the monitor. "They would've needed access to her prints. Then they would have had to sculpt the print, taking care to re-create every ridge and every swirl, using some material with the same contact properties as human skin."

"There arc people who can transcribe pages of the Bible onto the head of a pin."

"Only after decades of practice," Martin said. "And then there's the skin oils."

"Wait a minute," Joe said. "Is it possible to extract DNA from those oils?"

"Doubtful. We've tried to do it, but it's almost impossible."

"Almost?" Joe asked.

"Even if we were able to do that, we'd need a DNA sample to match it with."

"We could get it from my daughter. Angela's mother is still alive too. You can link it with family members. That would work, wouldn't it?"

Martin shrugged. "Yes, provided we could extract a usable strand from the print, but I'm telling you—"

"Try," Joe said.

"The labs that do this kind of thing are backed up for weeks, even months. It's very expensive, and I'm afraid that the department won't authorize—"

"I'll pay for it myself. Whatever it costs."

Carla patted his arm. "Come on, Bailey. You just need some time to get your head around this one."

"I mean it," Joe said. "Be careful with those print samples. Pull any favors that you have to, but I need this."

Suzanne Morrison gave Joe a wary look. "It's not nice to keep a lady waiting."

Joe stopped in the hallway near his apartment. Shit. In all the confusion, he'd totally forgotten that he was supposed to meet Suzanne. "God, I'm so sorry. It's been a hell of a night."

"I can see it on your face. Did you hear Angela's voice again?"

"Not exactly. I'll tell you about it when we get inside." Joe pulled out his keys.

"Where's Nikki?"

"At a friend's. She's absolutely convinced that her mother was here last night. It breaks my heart."

"I thought you were keeping an open mind these days."

"I'm trying to, but I don't want to see Nikki hurt."

"How about you?"

"There are more likely possibilities that I want to explore first."

"That's why I'm here."

Joe unlocked his apartment door and walked inside with Suzanne. "Before we do anything else, let me tell you what happened." Joe told her about his visitor and the fingerprint results.

Suzanne's eyes widened. "Okay, you're officially excused for being late."

"Thanks."

"How are you holding up?"

"I'm a little shell-shocked. I don't know how I'm going to explain this to Nikki."

"If you want me to leave, we can do this another time."

"No. I'll show you where I heard the voice." He led Suzanne to his bedroom and toward the walls opposite his bed. "It came from that general direction. I couldn't localize the sound. It appeared to be shifting in space."

Suzanne reached into the paper bag she'd been holding and pulled out a small box. "I bought this at a medical supply house today. It cost me eleven hundred dollars, so it'll be going back very soon."

"What is it?"

"It's a telephone amplification device." She opened the box and showed him a thick silver object approximately two inches in diameter. "Hearing-impaired people can take it with them when they travel." Suzanne walked to Joe's desk in the corner of the room, unscrewed the telephone earpiece, and replaced the receiver unit with the one she'd brought. She screwed the earpiece back onto the phone.

"Just like that?" Joe asked.

"Yep." She pulled out her cell phone, punched two

buttons, and Joe's phone rang. She picked up the handset and balanced it on the cradle.

Joe raised his eyebrows. "I'm still on your speed dial."

"So is a pizza delivery place that went out of business three years ago. Don't read anything into it, I'm just too lazy to update this thing." She spoke into her cell phone. "Hello, Joe . . ."

The sound filled the corner of the room.

Startled, he stepped backward. "Jesus. Is there a subwoofer connected to that thing?"

"Impressive, huh?" She was still speaking into the phone. "You can adjust the timbre to almost any frequency you want. With the bass turned up, it really adds presence. Is there any chance that your phone receiver was propped up off the hook last night? Whoever it was could've dialed your number and left the connection open until you went to bed."

Joe looked at the phone. "Very clever, but I don't think so."

"Why not?"

"Nikki used this phone line to call me at the office after she and Sam found that the apartment had been rearranged. If this phone was off the hook, she couldn't have dialed out."

"There may be a way around that."

"Maybe, but it just didn't sound like this. I'm telling you, the voice didn't come from down there. It was higher up and seemed to be moving. The sound was also much more full-bodied."

Suzanne turned off her cell phone. "Too bad. I once ran into a spiritualist in Lagrange who used this setup. I thought it might have been used here."

"I'll definitely remember this if someone tries to pull it on me. Any other ideas?"

"Not offhand." She glanced around the room. "I'll give it some thought though. I'm sure I'll think of something."

"Thank you, Suzanne."

She unscrewed the telephone earpiece and repackaged the receiver. "You want it to be true, don't you?"

"What do you mean?"

"You want it to be her."

"To be Angela?" Joe looked down. "Of course. But I can't let that stop me."

"There's a way we can find out."

"How?"

She stared at Joe. "You know how."

"One of your séances?"

She nodded.

"No, I've told you before. I'll never use her like that. Her memory is too precious to me."

"This is different."

"The hell it is. What would your séance prove?"

"It might prove to you that I'm not a fake."

"No. Most spiritualists I investigate have probably done a complete rundown of Angela, hoping I'll use her. Twice I've been tipped off by private detectives—ex-cops—who've been hired by these scam artists to put together files on her. It would prove absolutely nothing."

Suzanne shrugged. "I thought you'd say that. The offer's always open."

"Thanks, but let's keep things a little more earthbound, okay?"

"If you insist."

He glanced around the apartment. "I told Nikki I'd be seeing you tonight. She was happy about it."

"She's a great kid."

"Yeah. Think maybe you'd like to get together with us sometime?"

Suzanne didn't speak for a moment. "I'm not sure if that's such a good idea."

"Why not?"

"I think we need a better idea of where we stand with each other first. If you want me as your friend, that's fine. If you want more, that's something we should discuss. But it wouldn't be fair to her if you let me get close to her and then just cut me out of your lives again."

Joe stepped close to her. "It wouldn't be fair to you either."

"No, it wouldn't."

His face was only inches from hers. "I'm sorry. You deserved a hell of a lot better than that."

"I still do."

"I know." She held his gaze. "Joe, I'm not sure—"

A sudden strong knock at the door broke into her words. Joe walked over and checked the peephole. Before he could make out who it was, a deep voice boomed, "Are you waiting on a retinal scan, boy?"

Joe unlocked the door, opened it, and was immediately locked in a massive bear hug.

He struggled to catch his breath. "Hi, Dad."

Cal Bailey drew back. He had a head of thick silver hair, a chiseled face, and a muscular physique that would have been the envy of men half his sixty-eight years. "Why didn't you call, son?"

Joe gestured for his father to enter. "About what?"

"About the fact that the Hula Hoop is coming back," Cal said sarcastically as he strode into the apartment. He stopped when he saw Suzanne. "Hello there. I hope I'm not intruding."

"Of course not," Joe said. "This is Suzanne Morrison. She's a friend who's helping me on a case. Suzanne, this is my father."

Suzanne smiled as she shook Cal's hand. "It's very nice to meet you. I was just leaving, Mr. Bailey."

"Call me Cal." He turned back to Joe. "If I'm cramping your style, too bad. I hit the road as soon as I heard."

"Heard what?"

"About your visitor, the fingerprints, everything."

Joe checked his watch. "You must have heard about the fingerprints before I did. For you to drive all the way from Savannah . . ."

"In case you've forgotten, I have connections in the department."

Joe closed the door. It made sense. Dad still had a lot of friends on the force, and it was only natural that someone would have called him. "Sorry. I didn't want to bother you with it."

"Bother? When family members help each other, it's not a bother. It's what families do, right?"

"Right."

Suzanne excused herself, motioning for Joe to call her. He closed the door behind her.

Cal smiled. "A real looker. I'll get her story later, but right now I want you to tell me about everything that happened here."

"Do you want to take your coat off first?"

"Later. Tell me what happened."

Joe told him about the strange voice, his intruder, and the fingerprint results, but it was obvious that his father had already heard about them from one of his police buddies.

Cal shook his head. "You're looking at this the wrong way, boy. Don't worry so much about *how* they did it. If you can figure out who and why, the rest will follow."

"I haven't the slightest idea *who,* and I haven't the foggiest notion *why*."

Cal shrugged. "Unless it is a spirit of some kind."

"Come on, Dad." He frowned. "You'd better not talk like that when Nikki's around."

"How's she doing with this?"

"She doesn't know about the fingerprints yet. She's spending the night with a friend. I don't know what I'm going to say to her."

"Don't worry so much about Nikki."

"How can I not? She's just a—"

"—a smart kid who's more mature than you give her credit for," Cal interjected. "You need to take care of yourself, Joe, or you'll be no good for her. You look terrible. Have you slept in the past couple of days?"

"Not much."

"Look, I'm going to stick around for a while. I have someone who can look after the theater while I'm gone. I can only imagine what this has been like for you."

"Thanks, Dad. Nikki will be really glad to see you. And—*I'm* glad too."

Cal stood. "Well, I'll get out of your hair."

"What do you mean? You're staying, aren't you?"

"I got a buddy here in town I'm staying with."

"That's crazy. It's late."

"Ah, no problem." Cal walked toward the door.

Joe followed him. "Dad, this couch folds out. Why don't you just bring in your bags, and—"

Cal opened the door and gave Joe another big hug. "I got it covered. See you in the morning, Joe."

"Well, I—"

Cal was gone.

Joe stared at the door for a moment after it swung shut. Typical Dad. The first sign of trouble, and he'd come roaring into town in hero mode. But where in hell was he going at this hour?

Haddenfield ran to the end of the hallway and blocked Donna and Paul. "What's going on here?"

Donna shifted her canvas duffel bag from her left shoulder to her right. "We quit."

Paul nodded. "Outta here, adios, and farewell, Haddenfield."

"You can't do that."

Donna jerked her thumb toward the small room where they'd been staking out Monica Gaines's hospital suite. "All your gear is in there. We're finished. If any other jobs come up in the future, please don't bother to call us."

Haddenfield held up his hands to stop Donna as she tried to push past him. "Please. Think about this. At least give me time to find replacements for you."

She shot him a frosty look. "You already have to find a replacement for Gary. Just look for two more."

"Is that what this is about? Gary?"

Paul nodded. "He could be dead or dying out there."

"We looked everywhere."

"Not everywhere," Donna said. "The police could have looked everywhere, but you didn't want to call them. In the meantime, we haven't seen the guy he was tailing since that night."

"I told you I was handling it. You are both so important right now. Don't walk out."

"It's done," Donna said.

Haddenfield's tone grew desperate. "Do you want more money? It can be arranged. Give me a figure and I'll see what I can do."

Paul cocked an interested eyebrow, but Donna elbowed him in the chest. "Don't be a whore," she said.

Haddenfield leaned closer to him. "I can pay cash."

Paul appeared to be thinking about it, but he finally shook his head. "Sorry, Haddenfield. I have a real problem working for assholes. I guess that's something I need to work on."

He and Donna moved past Haddenfield and started down the stairs.

"Shit," Haddenfield muttered under his breath. He walked back into the stakeout room and kicked the empty containers of Thai takeout from the night before.

Bastards.

They could be replaced, of course, but not without attracting even more attention from the higher-ups. They thought he was a world-class screwup already, but it would look worse if it appeared that he couldn't even keep his own team in line.

No use delaying the inevitable. He picked up his phone and punched the number.

Monica Gaines's condition was obviously deteriorating. As Joe walked into her hospital room, he was immediately hit with how much worse she looked. He'd heard that her infection was spreading, and her swollen red face had rendered her almost unrecognizable.

"She's heavily sedated," the plump nurse whispered. "The pain got to be too much."

Joe looked at the nurse, wondering if the disposable camera was still in her locker. The little bloodsucker could probably taste her cash already.

"Is she conscious?" he asked.

"In and out."

Joe walked to Monica's bedside and spoke softly. "Monica, it's Joe Bailey."

Her lids fluttered.

Joe turned back to the nurse. "Thank you."

"I really should stay here to make sure she doesn't get too agitated."

"I'll come get you if there's a problem."

"I'll just stand right back—"

"Go. Please."

The nurse gave him an annoyed glance, but left the room.

Joe looked down at Monica. Was she smiling? "Monica, can you understand me?"

She nodded.

"Monica, you've occasionally disappeared for weeks

at a time. Nobody knows where you went. Can you tell me?"

She whispered something Joe couldn't hear.

He leaned closer. "What?"

"The crate . . . big crate," she slurred.

"A crate?"

She nodded.

"What does that mean?"

She closed her eyes. "Hurts so much. Christ almighty."

"Tell me about the crate, Monica."

"Hmmm?"

"The crate. Did you take a crate with you? Was there something special in the crate?"

"I was there."

"I don't understand. Explain it to me, Monica."

"Can't."

"Of course you can."

"No."

"Monica, if there's something you're not telling me that has some bearing on what happened to you—"

"No," she whispered. "Nothing to do with that."

"Let me decide."

"No."

Joe bent closer. "You need to tell me everything, Monica. If you're afraid that I'll expose something about you, maybe that your powers aren't genuine, that's not my focus here."

"All I have," she said. "It's all I have."

"What's all you have?"

"People's . . . memories of me." Her voice was weaker. "If I die here, that's all that will be left."

"Isn't it more important that we find out who did this?"

"Don't know who did this . . . or why."

"Maybe I can figure it out. But you have to help me."

"Hurts so goddamned much."

"Monica? Monica?"

She was unconscious.

Damn. He turned around to see the nurse standing in the doorway.

"I think you'd better go, Detective."

"Right." Joe took the nurse by her arm and led her into the hallway.

"What's wrong?" she asked.

He spoke quietly. "I know about the camera and your little get-rich-quick scheme."

She feigned innocence. "What?"

"Don't even try. You gave yourself away the other day. If she dies, you'd better make it your mission to see that not one scum-sucking photographer gets a shot of her body. If I see one tabloid with a shot of her, I'm coming after you."

"I don't know what you're talking about."

"How about I pull some phone records? And should we take a look in your locker?"

"You need a warrant for that."

"I do, but your supervisor doesn't. Shall we talk to her?"

The nurse's glance sidled. "No."

"Good. Because whatever you'd make from that picture, I don't think it would be worth destroying your career. If you do that, I'll make sure you never work as a nurse again. Do you understand?"

She nodded.

"Okay. Take good care of her."

Joe walked through the hospital's dim lobby, trying to make sense of Monica's ramblings. In her state
of mind, "the crate" might have meant anything. Or
nothing. There was no way he could—

"Detective Bailey?"

Joe turned. It was Raymond Fisher, an FBI agent
with whom he'd cooperated on two previous investigations. Fisher's stony face and gruff manner alien-
ated many of his fellow agents, but Joe appreciated
his dry wit and forthright manner. "Agent Fisher. Not
here as a patient, I hope."

"Wish I was. A colonoscopy would be a hell of a
lot less annoying."

"If you say so."

Fisher showed Joe a photo of a curly-haired young
man. "Have you seen him around here?"

"Afraid not. Who is he?"

"An out-of-towner named Gary Burgess. He's been
gone a couple days now and he was last seen around
here."

"Are you working with my department on this?"

"No. We've been asked to look into it off the
record, so I'd appreciate it if this could stay just between us."

"Sure. What's his deal?"

"I don't know who he is or why they're treating
this with kid gloves, and frankly, it pisses me off. I
might be able to do my job better with a little more
information."

"Do you get this kind of assignment often?"

"Once in a while. A cabinet member's kid might go on a bender or a senator's favorite prostitute might go on an unauthorized vacation with his stolen credit cards. A few discreet phone calls will be made and it's up to us to quietly clean up their messes. But with those cases at least we know what we're dealing with."

Joe studied the photograph. "And you say he disappeared around here?"

"He was last seen in the hospital."

"Hmmm." Joe studied the photograph. "Keep me posted, will you?"

"Sure."

Joe drove from the hospital to the *Monica Gaines's Psychic World* production offices, which occupied a building that had until recently housed the headquarters for a local restaurant chain. In Tess Wayland's cluttered office, he asked her about "the crate" that Monica had mentioned.

"The crate?" Tess shrugged. "She's probably out of her head. Maybe that's what the hospital brings her orange juice in."

"Please think about it," Joe said. "I'm sure I heard her correctly. 'The crate' has no special meaning for you?"

"Nope. Sorry." She turned back toward a small video monitor. "As one of the few who have seen the real thing, Detective, give me your opinion of this."

She pressed the play button on her remote, and a grisly, slow-motion re-creation of Monica Gaines's ac-

cident appeared on the screen. The actress imperson-
ating Monica spun around, twisting and screaming as
flames engulfed her.

Joe winced. "You're kidding, right? You're not going to put this on the air."

"We will if you won't let us have a copy of the real
thing." Tess froze the image. "What do you think?
Should we strip away the color and put a time stamp
on screen, to give it that 'security camera' look? It
might be more dramatically effective that way."

"Do whatever you want, but you're not getting a
copy of the real thing. I can't believe that Monica
would want you to do this."

"If you knew Monica, you'd understand that she'd
want me to do anything that would mean higher ratings for her show. Besides, her accident is the topic of
every episode we've been doing. We have psychics
from all over the world discussing it, and we need a
visual frame of reference."

"And have any of your psychics come up with a
convincing explanation for what happened to her?"

"Several explanations, in fact. And I'm sure they'll
come up with several more."

"I'm sure."

"What's important is that her show's ratings are
higher than ever. When Monica comes back, she'll be
at an entirely new level of success."

"What if she doesn't come back?"

"I don't even want to consider that. Monica needs
positive energy, not negative."

"Fine."

"We're a day or so from going public with this, but

there's something I'd like you to comment on, Detective."

"What is it?"

"Have you been getting some kinds of visitations from your late wife?"

Joe sighed. "Where did you hear that?"

"True or false?"

"I've seen no evidence of that. Where did you get your information?"

"My sources are confidential, but you should know that every cop in your department is talking about it."

"I wouldn't make an issue of this," he said. "In the end, you're only going to look foolish."

Tess shrugged. "We take that risk every time Monica makes a prediction."

"Don't run with this story. It's nothing, and it'll only make my job more difficult."

"Maybe I'll drop it if you'll do something for me."

"Like what?"

"Get me that security tape. This re-creation really blows."

"I can't do that, and I'm not knuckling under to blackmail."

"If I don't have that tape in hand by five P.M. tomorrow, we're going public with the story about your wife, fingerprints and all."

"That's your prerogative."

"I'm not bluffing." Tess jotted something on a Post-it note. "In the spirit of cooperation, I'm giving you this." She handed it to him.

He glanced at it. Two phone numbers. "What's this?"

"The top number is for a cell phone that Monica occasionally used. It was registered to the production company. I get the bill, and I noticed that she used it a couple of times when she'd dropped out of sight. Each time, she called that second number. Maybe it'll help you figure out where she was."

"Thanks."

"Five P.M. tomorrow, Detective."

"Grandpa!" Nikki ran across the apartment and threw her arms around Cal.

He laughed. "Hiya, pumpkin. Did you actually shrink since the last time I've seen you?"

"No, I've grown!" She giggled. "You're the one who's shrunk."

"Unfortunately, that's probably true."

"Not likely. You'll always be bigger than life." Joe closed the front door.

"Why did you come?" Nikki asked. "Daddy didn't tell me you were here."

"Isn't visiting you enough?"

"Yeah, but you have the theater to run." Her eyes widened. "Wait a minute. *I* know why you're here. . . ."

Cal placed a finger over her lips. "Shhh. Not now, honey."

Joe gazed at them curiously. "What's going on?"

"It's not important right now," Cal said. "I think there's something else you need to talk to her about."

They were definitely keeping something from him. "Okay, but we're coming back to this. I don't like secrets." He sat on the couch and patted the cushion beside him. "Come sit next to me, Nikki."

Joe told her about the fingerprints that had been found and their positive match with Angela's. He didn't mention the voice he'd heard in his bedroom. One thing at a time.

Nikki didn't look surprised. "It was her," she said quietly. "Mommy was here. Do you believe it now?"

Joe shook his head. "Honey, those prints could have been faked."

"How?"

"I don't know yet."

She turned toward Cal. "What do *you* think, Grandpa?"

"I think you'd better listen to your dad. He knows what he's talking about."

She gave them both a despairing glance. "You just don't get it. I *heard* her!" She jumped up and ran to her room. The door slammed behind her.

"Should we go after her?" Cal asked.

It was what Joe wanted to do too. "No. She needs a little time to absorb this. She'll be okay." God, he hoped he was telling the truth.

"But how about you, Joe? Will *you* be okay?"

"Okay as I can be, I guess." Joe looked toward Nikki's closed door. "I never realized how tough it must have been for you, Dad. When Mom died, you had three kids, all in grade school. You must've felt like your world had ended and we could think only of ourselves."

Cal shrugged. "Because I had you kids, my world *didn't* end."

"Yeah. I don't know what I would have done without Nikki."

"We should all go out to dinner tonight. There's something I need to discuss with you."

"Is that what you and Nikki were conspiring about?"

Cal stood up, smiling broadly. "Well, I don't know if 'conspiring' is the word for it. I'll meet you back here around six, okay?"

"You're going to leave me hanging, aren't you?"

Cal winked. "Yep."

Haddenfield climbed out of his car, wishing he'd insisted on a more populous area for this meeting. He and Dylan stood on a dead-end street near Spelman College, and there wasn't a soul around. Were the students on break?

"I really don't appreciate this," Dylan said. He leaned against his rented SUV and took off his sunglasses. "I thought we were going to keep our get-togethers to a minimum."

"Where is he?"

Dylan's expression didn't change. "Where is who?"

"My team member. I know you were onto him when he disappeared."

"How could I not? He made every mistake in the book." Dylan chuckled. "I told you I'd be staying close to Monica to make sure she didn't inadvertently give anything away. You said you could control your people."

"I wasn't there when he decided to go over. Where is he?"

"Dead, I'm afraid. I had to neutralize him quickly and quietly, and that was the only way. How was I to know that he was one of yours?"

Haddenfield closed his eyes. Shit. This couldn't be happening.

"Don't get squeamish, Haddenfield. Just keep your eyes on the prize."

"What the hell are you doing here? Why don't you just leave?"

"I will when you do. Some people in my government are suspicious as to why you decided to come here. After all, we're offering you far more funding than your government has ever given you."

"I know."

"Some believe that you're here trying to produce results that will encourage your government to increase your funding. Where would that leave us?"

"You're wrong. I'm just trying to finish my study."

"That's what you told us. Just know that I'm using my time here to do some research of my own. If I find that you're lying to me, that young man won't be your team's last casualty."

Joe slipped on his jacket and turned toward Cal. "Okay, Dad, are you going to tell me the big secret?"

Cal shot a glance at Nikki.

She smiled eagerly. She'd said little since emerging from her room a half hour before, but her grandfather always had a way of perking up her spirits. "Tell him," she said.

"Okay." Cal shrugged. "I don't know why I've felt so

funny talking about this. It's no big deal, really. Except that it *is* a big deal, at least to me."

Joe wrinkled his brow. "Well?"

A knock at the door. Nikki walked over, looked through the peephole, and opened it wide.

Carla stood in the doorway.

"Carla?" Joe stood and crossed over to her. "Is everything all right? You haven't heard anything else from the crime lab, have you?"

"Uh, no." She stammered and looked at Cal. "I—I guess you haven't told him."

Cal shook his head. "I was just about to."

"Told me what?" Joe glanced between them.

They didn't answer.

Instead, Cal joined Carla in the doorway, gently took her hand, and kissed her. He turned back to Joe. "*That's* what."

Joe was speechless for a good fifteen seconds. When he regained the ability to form words, he said, "Together? The two of you?"

Cal raised an eyebrow and mock-whispered to Carla, "Sharp. Real sharp. Can't get anything past my boy. They call him the Spirit Basher, you know."

Nikki giggled.

Joe still had trouble processing it. "How long?"

Carla snuggled close to Cal. "About eight months, hon. We got acquainted when I took Nikki down to stay with him in Savannah. I went back the next weekend and pretty near every weekend after that."

"Why didn't either of you tell me?"

"That was my fault," Cal said. "I just wanted to keep a lid on it for a while. You work with Carla, and I wanted to keep things separate."

Carla smiled teasingly. "Aww, listen to that malarkey. He just didn't want to complicate things if we turned out to be nothing more than a little fling."

"That wasn't it," Cal said.

"Sure it was, big guy. I didn't mind."

Joe wondered if the shock still showed on his face. He glanced at Nikki. "You knew?"

Still smiling, she nodded.

Cal patted Nikki on the head. "Carla joined us for dinner almost every night Nikki was in Savannah. I asked Nikki to keep it our secret for a while."

"Why didn't you tell me?" Joe asked.

"I'm telling you now."

Carla touched Joe's arm. "Are you okay, hon?"

"Sure. I mean, you're two of my favorite people. I just thought you'd scarcely more than met."

Cal gestured toward the open door. "Joe, you look like you could use a steak."

"And maybe a few stiff drinks."

Carla slipped her arm through Joe's. "By the end of the evening, I might even have you talked into giving me away."

Dylan slid his key card into Tess Wayland's hotel door lock and listened as the tumblers clicked. Perfect. He'd come earlier with his modified Palm Pilot and attached reader, which was all he needed to obtain the current magnetic code. With that, it had been a simple matter to encode the silver magnetic card he always carried with him.

He slipped inside the room and locked the dead bolt behind him. He didn't think Tess would be coming back anytime soon, but he couldn't risk her catching him.

He glanced around the room, looking for any portable alarm devices or motion detectors. Such gadgets were becoming increasingly popular among professional women who travel alone. They were rarely used during the day, however, when the house-keeping staff would be running in and out. And what could possibly happen in beautiful Atlanta, Georgia?

Nothing besides a few nasty serial murders.

No alarms, no cameras, no sensors. Dylan walked toward the cluttered dresser. He rifled through a stack of papers. He would've rather taken a look around the *Monica Gaines's Psychic World* production offices, but staffers had been working around the clock since their arrival. It wouldn't be impossible to get in and take a look, but there was far less risk here.

He found a stack of notes, torn from a hotel pad, next to the telephone. He squinted to see past the coffee stains. Nothing of use, he realized. Just the usual innocuous bullshit—a pet-sitter's phone number, rental car confirmation codes, address of a local talent agency, and—

Wait a minute.

Here it was. He raised the piece of notepaper and memorized the address written on it.

Jackpot.

Cal smiled. "Hey, I think the dazed look is starting to wear off."

Joe dropped down on the sofa. It had been a

strange evening, watching his father and Carla kiss-ing, holding hands, and exchanging their private little jokes. Carla had gone home after dinner and Nikki was now in bed. "I admit to being a little surprised, but I really don't have a problem with it, Dad."

"Not even a little bit? She's younger than you are, you know."

"That doesn't make any difference. You're both old enough to know what you want. I've never seen her so happy."

"I'm happy too."

"Well, I hope it lasts this time."

"What's that supposed to mean?"

"You're not exactly the relationship-longevity king. I don't want to see her get hurt. She's not like those Savannah tourists that you romance for a week, then drop off at the airport. Carla's taking this a little more seriously than a fling."

"So am I. Hey, did I tell you that one of those nice little women wanted me to live with her in North Dakota? Poor thing was pretty upset with me when I had to decline."

"That's what I'm talking about. Carla has no short-age of admirers, but I can tell that she really likes you."

Cal's expression sobered. "I know how lucky I am. I tried to tell her she'd be better off with a younger guy, but she wouldn't believe it. Trust me, I wouldn't do anything to hurt her."

"If you do, half the department will be coming down on you. And I'll be leading the charge."

"Got it. Lecture over?"

"For the moment." Joe emptied his pockets and

placed his wallet and keys on the coffee table. He stared at the phone numbers that Tess had given him.

"What's that?" Cal asked.

"A couple of phone numbers. The top one's a cell phone that Monica Gaines used. The second is a number that she called. She had a habit of disappearing for weeks at a time, and she phoned this number a couple of times during one of those disappearances."

"Have you called it yet?"

"No, I figure I'll wait and—"

Cal snatched the scrap of paper from his hand. He picked up the cordless phone and began punching numbers.

"Dad, don't do that."

"Why the hell not? I suppose you were going to run the number through a database and get the person's name first."

"It had occurred to me."

"Takes too much time. I've always liked the direct approach better."

Joe tried to snatch the paper, but Cal held it out of reach. "Dad, this isn't your investigation."

Cal finished punching in the number. "Consider it a professional courtesy."

"It's not the way we do things anymore. Hang up now."

Cal put the phone to his ear.

"It's after eleven," Joe said. "It's too late to do this."

"No, it's the perfect time. If we wake them up, they'll be less likely to censor themselves."

"Dad . . ."

Cal held up a finger and spoke into the phone.

"Good evening, ma'am. I'm calling on behalf of Atlanta Police Detective Joe Bailey. I'm sorry for phoning so late. Can you tell me how you know Monica Gaines?" He glanced at Joe. "She's your sister?"

Joe held out his hand for the phone.

Cal nodded. "I see. Please hold for Detective Bailey."

Joe took the phone. "I'm sorry for the disturbance, ma'am. What is your name?"

The woman spoke with a slight nasal pinch that reminded him of Monica's voice. "Lesley Burge. Are you calling to tell me Monica has—"

"No. Her condition is very serious though."

"I know. My daughter's been ill and I haven't been able to get away. I'm leaving for Atlanta tomorrow."

"Ms. Burge, I'm calling because Monica phoned you at a time when she wasn't in contact with anyone else. Did you know that she sometimes disappeared for weeks at a time, and no one knew where she was?"

"No, but it doesn't surprise me. She probably just wanted some peace. Wherever she goes, people hound her. They think she's the solution to all their problems."

"For all intents and purposes, she sometimes just ceases to exist. I ran a check and there were no credit card or ATM usages during these times and no phone calls except for these few to you."

"When were the calls?"

Joe looked at the scrap of paper. "Several days during the middle of May."

The woman paused. "I'd just lost my job and I was

very upset around that time. I think she said she was on a book-signing tour."

"She wasn't."

"I'm sorry. I wish I could be more help."

"I might need to talk to you after you come into town. Can you tell me where you'll be staying?"

"The Embassy Suites Buckhead."

"Fine. Thank you for talking to me, Ms. Burge."

Joe hung up and jotted down the hotel name.

Cal wore a self-satisfied smile. "See? Sometimes the direct approach is best. With all this Internet stuff and cross-referencing with this database and that, you can strangle yourself with too much information."

"Don't do that again, Dad. You're not on the force anymore."

"Aah, I could still show a lot of those guys a thing or two."

"Yeah, you could. But instead, you decided to go buy a movie theater."

"It was the right choice."

"I think so too."

Cal pointed to the phone. "Did she tell you anything?"

"Not really. She doesn't know where Monica was or what she was doing."

"Dead end, huh?"

Joe smiled. "She may be a dead end, but Monica's cell phone isn't."

10

A soft orange glow bathed Tess Wayland's nude figure as dawn broke over the city. Dylan looked at his watch. Six-ten A.M.

"Go back to sleep," Tess whispered. She pulled on a robe and wandered over to the large windows of her hotel room.

"You can't be going to work already."

"The show isn't going to produce itself. I slept late today. You're a bad influence."

Dylan smiled. The night before, he'd been on his way out of the hotel, when Tess spotted him. "Looking for me?" she'd asked.

Another few seconds and he would've been gone.

There was dinner, drinks, more drinks, and this. Why was it always so much easier with women who didn't know who he really was and the things he had done?

"You should come to a taping sometime," she said. "It might be fun."

"Sure. Maybe Thursday?"

"Good. We'll be in a studio by then."

"At one of the local TV stations?"

"No. A building downtown has its own studio with a satellite uplink. We're leasing it from them. I told you that the other day, didn't I?"

"Oh yeah, I think you did." Dylan stood and gently caressed her neck. This was the moment that some of his colleagues might have chosen to eliminate her— one quick twist and a potential loose end would be cleanly removed.

The risk of keeping her alive was minimal, he decided. Plus, her death or disappearance would attract unwelcome attention. He still wasn't finished with his work here.

"Well?" Tess asked.

His hands fell to her waist. "Sure. Sounds like fun."

Captain Henderson stared at the report that the cellular provider had just faxed to Joe.

"They got this to you already?" Henderson asked. "Didn't they need a court order?"

Joe shook his head. "The phone is issued to Monica Gaines's production company. They faxed Tess Wayland a waiver and she signed off on it."

"Good." Henderson held up the report. "Is this any help to you?"

"It's the nearest digital relay tower to where Monica made those phone calls. She called from the same place on two different trips."

"And where's that?"

"Just outside Remington, South Carolina."

"Where?"

"That was my reaction. There used to be a military supply distribution center there, but now it's pretty much dead."

Henderson handed the report back to Joe. "So you know she's been there at least twice. You think she went there the other times she disappeared?"

"I don't know. I doubt I'll be able to find out from her. I just called the hospital, and she's unconscious. She may not live until the end of the day."

Henderson nodded. "Howe and Carla are meeting with the crime lab guys today. How far away is this town?"

"Less than two hours' drive."

Henderson nodded. "Why don't you head over there and see what you can find out?"

"Will do."

Joe rolled into Remington, South Carolina, at a quarter past two. It had been a relaxing drive, but the tension returned when he saw the depressing town. An economic bomb had obviously detonated when the army supply depot withdrew.

Closed stores. Gutted buildings. Overgrown yards. The town was in the awful final stages of decay.

Joe glanced around the pothole-ridden streets. What could have brought Monica Gaines to this place?

The one area of activity revolved around a large bar called the Funky Tusk, which had faded Africa-themed murals on each exterior wall. It sat in the middle of a large gravel parking lot that obviously had been a drive-in movie theater.

Joe parked and walked into the bar. The Africa theme was less pronounced inside, where it looked more like the generic seedy bars in south Atlanta. A half-dozen customers were scattered throughout the establishment, some playing pool, some watching a tabloid talk show on a single dim television.

Joe turned to the bartender, a thin, blond-haired boy who couldn't have been more than fifteen.

"How old are you?" Joe asked.

"Older than you think." The kid spoke with a thick southern accent. "There's no prize if you guess my age, so you may as well order somethin'."

"Diet Coke."

"All we got is regular."

"Fine." Joe pulled out a photo of Monica Gaines and showed it to him. "Seen her in here?"

The kid studied the photo but finally shook his head. "Nah, but I usually only work during the day. Is she your wife? Did she run out on you?"

"Thanks for your concern, but no, I'm with the Atlanta PD." Joe flashed his badge.

The kid put a soda in front of him. "Oh. Your drink's on the house, then. Sorry I can't help you."

A jowly, gray-haired woman leaned against the bar. "Let me see her."

Joe showed her the photograph.

The woman's face lit up. "That's the psychic lady, isn't it?"

He nodded. "Her name is Monica Gaines."

"She's been here a few times."

"Are you sure?"

"Play me a game of eight ball and I'll tell you about it."

"I'm really not a pool player."

"I could tell that about you. That's why I said eight ball. It's a beginner's game. Give the bartender your driver's license and three bucks, and I'll meet you at the far table."

Joe did as he was told, and the bartender gave him a rack of balls. Joe walked back to the table and emptied the balls onto the table. "What's your name?" he asked.

"Deanna, after Deanna Durbin. Nobody remembers her anymore, so I'm stuck with this weird name."

"It's a nice name. I'm Joe Bailey. When did you see Monica Gaines in here?"

"I've seen her a few times over the past couple of years. I thought it was her, but when I asked, she wouldn't admit it. She wore a cap and didn't have her glasses on. I was pretty sure I was right, but the other people here thought I was nuts."

Joe lifted the rack and motioned for Deanna to break. "Why was she here in town? Any idea?"

"Nope. I'd go months sometimes and wouldn't see her. I don't know why anybody would be here if they had a choice." Deanna fired the cue ball into the cluster and sunk the four. "I'm solids."

"Did she come alone?"

"Usually."

"But not always?"

Deanna set up her next shot. "The last couple times I saw her, she was with somebody. I think she met him here."

"A local?"

"Nah. I never saw him before. Or since."

"What did he look like?"

"Okay-looking guy, dark hair, slightly overweight, maybe in his mid-forties."

"Do you think they were romantically involved?"

Deanna missed her shot. "No idea. It's not like I was watching them that close. The only reason I noticed is that I thought she looked a lot like the psychic. I spent nineteen bucks on her stupid hotline once and never even got to talk to her. All I got was some lame recorded message from her, then I got patched through to some dumb-ass girl who got everything wrong. It's your shot, Joe."

He sunk the eleven ball. "When was the last time you saw her?"

"I don't know, maybe a month ago."

"That recently?"

"Yep. You know, people usually come here to have a good time. But those two never looked like they were having any fun at all."

Joe left town via Old Fenton Road. The cellular telephone tower that had relayed Monica's calls was located north of the city, so he decided to take a look in that direction before circling back and heading toward Atlanta. After his conversation with Deanna, he'd stopped in the town's two motels and one Waffle House, but no one else had seen Monica during her visits. Hopefully, Deanna wasn't just yanking his chain for a free game of pool.

Within five minutes, Joe found himself on a dusty

rural road. Fine grains of clay blew in the wind, coating his car with dark red dust. Definitely the sticks, he thought. Except . . .

A tall fence in the distance. He gunned the engine.

Barbed wire and ominous warning signs. The old supply depot.

He drove alongside the fence, looking at the overgrown fields and weather-beaten corrugated tin shelters that had once covered hundreds, if not thousands, of military vehicles. The shelters went on for miles, almost like rows of tombstones stretching into the distance.

He followed the road around a thick cluster of trees until, on the other side of the bend, he caught sight of a brown two-story building with no windows. Distinctive horizontal panels jutted out from its side. It was an older building, possibly World War II vintage. He studied it. There was something odd about its shape. It almost looked like a—

He froze as the realization hit him.

It looked like a crate.

He cut the wheel hard right and circled back to the cluster of trees. This *had* to be what Monica was talking about. An unlikely spot for a love nest, but if isolation was what she wanted, this certainly fit the bill. He parked in the shade of a weeping willow and climbed outside.

He moved through the trees and took another look at the building. The wood panels were chipped and faded, and the surrounding grounds were as overgrown as the rest of the property.

He stepped toward the chain-link-and-razor-blade fence. Much newer than anything else in the vicinity.

The depot had been deserted for eight years, but the fence still had a chrome sheen that couldn't have been more than a couple of years old. He walked around the back of the building. There was a new blacktop driveway marked with a fresh set of red clay tire tracks. The tracks had been laid since the last rain.

He walked around the perimeter, studying the ground beneath the fence. He spotted a clump of pine straw and soft earth, which he kicked with his toe. It moved easily. He kneeled and dug at the earth, opening a narrow gap under the fence. He lay on his back and pushed himself along with his legs, turning his head to avoid the sharp ends of chain-link. After emerging on the other side, he stood and glanced around.

He walked across a clearing and climbed three rickety steps that led up to the door. Nailed shut by large slats of lumber. He looked down through the steps and saw that they covered a crawlspace beneath the building. He jumped to the ground, knelt on all fours, and crept underneath.

He paused to allow his eyes to adjust. The sun was setting, and his only illumination was a shaft of light spearing through the trees. Finally he saw a pipe jutting down on the other side of the building.

He crawled toward it, trying to avoid the chunks of rock and concrete that littered the hard earth. Perspiration covered his face as he breathed in the still, musty air.

Finally he reached the pipe. He gripped it and ran his hand up to where it penetrated the floor above. He lightly fingered the hardwood floor, feeling its smooth surface. Was there a seam here? He reared back with his elbow and struck the floor. The access panel flew off, and harsh fluorescent light jutted through the small rectangular opening.

He poked his head through the panel and found himself staring into a sparkling-clean bathroom that looked brand-new. A trace of pine scented the air.

He lifted himself up into the room, moved toward the door, and pulled it open. He peeked through the opening to see a long corridor that must have run the entire length of the building. The decor was sleek, with plush carpeting, subdued colors, and ornate sconces lining the walls. What the hell was this place? He may as well have been in the offices of a high-priced Buckhead law firm.

He moved down the corridor, glancing into the open doorways as he passed. Most were gray and institutional in their appearance, with a table, a scattered few chairs, and a mirrored one-way glass at the end. They reminded him of the marketing research labs he'd visited in his college days, where for a quick fifty dollars he'd sat with focus groups and discussed cars, clothing, or soft drinks.

Farther down the hall, the rooms were more cheerfully decorated, with bright colors, rainbows, and animal prints on the walls. A kiddie version of the observation rooms.

At the end of the hall, he stepped into an area that resembled a television studio's master control center. A large control board dominated the area, facing a bank of monitors. Three video cameras on mobile tripods rested in back. He was about to continue down the corridor, when he spotted a white, glossy board marked with a schedule of some kind. The names on the grid were familiar: DAY. ISSER. IVERSON. MILLS. COHEN. GAINES.

It took him only a moment to realize that the names all belonged to well-known psychics—Butler Day, Jake Isser, Jackie Iverson, Ramona Mills, Sharon Cohen, and Monica Gaines—and this was a schedule of traditional psychic tests to be performed in various rooms in the building. Joe nodded to himself. Of course. This was a paranormal testing center. He had visited several others, including the facilities in Atlanta's Landwyn University, but nothing as elaborate as this.

"Don't move."

Joe froze.

The voice came from behind him. "Turn around. Slowly."

Joe turned and saw two men standing in the doorway. Both wore plain gray security guard uniforms, and each held a .38 leveled at his heart. "I'm a police detective," he said. "I'll show you my ID."

The shorter of the two men, whose name badge read GRIFFITH, raised his gun. "Don't move."

"Does that mean you'll take my word for it?"

"No." He glanced at his partner. "Check him."

The taller guard, whose name badge identified him as HARRIS, unsnapped Joe's holster, lifted out his gun, and patted him down before removing his wallet and badge. He flipped open the badge cover. "It says he's with the Atlanta PD."

Griffith glared at him. "This isn't your jurisdiction. You have no right to be here."

"I'm investigating the Monica Gaines case." Joe

pointed to the schedule. "She's been here, hasn't she?"

Griffith glanced at the schedule, then shoved Joe out of the room. He pulled the door closed. "This place is off limits to you."

"Why? Is this some kind of control room?"

"The whole building's off limits. Now we have to figure out what to do with you."

"I'll make it easy. Just give me my gun back and answer a few questions. Who's responsible for all this?"

"You're in no position to be asking questions."

"Fine. Why don't you tell me what position I *am* in?"

Harris nervously spoke to his partner. "He's a fuckin' cop."

"I know."

"I didn't sign on for this. What are we supposed to do now?"

"I don't know. Shit. Let me think."

Joe stared at the gun barrels trained at him. He was reasonably certain that in three quick moves he could grab one of the guns and put a bullet into its owner. But that still left the other guy free to make Nikki an orphan. There had to be a better way. He'd never shot a man and he wasn't eager to start now. "Look, you can call my captain at the Atlanta Police Department. She'll back me up."

The short guard shook his head. "You don't understand our problem."

"Then help me understand."

"Shut up." Harris glanced at his partner. "We'll put him in one of the rooms upstairs."

The tall guard nodded uncertainly. "Then what?"

"Fuck if I know."

They led Joe up a small stairwell to the second floor. More open doors. Living quarters, Joe realized, decorated with plush carpeting, beds, sectional sofas, and entertainment centers. The guards shoved him into one of the rooms and closed the door.

Joe tried the knob. Locked, of course. He surveyed the room, and it appeared to be identical to the others. A dormitory for psychics?

It was all too surreal.

Who would have the money and influence to gather a "dream team" of psychic superstars to this godforsaken place? And why?

There'd be time to wrestle with that later, Joe thought. Now there was only one problem that needed his immediate attention.

Getting the hell out.

He had one major advantage—the building obviously wasn't designed to keep prisoners. It had been originally constructed as a supply warehouse. Then, more recently, renovated as some kind of testing center.

Surely he could do this. As a struggling nineteen-year-old magician, one of his earliest stunts had been an escape from a new juvenile detention facility in Alpharetta. A friend of his father's was the warden there, and he'd agreed to lock Joe in a cell until either he escaped or the center opened for business thirty-four days later.

Joe had escaped in an hour and twenty-six minutes. Sam typed up a press release, and within days the story was in newspapers all over the country. For the first time, Joe's magic act was in demand and he was able to leave behind the birthday-party gigs and corporate shows that had been his bread and butter.

Now, after all these years, it was time for an encore.

Forty minutes later, Joe took inventory of the materials he'd gathered in his prison: approximately thirty feet of heavy-gauge video cable from the television; coils of wire unwound from a spiral notebook; a can of hair spray; a sample-size bottle of shampoo from the bathroom, and a long-handled butane fire starter from the gas fireplace. He wished he'd taken a closer look at the building's exterior before barging in, but he hadn't expected to be staging an escape.

He cut slits in two small silk toiletry bags, looped his belt through them, and deposited most of the materials inside. He coiled the video cable and hung it from his shoulder.

He glanced up at the ceiling. Probably the best way out. He was sure he could pick the door lock, but if the corridor was rigged with motion sensors and/or security cameras, the two guards would pay him a nasty visit. Up and out made more sense.

He picked up a table lamp, yanked off the shade, and stood on a chair. He tapped on the ceiling, trying to find a hollow space between the joists. Easy enough. He swung the lamp's base upward, punctured a hole in the ceiling, then clawed down several chunks of chalky white drywall. He gripped the exposed wooden joists and lifted his head into the attic. Tiny, and covered with dust and rolls of pink insulation. He'd have to crawl.

He pulled himself up. It was now dark outside, but there was moonlight filtering through air vents on each end of the attic. He glanced at the criss-crossing beams that held the roof. Better to head west, away from the full moon. The building's shadow would offer at least some cover if he made it outside.

When, not if.

He pulled the fire starter's trigger, keeping the flame ignited as he wedged the tiny shampoo bottle into the trigger guard. He put the handle into his mouth and crawled on the narrow joists. Shards of fiberglass insulation pricked his exposed skin.

Crickets chirped outside. He was getting closer.

Slow down, man. Can't let the guards hear you thumping around. Focus on the vent.

He felt the cool, damp night air. Just a little farther . . .

Finally. He was there.

He tugged at the vent.

It didn't budge.

He held up the fire starter and saw that the grille was secured by four flat-head screws. He pulled a dime from his pocket, angled its edge into the screw head, and turned. He worked it loose, then tackled the other screws until the vent grille fell silently into a clump of insulation.

He stuck his head outside. Higher than he'd thought. Thirty-five, maybe forty feet. Shit. He glanced around, looking for a security camera. It was, as he'd suspected, at the roof's highest point, only six or seven feet away. He pulled out the aerosol can and sprayed its contents toward the camera, forming a dense film over the lens.

Typical nighttime condensation, they'd think. At least, he *hoped* they'd think. He'd seen enough diffused, cloudy surveillance tapes to know that outdoor security cameras were often worthless beyond the dew point.

He tied the coaxial video cable to the nearest cross beam, then tossed the other end out of the vent opening. He eased outside, legs first, wrapping the cable around his wrists. He glanced down. A long way to fall if the cable didn't hold.

He yanked on it. It *seemed* sturdy.

Only one way to tell.

He dropped from the vent, putting all of his weight on the cable. So far, so good . . .

He lurched downward.

Just the slipknot tightening, he realized. His lifeline was holding.

He moved down, inches at a time. He hadn't realized it was so damned windy. The gusts blew him back and forth like a clock pendulum.

Forget about the wind. Stay the course. . . .

He continued to move down, hoping that the guards wouldn't spot him. Here, suspended so far over the ground, he was completely vulnerable.

End of the cable. He looked down. Only ten feet to go.

He dropped to the hard earth, rolling as he landed. He jumped to his feet and hugged the side of the building.

Silence.

He moved away, inching toward his entry point at the fence. Another few feet, and he'd be—

A loud, high-pitched alarm sounded. The entire

area suddenly flooded with white, intense light. Either they'd discovered he was gone, or he'd tripped a motion sensor.

Christ.

He bolted for the fence.

Using the distant glow of Remington as his guide, Joe moved through the dense foliage and creek beds that peppered the landscape between the town and the old supply depot. No telling how many people would be looking for him, but his chances were much better if he stayed away from the roads.

After what seemed like hours, he finally emerged on a hilltop overlooking the town. Just below him was the good old Funky Tusk bar.

He half ran, half slid down the grassy hill and threw open the front door. The place was now packed. Joe glanced around for a pay phone as he pushed through the crowd.

The same kid was tending bar. He looked Joe up and down, his eyes widening at his ripped and stained clothes. "What happened to you?"

"Never mind. Let me use your phone."

The kid plopped a cordless phone on the bar, and Joe punched a number. To his surprise, Captain Henderson answered.

"Henderson, it's me, Bailey."

She didn't sound surprised. "Are you all right?"

"Yeah, but you wouldn't believe—"

She cut in. "Are you in Remington?"

"Yes, but you don't understand. I was just—"

"I *do* understand. It's going to be all right. Where in town are you?"

Joe hesitated. Something was very wrong here.

"Bailey?"

"Yeah. It's a bar called the Funky Tusk."

"Okay, here's the drill. The guys who grabbed you will be bringing your car and personal possessions there. Are you okay to drive?"

"Uh, sure."

"Come straight here."

Joe glanced at the clock on the wall: 9:05 P.M. "I won't be there until after eleven."

"We'll be waiting for you. See you then." She hung up.

Twenty minutes later, Joe watched as his 4-Runner entered the parking lot and rolled to a stop in front of him. Griffith was driving. He climbed out and handed Joe a padded manila envelope. "It's all here. Your wallet, ID, cell phone, everything. No offense, buddy."

"*Buddy?* What the hell happened out there?"

"I have a hunch you'll find out soon enough." The man turned and cocked his head toward a white pickup truck that had just entered the parking lot. "There's my ride. Have a good night."

11

Eleven-sixteen P.M.

Joe walked into Henderson's office to see the captain, Howe, Carla, and two men he didn't recognize.

Howe gave him a thin-lipped smile. "Okay, Bailey. Is this your revenge for us dragging you along with Monica Gaines in the middle of the night?"

Before Joe could reply, FBI special agent Raymond Fisher entered the room. It had seemed like ages since Joe had seen him at Grady Memorial, but it actually had been only the previous morning. "Uh-oh. Why are you here?" Joe asked.

"I was hoping you could tell me," Fisher said.

Henderson stepped around her desk and shook hands with Fisher. "Agent Fisher, thanks for coming on such short notice." She motioned to the two strangers. "This is Craig Oka, assistant director of Army intelligence, and Derek Haddenfield, project leader. They came to us a few hours ago with some interesting information. Gentlemen?"

Oka adjusted his wire-rimmed glasses. "Thank you. I regret you were inconvenienced earlier this evening, Mr. Bailey. I trust you're okay."

Joe nodded. "Fine. Now, what the hell is going on?"

Oka addressed the group. "As you probably know, in military intelligence we try to keep ourselves open to a variety of information-gathering techniques. We conduct studies that relate to surveillance methods, persuasion strategies, polygraph technologies, you name it. From time to time, our studies also explore extrasensory techniques."

Joe half smiled. "Don't tell me you're trying to groom psychic spies?"

"No," Oka said flatly. "But if we find evidence that true psychics do, in fact, exist, it obviously would be an avenue worth exploring. Our latest project, called the Narada study, has been taking place in a former military installation in South Carolina. Mr. Haddenfield is the director of that study."

Haddenfield was clearly uncomfortable. He didn't look anyone in the eye as he spoke. "It's been going on for almost two years. We gathered several world-renowned psychics and subjected them to a variety of tests. Monica Gaines participated several times over the past eighteen months."

Howe glanced at Joe. "That's where she was all those times?"

Joe nodded. "I found the testing center today. I was locked up there most of the afternoon."

Haddenfield crossed his arms in front of him as if bracing for an attack. "There was nothing sinister going on, no government conspiracies. It was just important that we maintain security precautions."

"Even from a police detective?" Carla asked.

"It took them a while to verify that's who he really was," Haddenfield replied. "This was a classified study."

Oka stepped forward. "With no offense toward Mr. Haddenfield's work, this study is just the type of thing that brings ridicule to the military and its spending policies. We knew that we probably wouldn't find anything there, but it was an idea worth exploring."

Haddenfield's face went red with anger.

"What *were* your results?" Joe asked.

Haddenfield glared at him. "That's classified."

Oka smiled. "The findings have been inconclusive, Detective, just like all of our previous studies."

"It's still ongoing," Haddenfield snapped. "Monica Gaines cut short her last series of tests to come here and offer her assistance to your department. We've never studied a psychic in action like this, investigating a crime. So, I gathered a team and came here to observe her. We stayed even after her accident. If there was some paranormal component to her attack, it could have been worth studying. It was going well until a member of my team disappeared a few days ago at Grady Memorial."

"That's the guy I've been looking for?" Fisher asked.

Oka nodded. "Yes. I'm sorry we weren't more forthcoming with the Bureau. He was working on a classified study, and we had to decide how many people to let in the loop."

"Which is what you're doing now," Joe said. "But would you be so forthcoming if I hadn't found your testing center? Or, even more to the point, if I hadn't escaped from your testing center?"

Oka took off his glasses and wiped them. "When you were caught, the personnel at the installation immediately phoned their superiors. This has been the subject of many meetings today, and ultimately, some sort of disclosure would have been made. We were trying to decide the best way to do that when you took your leave. So, yes, your escape pressed the point. I contacted your department immediately."

Joe stared at Haddenfield. "Would you like your trifield meter back?"

Haddenfield stared at him. "I'm not sure what you're talking about."

"You broke into my apartment with a trifield meter the other night. I chased you. Surely you haven't already forgotten."

Haddenfield smiled. "I think I'd remember that."

"I have the serial number. It shouldn't be too hard to find out if that unit was sold to your team."

Haddenfield let out a long breath. "Shit. Okay, it was me."

Oka wrinkled his brow. "What's this?"

Joe jerked his thumb toward Haddenfield. "Apparently, his research project extended to my apartment. I caught him in my place a couple of days ago and chased him. I didn't get a good look at his face, but there aren't too many other people around who would be sweeping my place with a trifield meter. It's down in the evidence room."

Oka glared at Haddenfield. "Explain."

"There was some unexplained phenomena at Mr. Bailey's apartment," Haddenfield said defensively. "It might have been related to what happened to Monica Gaines, so I thought it was important to—"

"I've heard enough," Oka said. "We'll discuss this later, Haddenfield."

Henderson stared daggers at Oka and Haddenfield. "Whatever your security problems may be, we're in the middle of a homicide investigation. Frankly, we don't have time for this shit."

Joe almost smiled. Henderson was famous for her short temper, though he'd never witnessed it first-hand.

She suddenly dominated the room, although she was a good six inches shorter than anyone else. "No more secrets, no more lies, gentlemen. We're not some Podunk sheriff's office that you can push around. I do have political connections who will make your lives miserable. Do you understand?"

Haddenfield turned to Oka. "Do we need to listen to this?"

"Yes, you do," Henderson said. "And I want full co-operation from now on."

Oka nodded. "You'll get it."

"Good. You can start by apologizing to Detective Bailey. It's up to him whether he presses charges or not."

Joe turned on the radio and pulled onto West Peachtree Street. Damn, he was tired. It had been a long day, and he couldn't wait to get to bed. He'd just talked to his father, and Nikki was in bed, asleep.

Carla was there with them, and Joe had visions of walking through the door and catching them making out on his sofa.

He was too tired to care.

He'd let the military intelligence guys off the hook. Haddenfield was no different from scores of other parapsychologists he'd encountered over the years, desperate to prove that their life's work wasn't a total sham. He actually felt sorry for the guy. Oka was decent enough, and he'd handed over Monica Gaines's complete testing schedule for the previous eighteen months.

The radio was on, and a familiar melody flooded the interior of the car. It was his and Angela's song, "Verdi Cries." He hadn't heard it in a long time.

Strange. It was an old Natalie Merchant/10,000 Maniacs song, and he didn't remember ever hearing it on the radio. During the soft piano solo, he felt emotion rising in his throat.

"Hello, old friend. . . ."

The whispering voice came from behind him.

Angela's voice.

He swerved to a stop and pulled out his revolver.

"Joe . . ."

He whirled around.

No one was in the seat behind him.

The song's lyrical, almost mournful violin struck a low note.

"Be careful, Joe. . . ."

Joe squinted at the stereo speakers. Was the voice coming from there?

He finally spoke. "Careful of what?"

The song suddenly broke up, overtaken by static

and finally, an Eddie Van Halen guitar riff. He turned toward the stereo and pressed the eject button. No tape. It was tuned to radio station 96 Rock just as it always was.

He wiped his sweaty hands on his shirt.

Jesus Christ.

He gripped the wheel hard and jammed his foot on the accelerator.

"I don't know whether to be flattered or pissed," Suzanne said as she joined Joe on the curb outside her home. She held a long extension cord that stretched back to her front door.

"I didn't know where else to go," Joe said. He lay on his side and rotated the handle of his car jack. "Sorry I woke you up."

"Hey, what else was I going to do at one in the morning? Except maybe get a good night's sleep." She held up the extension cord. "Where do you want this thing?"

Joe pointed to a work light he'd placed on the sidewalk. "There. Plug that in, will you?"

She plugged it in and angled the light beneath his 4-Runner. "What exactly are you looking for?"

Joe reached into his spirit kit and pulled out a digital camera. "What am I *always* looking for? Something that isn't quite right." He took a few quick shots of the undercarriage. Everything appeared normal.

"Joe, you're tired. You said it yourself. Maybe you heard the song and it brought back some memories."

"I didn't imagine it. It was too real."

"It wouldn't be a delusion if it wasn't."

"You think I'm delusional?"

"I think you're under a lot of stress."

"What kind of spiritualist are you? I thought you wanted to convince me of this stuff."

"You won't let me convince you."

"I came here because you're the one person I know who wouldn't think I was crazy. You know what these people are capable of and how ingenious they can be."

"The psychic scam artists?"

"Yes."

"But you think I might be one of them."

He slid out from under the 4-Runner. "But I don't *know*. A year ago I would've known, but now I don't."

"Is that so bad?"

"Right now it is. I really don't think it's Angela, but every fiber of my being wants to believe it. And because of you, a tiny piece of me *does* believe it." He stared into the open hatchback, where he'd taken out the trunk panels. "Shit. There's nothing in here."

"Call the radio station."

"Right." Joe grabbed his cell phone, called information, which patched him through to 96 Rock. The nighttime deejay had never even heard of "Verdi Cries" and assured him that it had never been played on his watch. Joe cut the connection.

"They didn't play it?" Suzanne asked.

Joe shook his head. "No."

"Well, there goes the idea of the song stirring up old memories for you."

"Maybe someone was following me."

She raised an eyebrow. "Following you with a hacked radio?"

He thought it through. "Yes. A low-power CB radio hacked to transmit on the FM band. This is the only station I listen to. If they were tuned to this frequency, they could have transmitted the song, Angela's voice, everything. Low wattage, so they had to stay close by."

Suzanne nodded. "Otherwise, everyone in the neighborhood would be listening to your wife's voice. But how did they know about your song?"

"I don't know."

"Who would do this, Joe?"

"I don't know that either." He glanced back at the 4-Runner. "I don't have one single bit of proof, but it's all I can think of."

"Sounds reasonable to me."

He turned toward her. "Thanks for helping. I thought I was going a little crazy."

"If it helps any, I thought you were too." She smiled. "But I'm glad you thought of me."

"Yeah."

She stepped closer. "Can I talk you into staying?"

God, it was tempting. "It would only make a crazy day that much crazier. You wouldn't believe all that I've been through."

She took his hand. "Come inside and tell me about it."

Haddenfield slammed on his brakes to avoid being run off the road. Christ. Dylan's monstrous SUV cut in front of him and squealed to a stop. They were on a dark street in Midtown, only a few blocks from the hospital observation center.

Dylan jumped out of his SUV and charged toward him. Haddenfield opened his door. "Hold on, Dylan. Let me just—"

Dylan pulled him out and threw him onto the hood of his car. "What the fuck did you tell them, Haddenfield?"

"Nothing, I swear. I just told them what they needed to hear."

Dylan applied pressure to Haddenfield's neck. "That's what I'm afraid of."

"No," Haddenfield rasped. "Bailey found our testing center. I had to explain what Monica Gaines was doing out there."

"And the Narada Study?"

"A complete failure as far as they're concerned. I didn't tell them anything else." Haddenfield gasped for air. "Please . . . You have to believe me."

Dylan released the pressure. "You didn't talk to them about what happened to your idiot team member? About Gary?"

"I didn't tell them anything. Why would I do that? I'm practically an accessory, for Christ's sake."

Dylan fixed him with a doubtful stare. "You'd better not be lying to me."

"I'm not."

Dylan stepped back.

Haddenfield sat up, gingerly stroking his throat. "The son-of-a-bitch cop broke into the testing center. We couldn't keep it a secret anymore."

Dylan nodded. "What do you know about Joe Bailey?"

"Just that I represent everything he's against. He's

good at his job, and most psychics won't go near him."

"Monica Gaines did."

"We both know that she's a special case."

"Is Bailey a threat to us?"

Haddenfield thought for a moment. Could his answer actually get Bailey killed? It should've given him a feeling of power, but instead it just made him sick. "I don't know," he finally replied. "We should wait and see how his investigation progresses."

"We don't want to wait too long, Haddenfield."

"You never give up, do you?" Suzanne smiled at Joe as she walked into her séance room.

"I couldn't sleep."

"Well, you could have at least put on a robe. It's chilly in here." She tossed him a throw from the back of the sofa.

"I needed to cool down a little." As usual, sex with Suzanne was fiery and passionate, yet incredibly tender. He'd never felt so connected with anyone else besides Angela.

Suzanne pulled her bedsheet tighter around her nude body and sat down on the sofa beside him. "If I were a little less secure, I'd think that you bedded me down to sneak another peek in here."

Joe shook his head. "You know better than that. You've never had a problem with my unexpectedly showing up for your séances, and you've always allowed me to impose any conditions I wanted."

"You're right."

"You've even allowed me to choose the time and

location of your séances with no advance notice. Not once have you used the lame excuses that almost every other spiritualist and psychic has used on me."

Suzanne smiled. "Oh, like your negative vibes are inhibiting my abilities?"

"Exactly. I've never met anyone like you."

"I hope you're not just talking about the paranormal stuff."

"Of course not." He gently touched her cheek. "You're amazing in every way."

"I've always felt the same way about you."

"Jesus, I'm sorry I shut you out for so long."

"I'm sorry too. I wondered if I'd ever see you again."

He looked away. "When I thought there was just a one-tenth-of-one-percent chance that your abilities were real, I liked it. Thanks to you, my door was cracked open to an amazing new world."

"So what happened?"

"The more I saw you, the less I could explain."

"Couldn't stand to lose your perfect record, huh?"

"It was more than that. You threw that door wide open. I wasn't only imagining that world, I had to find a way to *live* in it. It was harder than I thought it would be. When you spend your whole life thinking one way, it's not easy to change."

"Good God, you mean you actually believe in me now?"

"Let's just say that the scales have definitely tipped in your direction."

She nodded. "Good. I'm glad for small favors."

"And thanks for helping me out with this Angela stuff. It's been . . . difficult."

Suzanne reached out and rubbed his back. "What made you come in here?"

He glanced around the séance room. "I don't know. Maybe because it's where I first started to believe in you."

"Could there be another reason?"

"Like what?"

She hesitated. "Maybe you think you can speak to Angela here."

He opened his mouth to deny it but stopped himself. "Maybe."

"Are you ready for that? Because if you are, I think I can make it happen."

He instinctively backed off. "Not yet."

"I didn't think so." She leaned her head against his shoulder. "When you're ready, and one day you will be, the offer's always open."

12

"Are you fast enough to catch me, Joe?"

He ran faster. This time he could do it. He could catch Angela.

He'd been here before, chasing her in this white, sandy desert. The sand slowed him down, but Angela glided over it, moving like the wind.

"I need you to catch me. Hurry, Joe."

He tried to say something, but he was out of breath. He needed all his energy to chase her.

He heard only Angela's voice and the sound of his own breathing. Damn, it wasn't fair. Every time he got near her, she glided out of reach.

Was she taunting him? Was she being cruel?

No, of course not. There was nothing cruel about Angela. This was a dream. The dream he'd had almost every night when Angela was in the hospital. He forced himself to open his eyes.

Angela was still there.

She was on the television, laughing as she tried on

snow skis for the first time. It was a video of their trip to Big Bear, California, only three years before she died.

He checked his watch: 5:19 A.M. He'd come home from Suzanne's a little after four, popped in the videotape, and promptly fell asleep.

"She was a beautiful woman."

Joe turned to see his father leaning against the doorjamb. "Your note said you were staying at Carla's."

"Nikki's still there. Carla's going to take her to school. I thought you'd like some company." Cal came into the room. "Been thinking about Angela, son?"

"Always." Joe stopped the video. "I just wanted to—sort out some things."

"It's nothing to be ashamed of. We all need to spend some time in the past."

Joe stood. "It's not like that. This falls under the category of research."

"If you say so. But if you want to talk, that's why I'm here."

"Thanks, Dad." His father had always been there for him. "Right now I think I just need to go to bed."

Eight-fifteen A.M.

Joe awoke to the sound of the phone ringing. He was about to answer it, when he heard his father pick up in the next room. A few seconds later, Cal rushed into his room. "Come on, Joe. We have to go to Nikki's school."

Joe sat bolt upright. "Is she okay?"

"Yes, but her day is over. *Monica Gaines's Psychic*

World just went public with your so-called visitations from Angela."

That bitch Tess Wayland. He jumped out of bed. He had to get to Nikki before the media descended on her.

"What's wrong, Daddy?" Nikki stood up from a chair in the principal's office.

Joe hugged Nikki while Cal closed the door behind them. "Sorry to yank you out of your classes, honey."

Nikki shrugged. "No prob. You saved me from having to stand up and give a report on the agricultural revolution."

"You'll make it up later."

She made a face. "Great."

"What did the principal tell you?"

"He said that you were going to take me home and that you'd tell me why when you got here."

"Honey, remember the last time I investigated a murder case and all those reporters bothered us?"

"How could I forget *that*? It sucked out loud."

"Well, it's going to happen again. Monica Gaines's TV show is doing a story about the things that have been going on."

"What things?"

"The things in our apartment. The furniture, the fingerprints, maybe even the voices."

"The voices?"

Joe nodded. How could he tell her? "After you thought you heard Mommy the other night . . . I heard something too."

"Heard *what*?"

"Something . . . that sounded like Mommy's voice."

Nikki's lower lip quivered. "I knew it was her."

"I said it *sounded* like her, not that it *was* her. There's a big difference."

"What did she say?"

"Honey, I'm sure it wasn't really—"

"What did she say?"

Joe shared a quick glance with his father. "Just some stuff about me being careful. Nothing specific, nothing that proves anything."

"She's trying to warn you."

"Warn me of what?"

"Whatever hurt Monica Gaines. Whatever hurt those other people."

"Honey, we don't know what's going on here, but I wanted to talk to you before someone else did. Monica's show just did a story about it and they uplinked it to their syndicator on a satellite. Reporters are already starting to call my precinct with questions. They may be coming after us next, so it would be best if you came home. Grandpa will look after you."

"No."

"Sweetheart, it's only until—"

"I don't want to go home. If any reporters bother me, I'll tell them to bug off."

"It's not just the reporters. When this story breaks, the other kids and even your teachers will be asking you about it."

"So what?"

"They'll ask you a lot of things about Mommy. It might upset you."

"What's to be upset about? I know she's dead. It can't get any worse than that."

"They'll ask about the voice you heard. They might make fun of you."

"If they laugh or pick on me, that's their problem. Isn't that what you always say?"

Cal chuckled. "Yeah, Dad. Isn't that what you always say?"

Joe turned toward him. "Whose side are you on?"

"Yours, when we walked in here. Hell, it was my idea to come get her. But now I don't know. The girl makes sense."

Nikki gave him a curt nod. "Of course I do."

Joe wrinkled his brow. "I still think you should come home."

"I want to stay here. Please?"

Joe sighed. Nikki could be so damned stubborn, just like her mother. "Do me a favor. Don't talk about this to anyone, not even your friends or teachers."

"What am I supposed to say?"

"Say that it's a police investigation and you're not allowed to talk about it."

Nikki picked up her canvas knapsack and slung it over her shoulder. "You're afraid people are going to think I'm crazy. You're afraid they're going to lock me up like they did Suzanne."

"She told you about that?"

Nikki nodded. "When she was a kid, she spent a whole year in a special hospital because she heard her dead friend talking to her."

"That's right." Joe pushed Nikki's hair off her forehead. She had always liked Suzanne. "But that's not what this is about, honey. I just don't want you to talk about it until we have a handle on things, okay?"

"Okay."

"Leave it to the Spirit Basher to steal my thunder," Howe said as Joe entered the squad room.

Joe shot him a quizzical look. "What are you talking about?"

Howe grinned. "I proposed to Regina this morning, and she accepted. We're getting married in May."

"Hey, that's great. Congratulations."

"Of course, you're the only one that anybody's thinking about today. Timing was never my strong suit."

"Sorry about that."

"Apologize to the public information office. All the nutty calls about you are being directed there."

Carla walked into the room. "I just talked to the feds. The Narada Study has been officially disbanded, but the U.S. Department of Defense still respectfully requests that we maintain our silence about it."

Howe rolled his eyes. "About a half-baked study that yielded zero results? Fine."

"What's Monica Gaines's status?" Joe asked.

Carla shrugged. "Hanging in there. You gotta give her credit, she's a fighter. Doctors didn't think she'd make it through the night."

"Still unconscious?"

"Afraid so."

Joe sat down at his desk. "I wish I knew who she met in that bar. There was something interesting going on between them."

"What, you don't check your voice mail anymore?"

Joe turned to see Sam walking into the room, accompanied by a uniformed officer from downstairs.

Sam hefted a thick brown package under his arm. "I called you four times yesterday. You don't think I have better things to do?"

Joe motioned for the officer to leave. "Sorry, Sam. I was kind of busy." He pointed to the package. "What did you bring me?"

Sam tossed it onto his desk. "A gift, made to your specifications. I'm still not sure about this."

Joe tore into the paper and revealed half a dozen white terry-cloth robes. "Excellent. Thanks, Sam."

Howe grinned. "More hotel robes? Are you going to model those too?"

Joe carefully rewrapped the package. "Not yet. Tonight."

"Why tonight?" Carla asked.

Joe nodded at Sam. "We need to rehearse."

"You should have given me the security tape, Bailey." A faint tone of defiance tinged Tess Wayland's voice.

"Extortion is against the law." Joe fell into step with her as she hurried down the twenty-seventh-floor corridor of the Georgia Pacific Building. He'd come from Sam's shop and was amazed to find that the *Monica Gaines's Psychic World* production offices had moved overnight. The building's conservative atmosphere was shattered by the blue-jean-and-T-shirt attire worn by the dozens of technicians and assistants.

Joe ducked to avoid a boom microphone. "I told you that there was no way you were getting that tape. Is it true that you did a reenactment with actors playing me and my daughter?"

"We usually try to get the real people for our reenactments, but I had a feeling you wouldn't be interested. We found a good match for Nikki, but I'm afraid that the man who plays you is about thirty pounds overweight."

"Oh, this just keeps getting better," Joe said sarcastically.

"He's actually quite good. The look on his face when he hears his late wife's voice gave me chills."

"Are you sure it wasn't nausea?"

"You haven't seen it yet, Detective. It's tastefully done."

"Right. Like the Monica-Gaines-on-fire reenactment?"

"That's airing on tonight's show too."

"Can't wait."

"If you came here to try to pull your story, it's too late. It's already gone out to the stations."

"That's not why I'm here. I came to give you a different story."

"I see. A little gratitude for giving you cell phone info?"

"No. Any gratitude was instantly erased when you released that story. I may be fair game, but you have no right to upset my daughter. I'd like to break your neck."

"You'd have to stand in line. So what's the story?"

"Bring a camera crew to Monica's hotel at eight-thirty tonight. You'll see then."

"Give me a hint. How do I know you're not intentionally wasting my time?"

"In order to get back at you? Not a bad idea."

She studied him for a moment. "But I don't think you're doing it now. I'll be there."

"And, by the way, don't think I'm naive enough to think that you haven't already checked out that phone number she called."

"You mean to her sister? Okay, so I put a research assistant on it. Too bad it wasn't somebody more interesting or exotic. Are you sure you can't give me some idea why I'll be paying overtime for a camera crew tonight?"

Joe stepped aside to allow a crew member and a camera dolly to pass. "No."

"I *did* get under your skin, didn't I?"

"Don't push it. Listen, while Monica was away, she spent some time with a man. Fortyish, maybe a little chubby, with dark hair. Does that ring a bell with you?"

Tess shook her head. "No, and I thought I knew most of her usual boy-toys."

"It may not have been in one of her usual haunts. I traced the connection to a small town in the middle of nowhere. She and this guy spent some time together in an out-of-the-way dive."

"Ooh, now we're getting somewhere. You *must* tell me where this happened."

"South Carolina." He shook his head. "I can't be any more specific than that. Think about it, will you? Ask around with the people who knew her."

Tess scribbled on her yellow legal pad. "Believe

me, I will. If I have my way, he'll be our guest on Friday's show."

Exactly the reaction he'd hoped for. Let the self-serving witch do a little of his work for him. "See you tonight."

Shawn Dylan walked into his hotel room and looked around. Nothing fancy, but it would do. He'd been careful to avoid any of the hotel chains that he usually patronized. He didn't think he had any rivals on his tail, but with the stakes this high, one couldn't be too careful.

Dylan flipped open his leather satchel and spread its lethal contents on the bed. He'd brought a few of his favorites. He picked up his 7.65mm Beretta Brevetto and checked the ammo cartridge. Oiled and ready. He rested it on the pillow. Four packets of blasting gelatin were contained in flat, square-shaped packages that reminded him of condom wrappers.

He picked up a wrist-strap switchblade and fastened it to his left forearm. Its fiberglass construction proved handy for avoiding metal detectors, and the triggering mechanism was much more reliable than the earlier models, which had a nasty habit of unexpectedly ejecting into the wearer's wrist. He clasped his right index finger over the trigger and watched the brandy-colored blade spring across his watchband and extend midway over his palm. He pressed again and the blade retracted.

He'd used it on Haddenfield's assistant in the hospital stairwell the other night. The poor, stupid kid.

Dylan sighed. This was supposed to be a simple

assignment. Just a trifle, his superiors had told him, while he recovered from his hellish mission in Chechnya.

Chechnya, where he'd watched a busload of his countrymen blown to bits. He could have prevented it, but it would have meant destroying months of undercover work. Excellent decision, his commander told him.

Tell that to the people on the bus.

This was supposed to be his reward. An easy, low-stress assignment.

Nothing easy about it, he thought bitterly. Especially now, when he was about to come face-to-face with a serial killer.

In a hotel room directly two floors below Monica Gaines's suite, Joe raised his arms while Sam patted down the folds in the fire-retardant bodysuit.

"How does it feel?" Sam asked.

"Snug."

"Good. If you get an air pocket, the air could heat up and burn the hell out of you. I still think you should wait for the stuntman."

"He's working on a film in St. Louis. I'll be okay."

"Did you tell Nikki you were doing this?"

"No, I didn't want to worry her."

Sam raised his index finger. "That should be your barometer. If you're thinking about doing something risky, think about whether you'd want your daughter to know about it."

"She'll see it on TV tomorrow."

"And she'll be madder than hell at you."

"Probably."

"I don't know why in hell you invited the camera crews anyway. I'd like to pitch them all down the elevator shaft."

"So would I, but the captain wants to dispel as much of this mumbo-jumbo as we can. We need to shed some light on Monica Gaines's attack."

"Torchlight?"

"Very funny." Joe uncapped a tube of Zel-Jel, a product used by welders and other laborers who worked near open flames. He smeared the gel on his face and neck.

Sam pulled a polyester cap over Joe's head and handed him a robe. "They're waiting for you outside. It's not too late to back out, you know."

Joe smiled. "You said the same thing when I did that bungee-jump–straitjacket escape from the rafters of the CNN Center."

"At least this time you won't get arrested." Sam grinned. "Now get outta here."

Joe threw open the door and saw two dozen cops, reporters, and cameramen. He squinted in the camera lights' glare.

Howe and Carla stood front and center, standing near Captain Henderson. Howe shook his head. "Now I know why you became a cop. You wanted to give performances people were *forced* to attend."

Joe shrugged. "Whatever puts bodies in seats."

"Bodies," Henderson repeated dryly. "Unfortunate word choice. Show us what you got."

"Right." Joe addressed the group. "Before Monica Gaines was injured, she thought she heard a voice.

She was taking a bath, and she reached for the one article of clothing in the room—a terry-cloth bathrobe."

Sam raised the bathrobe for all to see.

"She put it on, and the voice threatened her."

A television reporter jabbed her microphone toward Joe. "Do you know where the voice came from?"

"I'm afraid I don't. At least, not yet." Joe slid the robe over his bodysuit. "But Monica did what almost anyone else would have done—run. She grabbed the doorknob—"

Joe gripped the knob and turned it.

"—threw open the door, and ran down the hall. She punched the elevator button, then grabbed the handle for the stairwell. I'm going to retrace her steps, so please move to the other side of the elevators."

The group moved toward the elevators, where two firemen stood with large extinguishers.

Henderson's gaze narrowed on Joe. "You aren't going to do anything foolish, are you?"

"It'll be fine," Joe said. "I promise."

The spectators walked to the end of the hallway. As the cameramen set up their new positions, Sam leaned close to Joe. "You're sure about this?"

Joe smiled. "You might not want to stand so close, Sam."

Sam recoiled. "Crap. You're right." He stepped back. "You're a walking time-bomb. Get it over with, will ya?"

Joe motioned toward the firemen. They raised the long extinguisher nozzles.

Joe took a deep breath and ran down the hallway, picking up speed as he neared the elevators. He pushed the elevator button.

He turned and moved to the stairwell door, the robe's tail billowing behind him.

He reached for the steel door handle.

Ignition.

A flash of white light, then the robe burst into flames.

He whirled toward the spectators, who watched in shock. All except Tess Wayland. She was enjoying it, the coldhearted bitch, probably imagining how it would cut into the next episode's on-air promo piece.

Jesus, were those firemen just going to let him cook? In a moment, he'd be frying alive in front of all these—

The firemen went into action. Within seconds, the flames were replaced with white foam, covering him from head to toe.

The journalists and cops stared in stunned silence.

Sam rushed to his side, joining the firemen in brushing away the foam. "You okay?"

"Yeah. Just call me the Pillsbury Doughboy."

"Well, it's better than burned toast."

"Get me another robe, will you?"

"Don't tell me you're gonna do it again."

Joe peeled off what was left of the charred bathrobe. "No way." He turned toward the others. "I believe that Monica Gaines's robe was treated with what magicians call flash powder. In its usual form, it's harmless. Depending on the type used, it's activated either by heat or a low-voltage jolt of electricity."

"Are we talking about static electricity?" Henderson asked.

"Exactly. Monica Gaines's robe could have ignited when she touched her doorknob, and that may have been the plan. But she may not have accumulated enough of a charge in the short distance between the bathroom and her front door. She ran down the hallway. The elevator button is plastic, so the charge still wasn't released. She grabbed the door handle, and that's when it happened."

Tess glanced back to make sure her camera crew was getting it. "The static electricity ignited the flash powder, but you said it's usually harmless."

Joe's chest itched. He scratched himself through the bodysuit. "It is. Flash powder alone couldn't have done this. It gives off very little heat. It was used as an activator for a much more flammable compound. We soaked my robe in alcohol, dried it in the sun, then treated it with the flash powder."

Carla nodded. "So the static charge ignited the flash powder, which in turn ignited whatever compound was in the robe."

"Yes."

"Have you found anything in Monica's robe that confirms this?" Tess asked.

"Not yet. Unfortunately, there was very little left of her robe, and it could have been contaminated by the solutions used by paramedics on the scene. The crime lab is running tests."

Joe scratched his chest again. It was now more than an itch; it *burned*. He unzipped the front of the bodysuit midway down his chest and rubbed the area. Tender.

Sam's face tensed. "Joe?"

"It's okay, Sam. It's just a little—"

"Holy shit." Tess Wayland's cameraman zoomed in on Joe's bare chest.

Joe looked down at what everyone else in the hallway had already seen.

A circle with two intersecting lines.

They arrived at the Grady Memorial Hospital emergency room twenty minutes later.

"Cut it off," Joe said curtly to Dr. Taylor Grant from the examination table. "Get as much skin around it as you can."

The doctor frowned. "Relax. We don't want you to bleed to death."

Carla and Howe stood in the doorway. "We have enough samples from the murder victims," Carla said.

Joe shook his head. "Not like this one. This sample is fresh. It might make a difference, right, Doctor?"

The doctor nodded. "Possibly, but we can find out what we need to know with just a thin layer of your skin. Please relax."

"Get as much as you need."

"Don't worry. Just lie still."

The nurse injected him near the mark.

"What's that?" Joe asked.

"A local anaesthetic."

"It won't contaminate the sample, will it?"

The doctor shook his head. "No."

Joe settled back and took slow, measured breaths. The doctor leaned over him with a gleaming scalpel that reflected the large examination room lights back to his forehead. Did the doctor ever blind himself from the glare? At the moment, it was probably better not to know.

"Did you see any sign of the marking before tonight?" Howe asked.

"None. I mean, I haven't given myself a breast exam lately, but I haven't seen or felt it. Sam saw me without my shirt right before I stepped out there, and I don't think he noticed anything. It may have been brought out by the heat."

Howe nodded. "The markings on the victims almost appeared to be an allergic reaction. From what, we can't tell. There was no trace of foreign matter on the skin samples."

Joe winced as the doctor's scalpel cut deeper. Evidently, the anaesthetic hadn't taken full effect. "It could have been laid there days before. That's why I think it's important to get this one right away."

"Laid how?" Carla asked.

Joe winced again. "Don't know. Kind of hard to think with a scalpel cutting into my chest."

It took only a few minutes for the doctor to finish cutting and bandaging, but it took another quarter hour for Joe to convince Howe and Carla that he was all right.

"Come on, I'll drive you home," Carla said.

"I'll rest a little, then take a taxi."

"But I really don't think you should—"

"Get going. I'll be fine."

After several more minutes of arguing, they finally left. Good. He needed some time to himself, and there was something he wanted to do before he left the hospital. His skin throbbed beneath the bandage. How had it happened? How in hell had he gotten the death mark? The same mark that the murder victims had worn. The mark that Monica Gaines had worn before bursting into flames.

The pattern was going to stop here.

Monica Gaines. He needed to check up on her.

If she was still alive.

He took the elevator to the hospital's third floor. He flashed his badge at the nurses' station and walked to Monica Gaines's ICU room. She was alive but still unconscious.

"How are you, Bailey?"

Joe turned to see Tess Wayland standing in the hallway outside Monica's room.

"Shit. I have no comment about what you saw earlier."

"I'm not asking you for one. I have a reporter and cameraman waiting outside the hospital for that."

He was surprised she'd told him. "Thanks for the warning. Why are you here?"

"I visit Monica every day. Why are *you* here?"

"I was in the neighborhood."

Tess walked to the bed and brushed Monica's hair away from her face. "She hates it when her hair covers her ears."

"Is that right?"

Tess nodded. "Monica is the only one who has ever really believed in me, you know that?"

"Have you worked for her a long time?"

"From the very beginning. When she started her show, I'd never worked in television in my life. I was a website designer. I designed her Internet site, and when that took off, she hired me to run it full-time. Then, when she got a shot at her own TV show, she insisted that I produce it. Two syndicators passed on it because they didn't trust me to run things. Hell, *I* wouldn't have trusted a website designer from Oregon to run a national television show. But Monica wouldn't have it any other way."

"That kind of loyalty is hard to come by."

"Damned right."

Her expression was amazingly soft, Joe saw in surprise. "Is there any way I can talk you out of using the footage of my branded chest?"

She smiled. "Nope."

"Didn't think so."

"I have to ask myself, what would Monica do? No question about this one. She'd run the hell out of it."

"I'm sure you're right."

"But, as always, you're welcome to come on the show and explain it."

"Right. Which will be reduced to one weak, out-of-context sound bite followed by ten minutes of commentary explaining why I don't know what I'm talking about. I think I'll pass."

"Your call. We're having Barry Roth and Alicia Dobal on tomorrow."

"I've met Roth. So *that's* what brought him to town."

"We're starting a new series, 'In the Footsteps of Monica Gaines.' " Every day, our guest psychics are going to use articles of Monica's to try to summon up her feelings and impressions in the last days before her accident. You worked with her most closely, so it might help if you were there."

"Help *who*?"

"The psychics, of course, but you too. It might help you in your investigation."

"I seriously doubt that, but I'll think about it."

"Fine, but while you're thinking, be careful." She lightly patted his chest. "That little mark on your chest isn't exactly a good-luck sign."

Dylan sat in the dark hotel room, watching the man fumble for the light switch. Finally. Face-to-face with the monster.

The light switched on.

"Rakkan?" He snapped the cartridge firmly into his Beretta.

The man whirled around.

"Be still," Dylan said. "Do as I say and you'll live. That's a promise. If I wanted to kill you, you'd be dead already. Do you understand me, Rakkan?"

"Why do you call me . . . Rakkan?"

"That's how you think of yourself, isn't it? A modern-day Rakkan, roaming the countryside in search of a worthy man?"

"I don't know what you're talking about."

"Let's not play that game. I've known about you for weeks, and I really don't care that you're a sick fuck. I need some information, and you're in a unique position to give it to me."

"Who are you?"

"That's none of your concern. Just know that you've been closely observed on an entirely unrelated matter, and that my colleagues discovered your nasty little secret." Dylan leaned forward. "Tell me what I need to know, and you can continue your sick game. Do we have a deal?"

Early the next morning, Joe woke Nikki to tell her about his fire demonstration and the mark that had appeared on his chest. Better to hear it from him than from a reporter, he thought. He was surprised and relieved to see how calmly she took it.

"Can I see it?" she asked.

He raised his T-shirt, and she ran her fingers over the unbandaged area. "Does it hurt?"

"No. It burned a little at first, but now I don't feel anything. Honey, some people are going to be saying some strange things, but I want you to know—"

Nikki cut in. "It wasn't an evil spirit."

Joe pulled down his T-shirt. "I'm glad you realize that."

"And I know that Mommy hasn't really been talking to us, and that she didn't move things around in here."

He looked at her, puzzled. "What changed your mind?"

"I just know."

"You don't have to say that to make me feel better, honey. I know that you may still have doubts—"

"No doubts. Somebody out there wants us to think she's been talking to us. Some bad person, maybe the same person who put that mark on you. But how could they do that?"

"I don't know, but I'm working on an answer." Joe

sat on the edge of her bed. "Just yesterday, you were convinced that Mommy was trying to warn me of something. What changed your mind?"

"Well, you told me it wasn't true."

"I've been telling you that for days, but you've never believed me."

Nikki shrugged. "I feel different now."

"Why?"

Nikki shrugged again. "Can't I change my mind? I've had time to think about it. I still wish you weren't working on this case. It's scary that somebody came in here."

"Well, we got Grandpa hanging around to watch over things."

Nikki nodded. "Yeah, I'm glad. He says he can still kick your butt."

"He did, huh? Well, he's probably right. He can still kick almost *anybody's* butt."

Nikki sat up. "I need to get ready for school now. Is there anything else?"

"I guess not."

"Okay." She bounded out of her bed and turned on the CD player on her dresser.

He was clearly dismissed. He supposed he should've been happy about her sudden reversal, but it filled him with uneasiness. Nikki didn't usually change her mind so quickly.

He stood listening as she hummed the Tchaikovsky Violin Concerto along with the CD. Everything appeared normal with her.

Too damned normal.

*   *   *

Joe was only a few blocks away from headquarters when he received a call telling him to report to the second-floor conference room. He arrived to find Haddenfield sitting alone at the long table. Half a dozen large white boxes were stacked in front of him.

"Mr. Haddenfield?"

"Finally. Can I go now?"

"Pardon the lapse in communication, but why are you here?"

Haddenfield gestured toward the boxes. "The Defense Department higher-ups wanted me to bring in all the data from our time here in Atlanta. I told them there wasn't anything here of use, but they insisted."

"And why did my department want you to turn it over to *me*?"

Haddenfield shrugged. "I guess you're the contact person for all of us paranormal nutcases." He stood up. "Now, if you'll excuse me, I have a career to salvage."

"Wait a minute. Tell me what you thought you could prove by coming here to Atlanta in the first place."

"I already told you. We've been studying intelligence-gathering abilities of psychics, and when Monica left our study to assist your police department, we thought it would be a rare opportunity to study a psychic in the field."

"You had the backing of the Defense Department?"

"I was given a lot of freedom to determine the parameters of the study. Instead of the military, it was law enforcement, but it was still relevant to our project. I pulled together a team, documented the crime scenes, and followed Monica."

"And broke into my apartment."

"I'm sorry. Monica spoke of dark forces at work, then we got reports of occurrences at your apartment. I wanted to investigate. When you came home and caught me, I didn't know what to do. I knew that if I got caught, I'd probably lose my job and maybe even get prosecuted. I understand that you're the reason there have been no charges filed."

"Yet. I'd better not find out that you were the *cause* of those occurrences at my apartment."

"If that was the case, why in hell would I go back with a trifield meter?"

"My thought exactly. That's what's kept you out of trouble. What are you going to do now?"

"Don't know. Try to get another teaching job. Write a book, maybe. Hey, maybe you and I can go on some afternoon talk shows together. Kind of a point-counterpoint type of thing."

"Don't count on it."

A knock at the door. Joe's father opened it and stuck his head in. "Hi, Joe. I was just up here visiting, and—" He noticed Haddenfield. "Oh, sorry. I'll just—"

"It's okay," Joe said. "We're finished here. Thanks for bringing this by, Mr. Haddenfield. I'll call if I have any questions."

Cal stepped aside as Haddenfield hurried past him. "Everything okay, Joe?"

"Yeah. I guess you heard about my new tattoo."

Cal nodded. "Why didn't you tell me last night?"

"You were asleep on the couch, and when I woke up this morning, you were gone."

"I wanted to go over to Carla's to give her a little wake-up present, Cal-Bailey style."

"Jeez, Dad, I don't really need to hear that."

"Breakfast in bed. Get your mind out of the gutter, will you?"

"You're a fine one to talk. Anyway, Nikki was surprisingly calm about everything this morning. Any idea why?"

"She's a smart kid. After the shock wore off, maybe she just figured things out."

"Maybe."

"Plus, I think your friend really helped her work through it."

"What friend?"

"The pretty one, with the long brown hair. Suzanne."

"Suzanne talked to Nikki?"

"I thought you knew. She came over late yesterday afternoon. She showed Nikki a lot of different ways that people can make it seem like spirits are visiting. She's a smart woman. She even had this gadget that she put in the telephone handset—"

"I've seen it. I just didn't know she came over. Funny that Nikki didn't tell me."

"Well, they spent most of the afternoon together. I wasn't around for a lot of it, but I think she did a good job convincing Nikki that those things weren't necessarily spirits. She's a terrific woman, Joe. You could do a lot worse for yourself."

"Yeah, I know." He shook his head. "I can tell Nikki this same stuff until I'm blue in the face and she doesn't listen. One afternoon with Suzanne and she's now a die-hard skeptic."

"What do you expect? She's eleven. When you're that age, everybody knows more than your parents. Just wait till she's fifteen."

"I can hardly wait."

Cal motioned toward the boxes. "What's this stuff?"

"Evidence. Probably not much use for me."

Cal opened one of the boxes and pulled out a pair of polarized glasses. "Sunglasses?"

Joe looked inside and pulled out another pair. "No, actually they're stereoscopic glasses. They must have taken some 3-D pictures."

"Oh, yeah. I showed a 3-D double feature of *House of Wax* and *Creature from the Black Lagoon* at the theater last year. Gave everybody headaches. Next time I do that, I'm selling aspirin at the concession stand. I'll make a fortune."

Joe put on the glasses and picked up a stack of photographs. "Wow. Next best thing to being there."

Cal put on the other pair. "The creature never looked *this* good." He flipped through the photographs. "What am I looking at?"

"I think that's the second Spotlight Killings crime scene. These guys were pretty thorough."

Cal flipped through a few more pictures, then stopped and stared at one. "I'll be damned. Joe, I think you should look at this."

13

"Haven't you grandstanded enough this week, Bailey?" Howe grinned as he entered the conference room. Joe, Cal, Carla, and a pretty Latino woman huddled around a TV/VCR combo unit in the conference room.

Carla glanced up from the monitor. "He's got something here, Howe. Let him grandstand all he wants."

Joe gestured to his father. "Actually, my dad deserves the credit for this one. We got the materials from the Defense Department research project, and there were several high-res 3-D photographs included. He spotted Councilman Talman on a pay phone outside Monica Gaines's room, appearing to be very emotional about something." Joe handed the photograph and a pair of 3-D glasses to Howe.

Howe put on the specs and studied the picture. "So? What does this prove?"

"By itself, nothing," Joe said. "But the team was very thorough. They also got video. Although they were concentrating on Monica's room, we can see the pay phone in the hallway. I had the A/V guys zoom in on Talman and output it to a new tape. Of course, there's no sound, so that's why I brought in Maria to look at it for us."

Maria stared at the screen as she typed onto the laptop computer, occasionally pausing the tape. She was a hearing-impaired woman in her mid-twenties and possessed a remarkable ability to read lips from seemingly every angle. She didn't just read lips, she maintained; the movement of cheeks, jawline, chin, body language, and even eyebrows factored into her "reads," adjusted for the each speaker's cultural background. The department had often tried to hire her full-time, but she refused to give up her teaching post at a local school for the deaf.

Maria printed out a page from the small portable printer. Joe picked it up. "Councilman Talman was talking to someone about what happened to Monica. There's something strange here. . . . Maria is going to tell us what's going on."

Maria scanned the video back to the beginning of the call. "Okay, I have it." She spoke with only the slightest trace of a speech impediment. "Are you ready?"

"I know the zoomed-in picture is kind of fuzzy," Joe said. "I'm surprised you were able to get it at all."

Maria smiled. "You should see some of the stuff Narcotics guys have me look at. This is a breeze, Detective. Let's start at the beginning." She pushed the play button. "Okay, he punches the number and whoever he's calling answers on the first or second ring. He talks a little about Monica's condition. It doesn't look good, she's not expected to live. Here's where he starts to get angry. He wants to know if he was a pawn."

"A pawn in what?" Carla asked.

On the screen, Talman pressed his mouth closer to the receiver as if he were lowering his voice.

"He wants to know if *this* is the reason why they wanted Monica Gaines to come here, so that they could hurt her."

Howe glanced at Joe. *"What?"*

Maria nodded. "He's getting even more angry here. He thinks they used him to help bring Monica Gaines to town. Then, after she arrived, they tried to kill her."

"Who is *they*?" Joe asked.

"Whoever he's talking to. It may be only one person. Now he seems to be getting some assurances that this person had nothing to do with Monica's accident. He doesn't look like he believes it though."

"Assurances from who?" Joe asked. "Does he say a name anywhere in this call?"

Maria shook her head. "No. I watched this three times just to be sure." She pointed to the screen. "Okay, he ends the call by discussing money. Talman feels he's owed some money."

"For helping bring Monica Gaines to town?" Cal asked.

Maria nodded.

"Those tapes are documented with date, time, and location," Howe said. "I'll get someone hopping on the telephone company to print out a list of all incoming and outgoing calls to this pay phone."

Joe nodded. "And I think I need to have a conversation with our honorable councilman."

*   *   *

A ten-second call to Edward Talman's office told Joe that the councilman was attending an afternoon rehearsal of the Atlanta Youth Orchestra in Chastain Park. As he descended the concrete stairs toward the music shell, Joe thought how Nikki would have loved hearing the orchestra play free of the venue's notoriously rude and talkative audiences.

Talman stood up from his table at the front of the amphitheater. "Welcome, Mr. Bailey. Aren't they glorious?" He gestured toward the teenagers performing on the stage in front of him. "Would you like some chicken? We have plenty."

"No, thanks," Joe said. "Is there somewhere we can talk?"

"Of course. My office called and told me you'd be coming here. Thanks for keeping me in the loop." Talman turned and excused himself from the others in his party. Joe didn't recognize any of them, but he assumed they were the local movers and shakers who helped fund the Youth Orchestra.

Talman joined Joe on the next level, about fifty feet from the stage. "What's the story?" he said.

"Who paid you to bring Monica Gaines to town?" Joe asked.

Talman went pale. "Uh, paid? Why—why would anyone pay . . . ?"

"You tell me. Don't make me haul your ass into the station while all those nice people are watching."

"Shit. Don't do that. Not here, not now."

"That'll depend how cooperative you are. Who wanted Monica Gaines here?"

"I don't know what you're talking about."

"We have you on videotape talking about it." Joe flashed his handcuffs. "Are you sure you won't help me?"

Talman flushed with anger. "Snap those things on me, and I'll sue you three ways from Tuesday."

"I've always wondered what the hell that means, 'three ways from Tuesday'? Is it just me, or does that make absolutely no sense?" Joe lowered his voice. "If she dies, that could make you an accessory to murder. If I were you, I'd be scrambling to get in front of this."

"Christ almighty, it isn't like that," Talman said.

"Tell me what it *is* like."

"Maybe we can talk later in my office."

"Now. Your friends are enjoying the music. They won't miss you."

"I had nothing to do with what happened to her, you have to believe me. I honestly thought she could help you."

"You still haven't answered my question. I'm afraid you'll have to come with me."

"Wait," Talman said, glancing back at his party. "Can we be civilized about this?"

"That depends."

"Okay. Shit." Talman tightly crossed his arms in front of him. "A couple weeks ago, I got a call. I have no idea who it was. He said that he was distressed by the murders here. He suggested that we enlist Monica Gaines's help in the investigation. I was told that she had offered her services to your department."

"An offer that had already been refused," Joe said.

"Yes, but the caller suggested I use my influence to allow her to join the police force's investigation."

"How much were you paid?" Joe asked.

"It wasn't quid pro quo exactly. The caller said some nice things about my leadership abilities and suggested that a series of large contributions would soon be made to the exploratory committee to elect me as mayor."

"Which will be rolled over into campaign funds as soon as you announce your candidacy," Joe said. "That explains why you were willing to put your reputation on the line for a psychic."

"It wasn't much of a risk. We did some polling, and most voters were in support of trying anything, even a psychic, to stop these murders."

"How much were you paid?"

"Eighty thousand dollars. I'm still waiting for the last twenty thousand."

"You have no idea who this was?"

"No. The contributions came from organizations I'd never heard of. I'll give you photocopies of the checks, bank account numbers, anything you want."

"Good. I'll need all of that. Do you have any idea why they wanted her here so much?"

Talman shook his head. "To be honest, I thought it might have been her idea. You know, for the publicity. It would probably be worth more than a hundred thousand to her when you factor in TV exposure and a possible book deal."

"So you both would profit from it."

Talman shook his head. "I did nothing wrong. I believe in Monica Gaines, and I honestly thought she might be able to help your department."

"Sure," Joe said. "But somehow I doubt you would

have rammed her down our throats if you weren't being well paid for it."

Talman glared at him. "I had nothing to do with what happened to her. When she had her accident, I was horrified at the thought that I might have been indirectly responsible—"

"You thought that your mysterious benefactor may have caused it."

"Have you found him?" Talman asked. "Is he trying to implicate me?"

"Let's not worry about that. If you thought this person might be to blame, why didn't you come forward? You might have helped us."

"I had no idea who it was. I couldn't have possibly helped you any more than I can now." Talman took a deep breath and let it out. "It could have destroyed me, you know. It still can."

"I'll need the check photocopies and all supporting documentation by the end of day," Joe said. "We'll decide where to go from there."

Dylan sat in his car, parked on a grimy downtown side street. European technopop blared from the stereo. Most technicians preferred to handle explosives in total silence, but his instructors had trained him to work in the most intense, chaotic conditions imaginable. It would feel strange to construct a bomb in a deathly quiet room somewhere.

He pressed his key-chain remote and watched the firing module's activation indicator light up. Perfect.

He'd phoned his superiors and given them his recommendation. No one liked the idea of taking a life,

especially on foreign soil. Too many possible reper-
cussions, especially in this era of U.S. homeland security. Ultimately, they'd left it to him to decide. In the
old days, that would have constituted an implicit order to kill the bastard. Now, however, things were
murkier, and maybe it really meant that it was up to
him.

Whatever. All that mattered is that a man would
soon be dead.

Dylan picked up the receiver pack, climbed out of
his car, and walked toward the vehicle parked around
the corner.

"Welcome, Bailey. Change your mind about appearing on our show?" Tess Wayland adjusted her
mobile telephone headset as she walked down the
twenty-seventh-floor corridor of the Georgia Pacific
Building.

"Sorry to disappoint you." Joe fell into step with
her. "Can I persuade you to stop walking and give me
your complete attention for at least a minute?"

"I have a show that's about to tape in nine minutes."

"It's not live. Can't you delay it for a bit?"

"Nope. We have guests who are being beamed to
us via satellite. It would cost a fortune to book more
time, and there's no telling if the bird will even be
available later."

"Then I'll make this fast," Joe said. "Whose idea was
it for Monica to come here?"

"Monica's, of course."

"Why?"

"Why do you think? She thought she could contribute to your investigation."

"Did you influence anyone to accept her help here?"

Tess stopped. "What do you mean?"

"Cash. Did you pay someone locally to facilitate Monica's working on this investigation?"

"Are you serious? Monica's a star. She didn't need this. We have requests from local police departments every day, begging for her help. We certainly don't need to pay for the privilege."

"This is a high-profile case. It would get her and the show a lot more attention than most investigations."

"Let's get this straight," Tess said. "You think someone in your department was bribed to allow Monica to come here?"

"No," Joe said, "but we know that someone wanted her here very much."

"Councilman Talman."

"Someone besides him," Joe said.

"But why?"

Joe shook his head. "You tell us. If it wasn't Monica or someone in your organization, who could it be? Who would have anything to gain by her being here?"

"Besides the entire population of this city?"

"It was especially important to someone. Do you know who that might be?"

"I'm sorry, but I have no idea. I'll put it on my ideas-to-explore-for-a-future-show list though."

"*That* makes me feel better," Joe said sarcastically.

Tess paused to listen to her headset. "Gotta run.

Feel free to hang around for the taping. I have a feeling you're going to be interested in this one."

"If I stay, do you promise not to try to drag me into the show?"

"Sure."

"Okay, but I'll leave if I see a camera turning my way."

"Fair enough."

Joe walked into the studio. He'd spent relatively little time with Monica's production team, and he was mildly curious to see how the show was run.

Although *Monica Gaines's Psychic World* was normally taped before a live studio audience, the shows since Monica's accident had taken on a lower-key, somber tone, without an audience present. A guest host, usually another well-known psychic, would take the stage, introduce taped pieces, and conduct interviews relating to Monica's tragedy.

Today there were two hosts—Barry Roth, wearing the all-black outfit that had become his trademark on the music video network, and Alicia Dobal, a Cuban psychic who hurled as many insults as predictions to callers on her syndicated radio show.

The program's lead story was, of course, Joe's demonstration from the night before. As the taped piece played on studio monitors, Joe noticed many crew members staring at him. As he'd predicted, only a few seconds of the fire demonstration was shown. Most of the story centered on the mark that had appeared on his chest. Eerie music and lurid voice-overs accompanied the slow-motion images.

Tess approached him and whispered, "Nice, huh?"

He grimaced. "If I'd known my chest would be getting this kind of airplay, I'd have logged more time at the gym."

The piece ended and the cohosts discussed its significance. A warning, Roth thought. A death sentence, Alicia countered. They broke for a commercial.

"*This* is what you thought I should see?" Joe asked Tess. "I was there, remember?"

She turned, spoke into her headset, then turned back to Joe. "The next segment." She smiled. "Just wait."

Roth and Alicia walked to a small table where several personal items rested—wristwatch, scarf, keys, eyeglasses. . . .

Those eyeglasses. There was no mistaking Monica Gaines's spectacles.

The stage manager silently fingered the countdown and pointed to the cohosts. Roth spoke with grim intensity. "Ever since the mysterious and tragic occurrence that befell Monica Gaines, the world has been searching for an explanation. Earlier, we saw the theory of an Atlanta police detective that raised more questions than answers. Today, using the same psychic tools that are Monica Gaines's stock-in-trade, we're going to try to reach our own conclusions. Live from San Francisco via satellite, we have Allen Simpson standing by."

Simpson, who looked considerably older than the photograph that adorned his "Psychic Vibrations" syndicated newspaper column, smiled from the remote studio. "Hello, Barry, hi, Alicia."

Alicia smiled. "Monica Gaines was here in Atlanta,

investigating a series of brutal murders that continues to baffle local law enforcement officials. Monica sensed that there may be dark supernatural forces at work, but tragically, her investigation was cut short. Today she lies unconscious at Grady Memorial Hospital, but with our coast-to-coast panel of psychics, we're going to try to discover what she sensed in those days before her attack."

Joe stepped closer to the cohosts.

Roth spoke to Simpson in a manner that was far less cheery than his colleague. His forceful demeanor practically dared guests to disagree with his readings, and he'd been known to scream at subjects he felt were holding back from him. "Allen, we've sent you a jacket that belonged to Monica. We understand that she wore it to some of the local crime scenes here. Are you picking up anything?"

Simpson held up the jacket. "Yes, and I knew what it was even before I opened the box. The vibrations were exceptionally strong. I sense a mixture of emotions from Monica. There was fear, confusion, sadness. . . . This was a new experience for her and it was absolutely terrifying. I think she knew this case could hurt her."

Tess gave Joe a self-satisfied smirk. Tell us something we don't know, he wanted to tell her.

Alicia held up Monica's scarf and wristwatch. She pressed the objects against her forehead and closed her eyes. "Monica *was* afraid. She was afraid that this evil presence would come for her. She felt it almost immediately after arrival here. She's a brave, brave woman. . . . She knew she was in danger, but she still insisted on staying here and helping the police."

"Extraordinary," Roth said.

Alicia nodded. "Whatever force, whatever entity it is, it's still trying to claim her. There's a battle going on in that hospital bed, but Monica's will is strong. The prayers and psychic energy of the viewers is making a big difference." Alicia opened her eyes and stared at the camera. "*You* are helping to keep her in this world. Keep it up."

Roth nodded. "We all will, Alicia. Thank you." He lifted Monica's distinctive eyeglasses into camera range. "We all recognize these, don't we? Well, if it's true that the eyes are the windows to the soul, these spectacles may have come closest to mirroring Monica Gaines's thoughts and feelings in the days before her accident."

"What do they tell you?" Alicia asked.

Roth frowned. "As we've discussed on other shows, Monica Gaines has always been an empathetic woman. She felt the pain of the murder victims. She feared for her own safety, but also for the safety of others. She was especially concerned for the police detective Joe Bailey, whom we saw on the tape a few minutes ago. I believe that not only is she fighting for herself, but also for him."

Uh-oh, Joe thought. Here it comes.

"For *him*?" Alicia asked.

"Yes." Roth paused. "He's been marked by the sign that marked Monica and the murder victims. We've heard reports that Detective Bailey has been hearing unexplained voices, which was also characteristic of the murder victims. Monica felt that she might be a target, and I suspect she knows Joe Bailey might also be in danger."

"From what?" Alicia asked.

Roth held the spectacles at eye level. "She's still not sure. But she knew that she was in trouble from the first moment she—"

He suddenly dropped the eyeglasses. "Oh God. Christ almighty."

Alicia leaned toward him. "Barry?"

He was panting, trying to get his breath. "We shouldn't be doing this. This is wrong, so goddamned wrong. Stop the tape."

The crew members looked toward Tess, but she shook her head. She made a circular "keep rolling" motion with her index finger.

Sweat beaded on Roth's forehead. "Goddammit, I don't want to do this anymore. Can we please stop?"

The stage manager stepped closer. "Do you need a doctor?"

Roth shook his head. "No, it's not that."

Joe studied him. Roth reminded him of Monica's terrified reaction near the swamp. The same wild-eyed look, the same expression of horror.

Tess called out from behind the camera. "Talk to us, Barry. Tell us what you're feeling."

"This isn't a game," he said. "Whatever it is, we can't stop it."

"Can't stop what?" Tess asked.

"She first felt its presence near Ernest Franklin's house. The moon was full, and the tree branches almost seemed to be reaching for her. Now I've touched its presence, just as Monica did. I wish I hadn't." He shielded his eyes from the studio lights' glare. "Detective Bailey, are you still here? Detective Bailey?"

Joe had had enough. He turned, pushed open the studio doors, and strode down the corridor, listening as Roth continued to call his name. He scratched the bandage on his chest.

Tess ran to catch up with him. "Where are you going, Bailey?"

"Work."

"Didn't you hear him?"

"Yes. That's why I'm walking away."

"His impressions were very strong. Aren't you a little concerned?"

Joe stopped. "Concerned that there's a killer on the loose? Yes. Concerned that someone is embellishing Monica Gaines's story and using it to further his own dubious career? Of course."

"He's terrified. Practically pissing in his pants."

"I didn't appreciate the attempt to pull me into your show. I told you I'd leave if anyone—"

"Listen, that wasn't part of the plan," she said. "I'm sorry. Barry's feelings were so strong, he felt he needed to warn you."

"This scar on my chest is all the warning I need, thank you."

"You think he was faking that?"

"Are you really interested in my opinion, or was that a rhetorical question?"

"Of course I'm interested. I know there are a lot of fakers out there. Some of them have even guest-hosted our show in the past week."

"I'm glad you realize that."

"I'm a believer, but that doesn't make me stupid."

Joe glanced back at the closed studio doors. "Barry

Roth strikes me as a self-deluder. Are you familiar with that term?"

"Of course. You think he actually believes in his powers even if they don't really exist."

"Exactly. Many so-called psychic detectives fall into this category. They honestly believe that they're helping police departments when they tell them to look for bodies in wooded areas near water."

Tess nodded. "And, of course, that's where a large percentage of bodies are found."

"Yes, and when it eventually turns up in a place like that, the psychic is hailed as a hero. Too bad they can't come up with a street name, huh? Anyway, these people are subconsciously spewing out generalities that often turn out to be true. They're not trying to fool anyone, they're just trying to help. They honestly believe that they have psychic powers, when all they have is imagination and a little common sense."

"You think that's Roth's story?"

"I don't know for sure, but he seemed to believe in what he was saying. You notice that none of your three psychics gave us any objective, verifiable facts. They extrapolated on Monica Gaines's impressions and put their own spin on them."

"I noticed," Tess said. "Very disappointing. But Barry Roth has come up with very specific findings in the past."

"Well, that might make him a semi-self-deluder. Someone who believes he's psychic but does his homework, bribes morgue attendants, police secretaries, and anyone else for additional information." The elevator doors opened, and Joe stepped inside.

"Even if you think you're psychic, you still want people to take you seriously. So, you help the process along a little bit. Believe me, I've seen it."

At the far end of the hallway, the studio doors opened. Roth staggered out, helped by two production assistants.

He froze when he caught sight of Joe. The assistants tried to move him along, but he didn't budge.

Joe stared him directly in the eyes. He pressed the button and the elevator doors closed.

Joe left the building and climbed into his 4-Runner. Shit. It was his own damned fault; he never should have stuck around for the taping, especially not today. It wouldn't be the first time that his curiosity had gotten the better of him. Another goddamned thing he'd have to explain to Nikki.

He checked his watch. Lunchtime. He turned right and drove toward I-85.

Fifteen minutes later, he climbed the front stairs of Suzanne's house and rang the doorbell. She opened her front door, smiled, and pulled him inside. "Unbutton your shirt," she said.

"Cool off, will you? I'm on my lunch break."

"Very funny. Let me see the creepy mark."

Joe slung his tie over his shoulder. "You realize that you're the fiftieth person to ask me that today."

"So I'm unoriginal. Let's see it."

He unbuttoned his shirt and peeled back the bandage.

She grimaced. "Looks like you had open-heart surgery."

"I just had a thin layer of skin removed. I wanted the doctor to cut away as much as possible. It's the freshest sample we have."

Suzanne picked up a digital camera and snapped a picture.

"For your scrapbook?"

"Hardly. I want to compare this against some other skin writings I've seen."

"You have experience with this kind of thing?"

"Not exactly, but I once had a session with a spiritualist who did something like this."

Joe pointed to the mark. "Like *this*?"

"No, but letters, numbers, and even names appeared on her skin during the séance. It was pretty eerie."

He buttoned his shirt. "So how was it done?"

"It took a few visits, but I finally figured out that she had written on her skin with an allergen-laced wax just before I arrived. I met her at the door with an ultraviolet battery lamp and the letters lit up like a neon sign."

He nodded. "Clever. So her body temperature softened the wax, which then released the skin irritant."

"Yep. The letters appeared on her skin just long enough, until the next sucker came along." She put down her camera. "But, as I recall, you're not a deep sleeper."

"Not deep enough for someone to draw pictures on my chest without my knowing about it."

"No." She bit her lip. "There had to be another way."

He sat down on the sofa. "I really didn't come here

about this, Suzanne. I wanted to talk to you about Nikki."

"I saw her yesterday."

"Yeah, my dad told me. It's funny, but Nikki didn't even mention it."

"I hope it's all right. There's been a lot on TV about you and the weird stuff that's been going on. I thought it might help Nikki if I talked to her about it."

"Well, it worked. I think she's a lot better now. Thank you."

"My pleasure. She's a great kid. I like your father too."

"He didn't hit on you, did he?"

She smiled. "No. He couldn't stop talking about Carla. He's crazy about her."

"Yeah, I guess he is. Miracle of miracles. He hasn't been serious with anyone since Mom died. Thirty years."

"I'm happy for him."

"Suzanne . . ." Joe took her hand. "I may have done a terrible job of showing it, but I feel the same way about you. I'd like you to spend some time with Nikki and me. Together. We always had fun. It felt right."

"Yes, it did."

"It can be that way again. Better even, because now I know it's the way it should be."

"You're going to have doubts, you know. You're too much the skeptic to give in completely."

"Probably, but there are issues in every relationship. You know, like leaving the toilet seat up, forgetting to take the garbage out, claiming to contact the dead. . . ."

"The typical stuff."

"I know I'm not perfect," he said. "Before, when I couldn't deal with things, I just ran away from you. I promise I won't do that again."

She smiled. "You'd better be sure about this."

"I am, Suzanne." He raised her hand and kissed her palm. "I really am."

An hour later, Joe entered Sam's narrow downtown magic shop. Empty.

"Sam?"

"I'm here," Sam called from the back room.

Joe walked back. "You should really put a bell or something on your front door. Anybody could just walk in and—"

"Hello, Joe!" a two-foot mannequin shrieked.

Joe stopped dead in his tracks. Sam stood in the middle of his storeroom. Beside him was a heavyset man with puffy cheeks who was holding the dummy.

"A ventriloquist," Joe said. "You asked me here to talk to a ventriloquist?"

Sam nodded. "You wanted a sound expert, and this is the guy. Joe, meet Frank Webb."

Frank extended his free hand. "Hiya, Joe. Nice to meet you. Sam tells me you've got yourself a knotty little problem."

Joe shook his hand. "Uh, yeah. But I'm really not sure a ventriloquist is who I need to—"

"Hey, don't let the dummy throw you. I was just showing Sam my newest creation. His name is Colin."

Joe looked at the dummy. "It looks like you."

"Everybody says that, but it's purely unintentional. I was trying to make him look goofy."

"You succeeded," Sam said. "That's why he looks like you. Now, put Colin away and tell Joe what he needs to know."

"All right, all right." Frank placed the dummy in a molded carrying case. "My whole life has been about studying sound, Joe. I don't think a ventriloquist is behind your weird voices, but I still might be able to help you out."

"I'd appreciate any insight you can give me."

"There are all kinds of ways that sound can be manipulated. You've heard about ventriloquists who can supposedly throw their voices."

Joe nodded. "It's mostly about directing the audience's focus with your eyes and body language, isn't it?"

"Right. If you want to make it seem like a voice is coming from a trunk, you have to sell the idea with your expression."

"Right."

"Help! Let me out!"

Frank turned and stared at a large packing crate.

"Let me out of here, you dirty jerk!"

Joe smiled. "Very good. I didn't see your lips move."

"That wasn't him," Sam deadpanned. "That was the new kid I hired. I keep him in there between shifts."

Frank turned back to Joe. "Now, in the past few years, there have been some interesting advances in audio-acoustical research. For about four hundred bucks, you can have a pair of Dolby Digital headphones that give the illusion of five speakers around you—three front and two rear."

"All from two tiny earphone speakers?" Sam asked.

"Yessiree. Sound waves take on different charac-

teristics depending on which direction they're coming from. It has to do with the shape of the ear, the
curvature of your head, all kinds of stuff. Well, researchers discovered that by electronically altering
those waves, they can fool your ears into thinking
that sounds are coming from somewhere they're
not."

"But it still has to come from *somewhere*," Joe
said. "I scanned my room only seconds after I heard
the voice. No magnetic coils."

"Tell me, did the voice have a specific quality to
it?"

"Other than the fact that it sounded like my dead
wife's?"

"Other than that, yeah."

Joe thought. "Her voice sounded . . . thin. Hollow,
somehow. It was difficult to localize in the room, and
it seemed to be moving in space."

"Sam said you'd bring pictures. Got 'em with you?"

Joe opened a manila envelope and spread out the
photos on Sam's desk. "I have police photos of my
place, Monica's hotel room, the recording studio, and
every other place where victims claimed to hear
voices."

"Good." Frank inspected the prints.

Joe leaned over the desk. "I've never seen them all
together like this." He froze. "There's one thing all of
these locations have in common."

Frank nodded. "You mean the glass window-
panes?"

"Yes."

"Joe, I might just have an answer for you."

*   *   *

Haddenfield threw in one last box and slid the van door closed. He'd spent the afternoon packing up the observation center, and the higher-ups had been too pissed to send anyone to help him. Within a week, the testing center in South Carolina would be dismantled and he'd be on his own. Who needs 'em, he thought. Soon, with Dylan's help, he'd begin work in a state-of-the-art testing facility just outside Moscow. Funny how the Russians had always been ahead of the curve in psychic research, even when they couldn't afford to feed their people. If only his own government could be so open-minded.

Haddenfield pulled away from the curb and glanced up at Monica Gaines's hospital room window. He wanted to see her one last time, but there wasn't time. What in hell had happened to her? He'd made a horrible mistake by bringing his team to Atlanta, but he couldn't resist the opportunity to study Monica Gaines in action. Damn. If only he *had* resisted.

Fifteen minutes later, on the I-75 expressway, he glanced in the rearview mirror. A black Jeep Cherokee was behind him. He wasn't sure, but he thought it had been on his tail since he left the testing center. Shit. Was it the feds? He wouldn't put it past the military intelligence guys to put a tail on him. But why? As far as they were concerned, he was just an embarrassing failure.

He sped up. The Jeep also sped up, but not in an obvious way. It hung back several car lengths.

Was he just being paranoid?

He fumbled for his cell phone and looked at the

top panel. OUT OF SERVICE AREA. He'd used his phone here dozens of times. Either the system was over-loaded, or . . .

He looked at the Jeep again. He'd heard that drug dealers could jam nearby radio and cell phone trans-missions with a device no larger than a briefcase. It wasn't a stretch to think that a government agent would have the same capability.

Or Dylan. Had he found out?

Haddenfield stepped hard on the accelerator, but the Jeep didn't follow suit. Relief flooded through him. Maybe he *was* just being paranoid. Goddamned cell phones cut out all the time. Maybe it was just—

BLAM!

A small explosion rocked the front of the van, and the vehicle jerked hard to the right.

Haddenfield struggled with the wheel. Mother of Christ.

The side rail raced toward his windshield. No, no, no, no . . .

He crashed through the railing. Silence. Pieces of the broken railing floated in air in front of him as he hurtled downward.

Holy shit. He was going to die.

Impact.

He opened his eyes. Water everywhere, spilling into the van.

The vehicle lurched forward. He was in the river, he realized. And he was alive.

He struggled with the seat-belt latch, now entirely submerged. The smelly water tickled the underside of his chin. Jesus . . .

He gulped the one remaining pocket of air as his

van plunged entirely underwater, rolling on the way down.

He was paralyzed. Snap out of it, he told himself. Get the hell out.

He pressed on what he thought was the seat-belt latch. Nothing. He jammed both thumbs downward, pressing everything and everywhere.

Success. He pulled free of the belt and tried to see in the murky water. No dice. He felt the passenger-side window's smooth surface and struck it with the heel of his hand. It held firm. Shit.

The door. Try the freaking door.

He pulled the handle. Locked.

His lungs ached. He couldn't last much longer. . . .

This wasn't rocket science. Just unlock the god-damned door. But would the electronic locks work down here?

He fumbled for the lock and pulled. Was that the sound of the door-lock mechanism? He gripped the handle and pushed. The door was opening! A bit more . . .

He was free. He wriggled through the opening, frantically crawling for the surface.

Oh God, he thought. His lungs were starting to pump involuntarily. He might not make it.

Just another few seconds . . .

He finally broke through. Thank Christ.

He swam for shore. His leg felt numb. Cold. It was probably bleeding.

He didn't care. At least he was alive.

14

Joe, Howe, and Carla watched Haddenfield through the large observation window. He sat in Interrogation Room C, wearing a sweat suit that one of the duty officers had scrounged up for him. His hair was slicked back and his lips were trembling.

"He *wanted* to stay here?" Joe asked.

Howe nodded. "He's scared shitless."

"Of what?"

"He won't say. But he thinks we're his only hope to stay alive."

Joe studied him. Although the accident had occurred more than two hours before, Haddenfield was still shaking.

"We thought you'd want to take part," Carla said. "You wanna go in with us?"

Joe nodded. "Definitely."

They unlocked the door and silently walked into the interrogation room.

Haddenfield glanced up warily. "You're not gonna make me leave, are you?"

"We have no reason to keep you here," Howe said. "There's nothing to suggest that your wreck was anything but an accident. Accidents happen all the time."

Haddenfield glared at him. "This was no accident."

"Why do you say that?" Joe asked.

"I'm not sure I can tell you."

Howe slapped the table. "We don't have time for this shit. Tell us now, or we're tossing you back on the street."

"You don't understand," Haddenfield said.

Carla leaned close to him. "Then make us understand. What are you afraid of?"

Haddenfield threw his head back and stared at the fluorescent lights above. Tears welled in his eyes. "I can't fucking believe it. None of this was supposed to happen. I screwed up."

"We can help," Joe said.

Haddenfield shook his head. "Not likely. This is so out of your league."

"We're all that you have," Joe said. "Try us."

Haddenfield finally looked down from the ceiling. "I'm fairly new to the parapsychology field. My background is in hypnotherapy."

"Like to help people stop smoking?" Howe asked.

"Well, I was involved on the research end of it. In one of my studies, I noticed that the subjects' perceptions seemed heightened. Hypnosis affects all kinds of behaviors and thought processes, and I became intrigued by the idea that we might be able to develop psychic abilities through a series of hypnosis sessions."

"That's what you were doing at the testing center?" Joe asked.

"Yes. I convinced the Defense Department to fund the study. I spent several months working on a hypnosis program that would foster psychic abilities."

Joe wrinkled his brow. "Why did you use subjects who already professed to have psychic powers?"

"It was just one phase of the study. We thought we may be able to increase the abilities they already had, and at the same time, learn from them. If we could study them, we might pick up on things we could use on later phases of the study."

"What were the results?" Carla asked.

Haddenfield sighed. "The early findings were inconclusive. I needed more funding to develop other variations of the program, but the Defense Department wasn't willing to go that far. When the study concluded, that would have been the end of it. I couldn't let that happen."

"So what did you do?" Joe asked.

Haddenfield shifted uneasily. "Well, as you can imagine, there would be enormous interest in the world's intelligence communities for this research. A Russian operative contacted me several weeks ago, and his government promised me a large budget to continue my research. I'd be allowed to conduct my study in a place of my own choosing. They promised me everything I could ever want."

"You sold out?" Carla asked.

"Remember, by this time our government had no interest. But the Russians needed some indication that my system actually worked. Only then would they be willing to fund more studies. So . . ." Hadden-field's eyes darted anxiously. "I arranged with some of my test subjects to improve their results."

Joe stared at him in disbelief. "They went along with it?"

"Yes. Some of them are quite well known, but they've never had scientific validation. I promised to give them that if they went along."

"Was Monica Gaines one of those involved?" Howe asked.

Haddenfield nodded. "We had all the best inten-tions. It was the only way to continue my research. Can't you see how important this is?"

"So what brought you here?" Joe asked.

"The agent—his name is Shawn Dylan—wanted to see Monica Gaines in action, working on an actual case. He wanted to show his higher-ups how her newly enhanced abilities could be applied to real-world situations. He influenced Councilman Talman to press for Monica's involvement."

"Influenced with a one-hundred-thousand-dollar donation," Joe said.

"I didn't ask," Haddenfield said. "But after Monica was attacked, he was afraid that she would let on about our scheme. So he kept a close watch on her. This man caught and killed a member of my research team, but it was an accident."

"An *accident*?" Carla was incredulous.

Haddenfield shook his head. "I haven't been able to think of anything else since. I was already nervous around Dylan, but then I was terrified that he'd find out that we were lying to him." Haddenfield anxiously bit his lower lip. "I think it's happened. I think he tried to kill me tonight."

Joe, Howe, and Carla sat in silence for a moment, letting Haddenfield's story sink in.

"We're going to bring in this Dylan," Joe finally said. "And *you're* going to help us."

"You're gonna be my goddamned bodyguard, Dylan. You owe me."

Dylan sat in his car, listening incredulously to the voice coming through his cell phone. He'd triggered the charge that sent Haddenfield's car into the river, then watched as the lucky bastard swam to shore. If it hadn't been so important to make it appear to be an accident, Haddenfield would be dead now.

"Of course I owe you, Haddenfield. But why do you need a bodyguard?"

"Someone just tried to shoot me on the expressway. They blew out my tire and I lost control. I almost drowned."

Good God. It didn't sound as if Haddenfield even suspected him. "You're lucky."

"This kind of luck I can do without."

"I told you that your research might make you a target. Another nation may be close to a similar breakthrough, and they don't want you to complete your work."

Dylan paused. Was Haddenfield buying this bullshit?

"That's what I thought. That's why I need you to take me back to South Carolina."

Yes, he was buying it. "When do you want to leave?"

"As soon as possible. Can you meet me at the Georgian Terrace Hotel at six-thirty?"

"Why there? I'd suggest another place, perhaps a bit less conspicuous. How about—"

"No way. Until I'm with you, I'd feel safer there. I'll see you at six-thirty."

Click.

Dylan turned off his phone. Okay, fine. There were plenty of places to dump Haddenfield's body after they were on the road to South Carolina.

That miserable fuck. Who the hell did he think he was, stringing everybody along with his lies? Did Haddenfield really think he wouldn't eventually find out?

He'd convinced his superiors that Haddenfield represented a security risk and needed to be eliminated. He wasn't sure if that was true, but that bastard had to pay.

Dylan turned the wheel of his Jeep and headed for downtown.

Six-eleven P.M.

Joe, Howe, and Carla arrived at the intersection of Peachtree and Ponce De Leon Avenue, half a block from the Fox Theater. Special ops section commander Hank Barbour was already there with four other plainclothes officers.

Barbour squinted at Joe. The man's neck was so big that it was difficult to see where his head began. "What are you doin' here, Spirit Basher?"

"Backup," Howe cut in. "This is related to a case we're working."

"Don't worry, I'll keep him from getting into trouble," Carla said from behind Joe. He turned to see her smiling at him as she tightened the strap on her flak jacket. "Betcha you don't get this much excitement in bunco, huh, Joe?"

"So, Barbour," Carla asked. "What are *you* doing here? I thought you usually handled hostage situations."

Barbour shook his head. "I was told that our suspect may have some specialized training. They sent me to keep you children nice and safe. By the way, he's already in the lobby."

"What?" Howe said. "I thought you were going to get him before he went inside."

Barbour nodded. "Plan's changed. He managed to slip in somehow. I guess he's scoping things out. Reinertson and Clune will enter and ask him to leave with them."

Howe nodded. "And if he's not so inclined?"

"The rest of you will already be in place. We move against him in three minutes."

Dylan sat twelve feet from the front windows, scanning the faces of the passersby on the sidewalk. He was across the street from the Fox Theater, where he'd first made the acquaintance of Councilman Talman a few weeks before. Talman's favorite charity had been holding a fund-raising dinner in one of the reception halls.

Dylan shook his head. He hated politicians. It was almost enough to make a man want to—

What the hell?

Dylan leaned forward. Someone on the sidewalk had been staring at him. Staring and talking into a cell phone . . .

The man turned his back.

Dylan glanced up the street. Another man was about sixty feet away, doing absolutely nothing. Yet another man was standing casually near the corner restaurant.

Tactical positions.

He turned and glanced around. Shit. He was alone in the lobby; the area had been cleared.

The police. They undoubtedly had the exits covered. Haddenfield wasn't as stupid as he'd thought.

Dylan took a deep breath. Keep calm. As a matter of habit, he'd mapped out three possible escape routes each time he visited a new locale. It was a routine that had saved his life on many occasions. He'd automatically run through the possibilities in his first five minutes there. Christ. Now he wasn't sure if any of them would work.

Well, perhaps one.

He glanced at the elevator. A dim readout told him that it was headed downward. Another few seconds . . .

Two men walked through the lobby's main doors. They were trying to look relaxed and casual, but he could see their tense expressions.

Not to mention the slight bulges of their shoulder holsters.

The elevator car arrived with a sharp "ping," and

Dylan jumped to his feet. The two men reached for their holsters.

Showtime, boys.

Dylan bolted for the elevator, leapt through the open doors, and punched the button for the highest floor. He drew both of his guns and fired repeatedly as the cops dove for cover. The doors finally slid shut and the elevator lurched upward.

Dylan glanced around the cramped little car. How many seconds would he have until—?

The elevator stopped and the lights cut out. An emergency battery lamp switched on.

The cops had cut power to the elevator.

Precisely as he'd anticipated.

"All units, suspect has been contained. Convene to lobby area immediately."

"Copy that," Carla said into her radio. She and Joe stood in the back alleyway, near the service entrance.

"Contained, not apprehended," Joe said.

Carla drew her gun. "Guess they're waiting for us to save the day, huh?"

They ran to the lobby, where Barbour was assigning positions. "We're bringing the elevator down. Maintain your defensive positions until I give the word, got it?"

Joe and Carla took cover behind adjacent pillars. Howe nodded to Joe from behind a sofa.

Barbour turned a key in the elevator panel and stepped back. "Get ready."

The elevator chimed. Joe angled his revolver

toward the doors. After what seemed like forever, the doors finally slid open, and—

"I don't fucking believe it," Barbour cursed through his teeth.

Blood drizzled from Dylan's hands onto the carpet as he ran down the second-floor corridor. It had been simple enough to climb through the elevator's flimsy ceiling, but the steel lift cables had sliced his palms and fingers to ribbons.

He peered through a window at the alley below. A Mercedes was parked underneath. Too strong a frame. He ran to the next window. A Volvo. No good, built like a tank. A Sentra was parked beneath the third window. The perfect air bag.

He pushed open the window and leapt outside, tucking and rolling as he plummeted downward. He landed on his backside, crushing the Sentra's roof. He sat up and checked for damage. None. The car's paper-thin frame had absorbed most of the impact. Nissan hadn't let him down yet.

"Freeze!"

Dylan glanced over. A plain-looking woman leveled her service revolver at him.

He rested back on the crumpled car roof. "I think my back's broken. Jesus, I can't feel my legs."

He studied her, looking for any sign that she was lowering her guard. None so far.

She raised her gun. "Show me your hands. Now!"

He grimaced and showed her his bloody palms. His lids fluttered as if he were about to lose consciousness.

She slightly lowered her gun.

That's it, you ugly bitch. Now go for your radio.

"Keep your hands where I can see 'em," she said. She cast a glance back toward the end of the alley.

No one's there yet, little lady. It's just me and you.

Her left hand fumbled for the walkie-talkie at her waist.

Gunshots rang out from behind the hotel.

Joe's head jerked back. *Carla . . .*

He bolted from his post at the side entrance. He drew his gun and ran toward the alley.

More shots. Jesus.

Joe raced around the corner. Not Carla, please not Carla . . .

First he saw the crumpled car with the blood-soaked suspect sprawled on top. The man's head had been practically blown off, but his twitching, bloody hands still gripped a pair of Beretta automatics.

Oh God. Carla. She was bleeding on the ground, her revolver extended in front of her. "Christ," she whispered.

Blood oozed from a wound on the side of her neck. Joe tore off his jacket and pressed it against the wound. "Hang on. Help is coming." He yelled into his radio. "Officer down at the rear service entrance. Get a goddamned ambulance here!"

She looked at the body on top of the crumpled car. "Bastard faked me out. He got two shots off before I unloaded on him."

"You nailed him, Carla."

"Hard to breathe . . . can't catch my breath. God, Joe, I wish Cal was here."

"I'll call him as soon as we get you in the ambulance. Just relax."

Her lids fluttered. "I've never been shot before. I didn't think it would feel like this. . . . Hot and cold at the same time."

Joe glanced down the alley. What the hell was taking so long? "You're gonna be all right. Just fight." He tried to smile. "You don't want to get me in trouble, do you? Dad would never forgive me if he thought I didn't take care of you. He loves you, Carla."

"I love him," she whispered. "So much . . ."

Cal sat quietly in the waiting area of the hospital emergency room, staring at the tiled floor. To Joe, it looked as if his father had aged twenty years in the hour and a half since he'd been told about Carla.

"It's taking a long time," Cal said.

"She's in surgery. It could be hours."

Cal glanced around the waiting room, crowded with over a dozen cops. Several more were standing outside. "Looks like half the force is here."

"Carla's a special person. I don't know anybody who's better-liked than she is."

"All those years that your mother worried about me, I never had any idea what she went through. These past few months, whenever I've known that Carla was on a shift, my stomach's been in knots. I don't know how your mother took it."

"She took it because she knew you loved your work. Just like Carla loves hers."

"Carla's the real thing, Joe. She's all I need for the rest of my life."

"I know."

"I always thought your mother would outlive me. It never occurred to me that it could happen any other way. When she was taken from us, I thought it was such a cruel trick." He hit his knee with his fist. "How in hell could it happen again? Not to Carla. She's so young, she doesn't deserve it."

"I thought the same thing when Angela died. I wish I had the answers."

Howe walked into the waiting room. "They think they've found the suspect's car. It's on West Peachtree, a few blocks from the Georgian Terrace."

Joe stood. "Any idea who he was?"

"No. He had no ID on him, and the car's a rental. The fingerprint guys are dusting it now. Wanna go over and have a look?"

Joe glanced at his father. "Not right now. I'd better stay here and—"

"Go," Cal said. "Find out why that bastard did this. Make some sense of it."

"Are you sure?"

"Yes. If I need moral support, I have about twenty of Atlanta's finest here to back me up."

Joe peered into the rear window of the Jeep Cherokee. It was parked near the AT&T building on West Peachtree Street. "Any info on the renter?"

Howe checked his notebook. "Jonathan Hemet, which matches the New York driver's license we found in the glove compartment. We ran a check on it, and it's a fake."

Joe nodded. "Have they printed the corpse yet?"

Howe nodded. "The hands are cut up pretty bad, but forensics thinks they can get enough to work with."

Joe walked around to the open passenger-side door and pointed to a pile of books on the floor. "Has anybody looked at those?"

"Only to dust for prints. Looks like Oriental folklore stuff. Could we be lucky enough to have nailed the Spotlight Killer?"

"Doubtful. The killer's been doing this for years, and these books look brand-new. This guy may have known something though. Anything else?"

"A laptop computer."

"Where is it?"

"Ask your pal Fisher."

"*FBI* Fisher?"

"He and some fed technogeek are in that white car three spaces behind us. Maybe they'll let *you* in on the secret."

Joe walked back to the white Ford Taurus, where Fisher and a young bushy-haired man sat in the front seat. Joe rapped on the rear passenger-side window. The doors unlocked, and Joe climbed in back. "I thought you guys were off this investigation."

"Detective Joe Bailey, meet Special Agent Dorn Whitaker."

Whitaker never took his eyes from the notebook computer screen. He raised his hand in greeting.

Joe crossed his arms over the seat backs. "What the hell is going on, Fisher?"

"We've decided to take a closer look at this guy. If he killed someone who was engaged in a Defense Department research project, it could possibly fall under the purview of national security. You should have told us you were on to him. My feelings are hurt, Bailey. You know what a sensitive soul I am."

"Yeah, and by the time you went through all the channels with the Bureau and the CIA, he might have gotten away. We know he killed the kid at the hospital, and we didn't feel like waiting."

Fisher nodded. "How's your officer?"

"Fighting for her life. We want that computer."

"Won't do you any good," Whitaker said. "Everything's encrypted."

Joe shrugged. "We have people who can get around that."

"Not like *our* people," Fisher said.

Whitaker made a face. "Actually, *our* people may have a problem with this one. This is a high-level encryption scheme. I've never seen anything like it."

Fisher glanced at the screen. "Surely there's some way—"

"I'm sure there is, but we have to be careful. If we go about this the wrong way, the hard drive may wipe itself clean. We need to take this in."

Fisher turned back to Joe. "My boss has already spoken to your boss. We're taking the computer, but I promise we'll keep you in the loop." He paused. "I know what it's like to lose a fellow officer."

Joe opened the car door and climbed out. "We haven't lost her yet."

*   *   *

Joe drove back to the hospital and walked past the off-duty cops chain-smoking on the sidewalk outside the emergency room's large double doors. No news yet, they told him. Inside, his father was surrounded by officers who were doing a good job offering him comfort and companionship.

"Why didn't you tell me that your father was such an attractive man?"

Joe turned to see Tess Wayland. Just what he needed. "Ms. Wayland, I'm really not in the mood—"

"Relax, I'm off the clock. I heard about what happened, so I came by with some food." She motioned toward dozens of containers resting on chairs. "It's from Mick's. About five hundred dollars' worth, courtesy of *Monica Gaines's Psychic World*. I think there's still some good stuff left."

"That's very generous," he said warily.

"Just our way of showing our appreciation to the Atlanta PD. By the way, Monica has taken a turn for the better."

"Are you serious?"

"Yes. She's not out of the woods yet, but it looks like her body is fighting the infection. The doctors say it's a miracle."

"Well, you always said that miracles were her stock-in-trade." Joe glanced back at his father. "If she has any left over, we can sure use one down here."

An hour later, Dr. Dale Fuller emerged. His expression was not encouraging.

Cal moistened his lips. "I hope the news is better than the look on your face, Doctor. Well?"

"She survived surgery, but it wasn't easy for her. Her heart stopped on the table. She was nicked on the anterior branch of the external jugular, and she lost quite a bit of blood."

Cal's voice wavered. "What's the prognosis?"

"Difficult to say. If she survives, it could be a long recovery."

"*If* she survives?" Cal said. "You make sure that she comes out of this. She has to live. *When* she comes out, I'll take care of her. However long it takes."

"It could be a long road back. She's in recovery right now, and as soon as she's stable, we'll move her up to ICU. You can see her then. Does she have any family?"

"A sister in Savannah," Cal said. "She's on her way."

"Good. If she has any questions, I'll be available to talk to her." The doctor gave them directions to Carla's ICU room and left.

Joe checked his watch. "Dad, I have to pick up Nikki. She's staying with a friend, and I don't want her hearing about this from someone else. Do you want me to bring her back here?"

"No, hospitals scare Nikki. Too many bad memories. Take her home and talk to her."

"Can I get you anything?"

"My toiletries kit and a change of clothes. I'm not setting foot outside this place until I can walk out with Carla."

After all those years, his masterpiece was finally coming to an end.

Rakkan stepped toward the floor-to-ceiling windows and stared at the illuminated Atlanta skyline. He'd been looking forward to this day for so long, but now it only filled him with sadness. Funny, he hadn't expected to feel this way. It was a time to celebrate, not mourn, yet there was a terrible emptiness growing in the pit of his stomach.

The original Rakkan wouldn't have let such feelings overtake him. He was the perfect hunter, sleek and pitiless, without need for such simple emotions.

But how could he not feel a twinge of regret? It had been an exhilarating journey. He'd almost been apprehended in San Antonio, and the experience had so rattled him that he'd abandoned his masterpiece for almost two years. He didn't need this, he'd thought. The risk was too great.

Ah, but he did need it. His magnificent symphony was unfinished, and he needed to compose one final movement to bring it to fruition. It couldn't have gone better—his last-minute embellishments had only improved his masterpiece, surely the mark of a true artist. As if there was ever any doubt.

Even that brutish Russian with the gun couldn't bring himself to disturb such a perfect creation. Once the man had the information he desired, he went about his way.

Rakkan stroked the smooth back of the panther statue on the coffee table. No, there was no cause to grieve.

Not on the eve of his grand finale.

15

"Councilman Talman is missing."

Joe gripped the cell phone harder. *"What?"*

Howe's voice was grim. "You heard me right. He didn't show up for work today, and he's missed all of his appointments. Apparently, that never happened before."

Joe stood outside the hospital's side entrance. It was three-thirty P.M., and he'd phoned to give Howe an update on Carla's condition. Critical but stable. "Jesus, you don't think—"

"No idea. I'm about to head over to Talman's office."

Joe thought for a second. "I'll meet you there."

"Are you sure?"

"Yeah. Wait outside for me."

Joe cut the connection and walked back to the intensive care waiting room. Christ.

He'd spent all day with his father at the hospital, save for the few minutes it had taken to pick up

Nikki. Despite his father's warning, Nikki had insisted on coming to the hospital after school. It had been a miserable night for her. He'd broken the news to her after they returned home, and she'd cried on and off for hours. "Why?" she repeated. "Why did it happen?"

If only he knew. Nikki had known too much tragedy in her young life. None of it could ever make sense to anyone, much less an eleven-year-old girl.

Joe walked into the waiting room. Nikki was putting up a brave front, trying to cheer up her grandfather with a story about her triumph in choir class. What an amazing kid.

"Guys, I have to take off for a little while. Will you be okay without me?"

Concern etched Nikki's face, but she said nothing.

Cal nodded. "Is everything all right?"

"Yeah, there's just something I need to check on."

Nikki obviously knew something was up. "When will you be back?"

Joe kissed her on the forehead. "Soon."

She hugged him close and whispered into his ear. "Be careful."

Joe met Howe outside Talman's Colony Square office building, and together they went in and pelted the councilman's attractive young assistant with the usual missing-person questions. Talman's schedule was packed with appointments, yet he hadn't called to cancel. He was unreachable by phone, fax, or pager, and the assistant had even driven to his house and found his car missing and home empty. The last time anyone had seen him was at ten the previous evening, when he'd left a social gathering at a Peachtree City restaurant.

The secretary escorted them into Talman's cherry-wood-paneled office. "It's totally unlike him to just drop out of sight like this," she said. "I know you're supposed to wait twenty-four hours for a missing person's case, but I was worried. You know, with these terrible murders. He fits the profile of the victims, doesn't he? Well known and all?"

"Yes, ma'am," Joe said. He glanced around the office and examined a group of tiny origami figures resting on the edge of Talman's desk. "Did he make these himself?"

The secretary stared at them. "I don't know. I've—never noticed those before."

"Look around," Howe said, "See anything else different, or maybe something missing?"

She moved around the office, inspecting each wall and piece of furniture. "I don't think so. Everything else looks the same." She gestured toward the origami figures. "Somebody could have given him those. He gets gifts all the time."

Joe took out his pocket digital camera and snapped a few quick shots of the office.

Howe turned toward the secretary. "How did you know his house was deserted? Do you have keys?"

She nodded. "I run errands for him sometimes, and he occasionally has me get things for him there."

"Does anybody else have a set?"

"I don't think so. He's divorced."

"It might be helpful if you took us to his house and let us look around," Joe said. "I know it's getting late, but would you be willing to do that?"

Her only response was to reach into her purse and pull out a set of keys.

They followed her to Talman's large Northside Drive home. It was a two-story colonial, hidden from the street by clusters of oak trees.

Joe turned toward the secretary as they walked through the front door. "Keep your eyes open for anything unusual, anything that may have changed."

They went to the kitchen, where Howe logged the answering machine messages. Nothing notable.

They moved through each room, looking for some sign of a struggle. There was none. They finished their tour in Talman's upstairs study.

"Okay," Howe said, "are we absolutely sure there are no girlfriends, boyfriends, love nests, vacation homes, or whatnot? This isn't the time to try to protect your boss from negative publicity."

The secretary shook her head.

"It's the 'whatnot' we really need to find out," Joe said as he raised his digital camera and took a shot of the study. "Think about anyplace that he—" Joe froze.

Howe picked up on his startled reaction. "Bailey?"

Joe turned to the secretary. "Will you excuse us for a moment?"

She furrowed her brow. "Well, I—I let you in here, so I think that I really should stay and—"

"We won't touch a thing." Joe led her to the door. "We just need to discuss some police business. Thanks for understanding."

The "police business" line usually worked wonders, and Joe was relieved that it did in this case too. The secretary nodded and left the room.

Howe spoke quietly. "What is it?"

Joe pointed to a small sculpture on a wood pedestal. "Look at that."

Howe examined it. "Is that a—"

"A panther," Joe said. "Mean anything to you?"

Howe nodded. "Rakkan's original form in the legend."

"Am I reaching?"

"Don't underestimate the value of a long reach."

As Joe stared at the sculpture, something occurred to him. He pulled out his digital camera and cycled through his shots on the back-panel LCD screen. "Shit," he whispered.

"What?"

Joe held up the camera. "Look at the origami figures from his office."

Howe looked at a few of the photos. "I'm afraid you're going to have to help me with this one."

"Those figures represent the various forms that Rakkan adopts in the last town—a horse, a cloud, a whale, a pushcart, a dog, and a tree."

Howe squinted at the screen. "Kind of a bizarre-looking cloud, but I think you're right."

"You have to be looking for them, but they're there. Look." Joe displayed each of the pictures. "They match with the guises in the legend."

Howe looked dazed as he pulled out his cell phone. "Jesus."

*   *   *

Thirty-five minutes later, Joe floored his accelerator and turned onto a small access road. Moments after Howe's call to Henderson, the captain had dispatched manpower to each of Talman's usual haunts. Joe and Howe were heading to Talman's dinner cruise boat, the *Carlotta*, at its dock on Lake Lanier. Joe drove while Howe talked to Henderson.

Howe cut the connection. "Okay, officially, we're doing this because of the department's concern for the councilman's well-being."

"And unofficially?" Joe asked.

"We're taking him in for questioning. Forensics is going over his house and office. It's incredible. . . . Talman may be our killer." Howe turned to Joe. "How long has it been since you've been on a stakeout, Bunco Boy?"

Joe frowned. "It doesn't seem right."

"What doesn't?"

"Why would Talman just leave those things lying around?"

Howe shook his head. "It may have given him a thrill. You know, a whiff of danger. Some serial killers get bored after they do it a few times. It doesn't give them the same charge, and they need to ratchet up the intensity."

Joe sped down the access road toward the lake. The sun had set behind the forest of tall pines, and lights from the cabins and houses dotted the surrounding hillsides.

Howe looked ahead. "The *Carlotta* doesn't do dinner cruises on weeknights, does it?"

Joe shook his head. "No. Why?"

"Because it's not here."

16

Joe and Howe climbed out of the car and stared into the darkness. "It's the biggest thing on the lake," Howe said. "Shouldn't we see it?"

Joe nodded. "Unless it's running without lights."

Howe glanced around the empty parking lot. "I don't like this."

"Me neither." Joe gestured toward the dock, where several small motorboats were moored. "Let's go find it."

They quickly surveyed the crafts before climbing into the only one without a lock. The small open boat reeked of dead fish and marijuana. Joe started the engine in three yanks of the ripcord, and they set out for the middle of the lake.

Howe turned on a battery lantern and aimed it into the void ahead. "Kind of a lame getaway, if that's what this is. We're landlocked, and once daylight hits, that boat is about as inconspicuous as an elephant in a broom closet."

"It's not a getaway," Joe said, staring at the cloud-like mist before them. "It's the end of the legend."

"What?" Howe asked.

"Unable to find a worthy man, Rakkan finally destroys himself in a magnificent funeral pyre in the Yellow Sea."

Howe pulled his jacket closer around him. "It's a nice ending, Bailey, but serial killers are rarely so obliging."

Joe moved the tiller. "See anything?"

Howe shook his head. "No, and the fog isn't helping. We're in serious danger of running into something. Looks like we got a full moon on our side, but it's no good to us in this fog."

Joe reacted with a start. "A full moon."

"Yeah. Don't tell me you're choosing this moment to get superstitious."

"No." Joe thought for a moment, then pointed ahead. "What's that?"

Howe aimed the lantern to reveal a large white hull three hundred yards away. It appeared to be dead in the water, drifting without engines or running lights.

"It's the *Carlotta*," Joe said. "I'll take us closer."

He steered toward the bow. Twenty yards away, he cut the motor. "Turn off your lantern," he whispered.

Howe switched off the light, and they sat still as waves lapped around them. No sign of movement on the *Carlotta*. Joe picked up an oar and sculled the boat around to the port side. He almost collided with a small powerboat tied to a deck cleat. A rope ladder dangled from the *Carlotta*'s lower railing.

Joe pointed to the rope ladder, and Howe nodded.

They moved alongside. Joe held the ladder while Howe grabbed the lower rungs and pulled himself up.

Howe stood on the deck and leaned over the railing. "Just like being back at the academy," he whispered. "Never thought I'd actually have to climb one of these—"

Boom.

The *Carlotta* exploded in a thunderous roar and a blinding flash of light.

Joe gripped the ladder as shock waves almost capsized his motorboat. He closed his eyes.

Let go, he told himself.

He couldn't. Not while Howe was up there.

Fiery splinters and debris rained down on him. His skin burned. His ears throbbed.

A low moan, and a splash in the water next to him.

Joe opened his eyes and peered into the dark water. Howe was motionless, lying face-up. Chunks of burning wreckage floated around him.

Joe looked up. The upper deck was on fire.

He jumped into the water. Holy shit. Fire and oil all around. Where in hell was Howe? Just five seconds before, he was—

Howe broke the surface and grabbed his arm. Joe lifted his head up. "It's okay. Relax."

Howe squinted up at the burning boat. "Jesus. Like a truck ramming into my back. I'm numb. I can hardly move."

"I've got you."

Joe looped his arm under Howe's armpit and swam back to the motorboat. Howe squinted up at the burning deck. "We were too late. Talman finished his tapestry."

Joe handed Howe a mooring rope and climbed into the motorboat. He leaned over and pulled Howe aboard.

"You're bleeding," Howe said.

Joe felt the cold stickiness at his forehead. "Glass from the windows. I'll be okay. You just lie back and we'll—"

A scream.

Deep within the bowels of the *Carlotta*.

Joe grabbed the rope ladder and turned uncertainly back toward Howe.

Howe squinted at him. "You're not seriously thinking of going in there, are you?"

"That depends on you. How bad are you hurt?"

"I'll be fine. But, Bailey—"

Joe climbed the ladder. "Call for backup!"

"Bailey!"

Joe threw his legs over the railing and ran past the smoke billowing from the downstairs dining room. The fire was confined to the aft section of the boat, but he knew it was only a matter of time before it spread.

Where had the scream come from?

Below. Somewhere below.

Joe drew his gun and bolted down the stairway. He peered through the glass doors of the cigar lounge. Empty.

Crew quarters. Galley. Bathrooms. All deserted.

He turned down a narrow hallway and almost stumbled over something. A body.

Joe knelt over him. Christ. Edward Talman dead, his chest oozing blood.

Footsteps pounded on the deck above.

Joe stood and ran for the stairs. He pulled himself up, listening as the roaring flames grew louder.

The earsplitting fire alarm kicked in. About damned time. Half the boat's gone, and *now* the alarm sounds?

The footsteps again, coming toward him. Of course. The other way could only lead into the fire. He held up his gun.

Joe stepped from the stairway and a gunshot whistled past his head. He ducked behind a wood-paneled arch and stared into the decorative mirrors over the bar. There, reflected hundreds of times in the myriad designs, he saw the server's station on the other side of the archway. A man stood there, holding a handgun.

"Only one way out," Joe shouted. "It's over, Roth."

Barry Roth flattened himself in the server's station. He stared at Joe in the same mirrors. "It's getting warm, isn't it, Mr. Bailey?"

"You want to step outside and cool off?"

"You first."

"You didn't come here to kill yourself, Roth. Even if that's what the real Rakkan did."

"You've made the connection. I'm impressed."

"Kind of hard to miss after you carved the name into my dining room table."

"There's no evidence that I did that."

"Or of rigging Monica Gaines's robe to ignite?"

"Again, no proof."

"Then how did you know what was in the sketches in her closet?"

"What are you talking about?"

Joe steadied himself as the *Carlotta* listed. "On the

television show, you gave us Monica's impressions of Ernest Franklin's murder scene. You said there was a full moon, but there wasn't. The only full moon was in Monica's preliminary sketch. She didn't show it to anybody, but you saw it, didn't you? You saw it in her closet when you were rigging her robe."

"That means nothing."

"Not by itself, but what if I looked in that file of your so-called triumphs? How many of those murders would fit the pattern of Rakkan's killings? I'd imagine it would be very easy to help the police on murders that you committed yourself. The only trick would be in not giving away too much information, right?"

"The fire's spreading belowdecks, Detective."

"You thought you'd be long gone by now, didn't you? But you saw us climbing aboard and you decided to set off the charges early and blow us to pieces. You figured you could still finish off Talman and make your escape before the boat burned itself out, am I right?"

Roth didn't reply.

"Forget it," Joe said. "My partner has already called for backup. The lake will be surrounded."

"It's a big lake."

Joe looked down. Smoke snaked up between the floorboards. "Time's running out. Let's get the hell out of here." Joe strained to see through the smoke. "You failed, Roth. You didn't have the guts to finish it right."

"Shut up!"

He'd hit a nerve. Good. "Face it, if you had the courage to destroy yourself the way Rakkan did, you would have already succeeded. Instead, you tried to

frame someone else and let him die for it. You planted
the panther sculpture and those origami figures."

"*I didn't fail.*"

Joe raised his gun. Roth was still protective of his
grand tapestry. "You knew I'd unravel your pathetic
little scheme. You knew I'd expose you for the fraud
that you are. You wanted to scare me off and thought
you could use the memory of my wife to do it. It
didn't work. You're an amateur, Roth."

"Fuck you!" Roth fired twice at the wall between
them. The wood panel splintered, but the bullets
didn't penetrate.

Joe grabbed a railing to steady himself as the decks
whined and groaned. He could keep pushing Roth's
buttons, but it wouldn't do him any good if the boat
went down with them inside. Black smoke poured
from the vents. The alarms were almost deafening.

"Throw down your gun and let's get out of here!"

The aft deck collapsed. Burning cinders flew, and
the entire boat shook.

Joe glimpsed the fireworks show through the bar's
rear windows. "The fuel tank is next, Roth."

The windows blew out, and bottles of alcohol lining the bar exploded.

Three shots rang out, shattering the mirrors across
from them. Joe ducked as another bullet whizzed
past him.

Footsteps. Roth was making his break.

Joe raised his gun and bolted around the corner.

Roth hurtled though the lounge, dodging the flam-
ing rivers of alcohol. His jacket caught fire. He tore it
off as he hurtled toward the doorway.

Joe took aim. "Roth!"

Roth spun around, gun in hand. His lips curled into a twisted smile. He raised his gun.

Joe's finger tightened on the trigger, and . . .

The burning floor opened up and swallowed Roth.

Joe stared in shock at the spot where Roth had disappeared. Half the lounge was gone.

Screams from the burning deck below. Roth. Horrible, frantic screams from a man who knew he was already dead.

Joe ran to the edge of the floor and stared down. Nothing but fire and Roth's screams.

After a few seconds, only fire.

The boat shuddered and listed even harder. Joe pulled himself toward the glass door and pushed.

It wouldn't open.

He grabbed a chair and hurled it toward the door. The glass cracked.

He struck it again. And again. Finally the door shattered and he threw himself onto the deck outside. He turned. Something rumbled deep within the *Carlotta* as flames shot high into the night sky.

He jumped into the water.

Boom.

Another explosion, more intense than the last. The shock waves rammed through the water, pummeling him.

He broke the surface, dodging chunks of burning, floating debris. His lungs hurt. He couldn't breathe.

Relax, he told himself. The blast had only knocked the wind out of him. He threw back his head until the pressure on his chest eased. He inhaled deeply.

He turned toward the boat. He swore he could still

hear Roth's tortured screams inside, echoing in the burning hull. Impossible, he thought. It had to be the twisting, groaning bulkheads.

At least that's what he hoped it was.

The burning hulk of the *Carlotta* dipped lower into the water, crackling and rumbling as it slid beneath the waves.

17

Joe stood in the city hall media relations room, where he'd seen the mayor and other city officials conduct numerous press conferences over the years. He never thought *he'd* hold one there.

It had been three days since Roth's death and the fiery destruction of the *Carlotta*, and Joe had worked feverishly to tie up the case's loose ends and come up with some answers for the department's higher-ups and the media. Wrap it up, Henderson urged. Put an end to it.

Joe checked his notes one last time. Howe was giving a brief recap of Roth's deadly homage to the Rakkan legend. Howe had been discharged from the hospital the day before and would soon be his old self. He was concerned, however, about the likelihood of his eyebrows growing back.

Howe finished his presentation and left the podium. He whispered to Joe on the way back to his seat, "I warmed 'em up for you, Bailey. You can thank me later."

Joe smiled and stepped forward. "Good morning. There have been a lot of questions about things that have happened recently, and I have some answers." Joe hit the button on his remote, displaying slides taken from the victims. "A lot has been made of the bizarre markings on the victims' skin, a mark that later appeared on my chest. This corresponds to the brand that Rakkan burned into his final set of victims. The appearance of the brand isn't specified in many versions of the story, and we assume that Roth designed his own pattern. He was very meticulous in laying the groundwork for each set of killings. This was his grand finale, and he laid clues that would enable us to finally make the Rakkan connection. This symbol was one of the clues."

"How did he do it?" a reporter called out.

"Well, we figured out that the marks were an irritant contact dermatitis, but we didn't know how it was done." Joe pointed to a rack of shirts left of the podium. "Those are mine. We ran some tests and discovered that almost all of my dress shirts were treated with a lye solution, colorless and almost odorless. It won't even appear on standard toxicology tests, and it was in such a diluted form that it took several days of contact before it would cause a reaction. Roth entered my apartment and drew the pattern on my shirts, which then triggered the reaction on my skin. Of course, the symbol would fall slightly differently depending on how the various shirts fit. That explains why the mark was never sharply defined on the skin. We're testing the clothes of the murder victims, and so far the results have been positive."

Tess Wayland, standing in front with her camera crew, called out, "That doesn't explain the voices, Detective."

Joe walked into the crowd and handed her a cordless microphone. "Care to say that again?"

She gave him a puzzled look, then spoke into the microphone. "What about the voices?"

The sound seemed to emanate throughout the room, booming and distorted. The reporters glanced around, looking for the source.

Tess smiled and spoke again. "Is this really me?" Again, her voice boomed through the room.

Joe took back the microphone. "If you're looking for speakers, they're all around you."

"Where?" Tess asked.

Joe pointed to the tall windows lining the walls. "There."

"I still don't see them."

"The windows."

She stared at him. "The *windows* are the speakers?"

"Yes. I was looking at photos of places where these voices were heard, and I noticed that the one common element was the presence of large glass surfaces. Olympia Technologies recently patented a speaker technology based on a material called Terfenol-D. It was originally developed by the U.S. military for sonar applications. Metal strips of this material can conduct vibrations through any flat, glossy surface, creating specific sound waves. Roth used the same technology, applying small metal conductors along the edge of glass surfaces such as window-panes and mirrors."

Diana Schroeder, a reporter from *The Atlanta Journal-Constitution,* appeared skeptical. "There's no way you could get the same sound from a room window as you could from a precision-engineered glass speaker."

"You're right. There are too many variables—the size and thickness of the window, the build quality of the frame, and how tightly it's mounted. But remember, Roth wasn't trying to re-create the sound of a symphony orchestra. He only needed to produce the sound of one creepy-sounding voice, which is probably the best you'll get no matter how much you fine-tuned this setup."

The reporter nodded. "Creepy like your wife's voice?"

"No," Howe said coldly. "Creepy like you suddenly finding yourself outside, facedown on the sidewalk."

Joe glanced reassuringly at Howe. "It's okay." He turned back to the journalists. "Like many in his profession, Roth made a career out of deceiving the public. He was a talented illusionist even if he didn't call himself one. He may have been trying to throw me off my game by conjuring up the visits from my deceased wife and branding me with his mark, but I think there was more to it than that." Joe stared at the slide taken of his own chest. "I've made it my career to expose paranormal scams like his, and I think he saw me as a special challenge. What better way to finish his masterpiece than to bring me down at the same time?"

Joe changed the slide to a police photo of his

altered apartment. "He used this technology to reproduce my wife's voice, but he still needed to get the background information. After my apartment was rearranged, I tried to figure out how anyone could have known how things looked when my wife was alive. My first thought was photographs, but I've never had many of those. Then, later, I remembered that I used to shoot video, especially around the time that my daughter was born. I pulled the tapes out and saw that he could have gotten everything he needed from those. It would have been simple to borrow them when he was tampering with my shirts, copy the tapes, then replace them. I've been rewatching the videos and confirmed that Angela said every single thing that I heard in my apartment. She told me to be careful when I was filming her from the edge of a balcony, and there are several other phrases that Roth sampled and transmitted. Our wedding video was there, so he even knew our song. We found a hacked transmitter in his rental car that he used to transmit that song and Angela's voice to me on my radio station's frequency."

Joe hesitated. God, it felt strange to discuss Angela so coolly, so analytically, as if she were just another piece of evidence. "Anyway, these metal strips, attached to a tiny radio receiver and power source no larger than a hearing aid mechanism, could be easily placed along the edges of a mirror or windowpane, then quickly removed. They could even be placed on the outside of a window as I suspect they were at my apartment. If there were two or more windows rigged, it would be possible to create imaging effects to make it seem like the voice was coming from somewhere in the middle. That's what I've done in here."

Joe displayed another slide. "These are fingerprints lifted from the scene. They appeared to be Angela's, but when the crime lab analyzed the skin oils for possible DNA extraction, they discovered it wasn't skin oil at all. It was cocoa butter." Joe nodded to forensics specialist Graham Martin, who stood near Henderson at the front of the room.

"With a trace of pineapple," Martin added.

"We determined that Roth probably used an engraving press to create the prints. I wondered where he could have gotten copies of her fingerprints, but I knew there are certain professions that require a complete set to be taken. One of those professions, I discovered, happens to be the real estate industry. Angela was a leasing agent in Florida before I met her, and in that state, fingerprints of all agents are kept on file with the licensing authority. Roth most likely bribed a temp or someone else there for a copy. There's a light scratch on her right thumbprint that matches a scratch on her print in Florida. Roth scanned her prints into the press and engraved them on thin pieces of vinyl. He lightly oiled the vinyl and left her prints on my dining room table."

A CNN reporter stood up. "Did he own an engraving press? I assume that most people don't have these things lying around."

"No, but his employer did. The internal publications department at his music video network had one, and he would have had easy access after hours. Plus, our friends at the New York City Police Department found vinyl sample sheets in his apartment. He

may have been contemplating an especially bad redecorating project, but this is more likely."

A barrage of questions erupted from the journalists, but Joe shook his head. "I'm sorry, but I can't take
any more questions right now. I hope this has been
helpful." The questions continued as he gathered his
notes and quickly headed for the door. He knew he'd
be fielding calls from these reporters for the next
several days, but that didn't matter. There was somewhere he had to be.

Joe drove to the Charlie Brown airport and parked
his car. He hoped he wasn't too late.

He walked past several small charter planes until
he spotted an ambulance parked next to a Gulf-
stream jet. It had to be her. He strode to the ambulance's rear doors, where two attendants pulled out a
gurney and extended the wheels.

Monica Gaines looked up at Joe from the gurney. "I
thought the mayor might come to see me off. Oh,
well. I suppose you'll do."

Joe smiled. "Hello, Monica. You look much better
than you did the last time I saw you."

"Considering that I was at death's door, it's not
much of a compliment."

"I just got back from the press conference. You
could have appeared there too, you know."

She smiled. "Too many unpleasant questions. I'll
have one of my own when I feel better and can put
the correct perspective on things."

"I'm sure you will." Joe spoke to the attendants.
"Will you excuse us for a minute, guys?"

The attendants hesitated but stepped away after Monica waved them off.

Joe leaned close to her. "The feds cracked that Russian agent's laptop. It was very enlightening."

She looked away with apparent disinterest. "Is that right?"

"Yes. The agent had all of you test subjects under close observation. He knew Roth was a killer, but he didn't care. With Haddenfield's program, he thought he had the Holy Grail of psychic powers. You and Haddenfield led him to believe that, didn't you?"

Monica sighed. "Do I need my lawyers present, Detective? Because if I do, we should—"

"Not necessary." Joe leaned closer. "Haddenfield had a psychic 'dream team' there at the Crate. He conspired with you and a few others to convince Haddenfield that the program was a success. He even got the agent to grease the wheels—by bribing Councilman Talman—for you to come here and impress him with your patented serial killer investigation routine. The 'paranormal killer' angle was guaranteed to get you big headlines, wasn't it? It worked for Arthur Lanska in Poland in the sixties, and Tricia Dere in Holland in the seventies. Plus, it fit in with the fact that the victims heard eerie voices in the days before their deaths. You make headlines with your 'spirit killer' readings, and then, if the killer is found, you just say that the spirit was working through a human instrument. That's what the other psychics did. Is that how it was supposed to go?"

Monica smiled. "Utter nonsense."

"Roth may not have not thought so. Did you ever see him at the Crate?"

"A few times last year. Our test sessions hadn't co-incided recently."

"Well, it's possible he thought you were hitting too close to his Rakkan killings, patterned after a super-natural being wandering the countryside. He may have thought you *were* real, and it scared him. So he made you his next victim."

"Maybe he had good reason to be afraid of me."

Joe shrugged. "In any case, tell your producer to be more careful who she spends time with. This Russian agent knew Roth was the killer, and he used your producer to find out where he was staying locally. He blackmailed Roth into admitting that Haddenfield was cooking his results."

Monica nodded. "The FBI told us that. But how did he know that Roth was the killer?"

"During the course of the study, his agency had you all under close observation. It was a big deal to them. That's how they happened to find out that Roth was our serial murderer."

"This is all very interesting, but I've already given the FBI my full cooperation."

"Without telling them much of anything. Don't worry, Monica. They want to keep the Defense De-partment study classified, so they're not going to make a big fuss about this. They didn't even want me to discuss it at the press conference."

"That must have been torture for you."

"Not really. We stopped a killer, and that's what matters." He smiled. "I'm glad you're going to be okay."

"Much to my nurse's chagrin. She'll have to find another ghoulish subject for her camera."

"You read her lips, didn't you?"

"Pardon?"

"I have to admire you. You were in so much pain, but it must have been second nature for you. We used the same trick on Talman. We read his lips when he talked on the pay phone outside your room. You read your nurse's lips, didn't you?"

Her eyes twinkled. "Is that what you think?"

He nodded. "You're in good company. Some of the greatest supposed psychics in history were skilled lip-readers. It comes in handy before performances when you scan the crowd from behind the curtain. You can pick up all kinds of things, can't you?"

Monica nodded. "I imagine you would."

"That's how you found out about my argument with my daughter, and maybe even about Carla's secret romance. I've determined that each of us had telephone conversations within sight of you—conversations that would have tipped you off to these things. Add a few good research contacts—including a source at one of the credit reporting bureaus—and you could come up with all kinds of information about people. Like the fact that Howe had recently spent six thousand dollars at a jewelry store. When an unmarried cop spends that much at a place like that, there aren't many other possibilities. You also could have found out that I'd recently dropped seven hundred at an auto repair shop. You filled in the blanks with some educated guesses."

"Well, will you at least give me credit for the name of the song that Glen Murphy was working on?"

" 'Nothing but the Stars'? I was impressed until my daughter showed me Glen Murphy's fan website.

There were daily updates on the making of his new album. If you had read that, you could have seen that Murphy was working on 'Nothing but the Stars' during the last week of his life."

"*If* I'd visited the website."

"That's the funny thing. Murphy's people were very accommodating, and they gave us the website visitor logs. A few of the IP addresses were from Canada, and a guy at the station checked them out. One of them belongs to you. You visited the website just before coming to Murphy's murder scene that morning."

Monica shook her head. "It must have been someone at my production company."

"If you say so."

She patted his hand. "I'm sorry, Joe."

"For what?"

"For disappointing you."

"I'm used to it, Monica. It's my job."

"I'm not confirming anything you said, but it's obvious I haven't made a believer of you. Maybe you'll give me another chance someday."

"You never know."

"It was nice meeting you, Joe Bailey."

"The pleasure was mine."

She looked at him quizzically.

He smiled. "At least it's been interesting."

"You're right about that. By the way, my offer stands. Anytime you'd like to be a guest on my show, we'll be happy to have you."

"I'll keep that in mind. Have a good flight."

"Good-bye, Joe."

Joe motioned toward the attendants, and they

came and lifted Monica onto the plane. He wasn't close enough to hear, but he thought she was giving them an impromptu reading as they helped her aboard. He chuckled to himself. The lady definitely had spirit.

He stayed and watched as her jet taxied to the end of the runway and took off into the cloudless sky.

Epilogue

I s there something wrong, Daddy?"

Joe stood on the riverbank, taking in the bright red-yellow leaves and breathing the crisp morning air. He turned toward Nikki. "Nothing's wrong, honey."

"So can we go now? I don't want to miss the parade."

"We won't."

Joe looked up at the path that overlooked the riverbank. His father was pushing Carla in her wheelchair, talking a mile a minute about all the plans he had for them. Not only was Carla expected to make a full recovery, she'd emerged from her coma with an engagement ring on her finger. She planned to move to Savannah by Christmas and join the local police department.

Joe, Suzanne, and Nikki had driven Carla from Atlanta the night before, and they'd all risen early to see the town's Veterans' Day parade.

Joe gently pushed back Nikki's hair. "You're getting to be so grown-up, you know that?"

"I don't feel grown-up."

"Well, you are. You really handled yourself well these last couple of weeks. Barry Roth tried to hurt us in the cruelest way imaginable, and you held it together. I'm proud of you."

Nikki hugged him. "Suzanne helped me. She's awesome."

"I think so too."

Nikki pulled away. "I knew it wasn't Mommy doing and saying those things. I thought it was at first, but later I knew."

"Suzanne explained it to you really well, huh?"

"Not just Suzanne."

"Who else?"

She didn't answer.

"Nikki?"

She looked away from him. "I knew it wasn't Mommy because . . . Mommy *told* me it wasn't."

Joe felt as if he'd been kicked in the stomach. "What?"

"Suzanne came over that day, and after Grandpa left, she helped me talk to Mommy."

"How?"

"Please don't be mad. Suzanne said you'd be mad if you knew."

"I'm not mad. Just tell me what Suzanne said."

"Suzanne talked to her friend, the one who died when she was a little girl. Her name is Daphne. Daphne talked to Mommy."

"You believed her?"

Nikki nodded. "Mommy told me not to be scared.

She said that you'd take care of me. She knows that I still sing 'Breakout' in my head when I get scared. I've never told anybody that, not even you." Her gaze searched his face. "I knew you wouldn't believe me, but it's true . . . it's true, Daddy."

"Are you . . . sure?"

"Yes. Mommy misses you. She's happy, but she still remembers us and the things we did. And she knows about Lillian."

Joe stopped breathing. "What?"

"There's a statue you like to look at. It's in the window of an antiques store. It's a statue of a pretty lady named Lillian. It reminds you of the way Mommy looked one summer when she got her hair cut short. You've thought about buying it, but it's expensive and you're afraid it will make you sad. Mommy doesn't want you to be sad."

Joe felt light-headed. He'd been looking at that statue for months, but he'd never breathed a word about it to anyone.

No one could possibly know this. Unless . . .

"Joe?"

He turned and saw Suzanne standing on the path above them.

He and Nikki climbed the embankment and stopped a few feet away from her. Suzanne studied his expression. "She told you, didn't she?"

He nodded.

"I knew I should have asked your permission, but I had to keep Nikki from hurting. I'm not sorry I did it. Do you want me to leave?"

He shook his head.

"What do you want to do?"

Joe's eyes stung, but for once he didn't care if Nikki noticed. He wanted to say something, but the words wouldn't come.

That's okay, he thought. He had a lifetime to find the words.

He took Suzanne's hand and kissed it. "Let's go watch a parade."

ACKNOWLEDGMENTS

As with my previous Joe Bailey mystery, I owe a debt of gratitude to the skeptics—past and present—who have influenced me through the years. Many of history's most effective debunkers have been magicians—from Harry Houdini to James Randi to Penn & Teller—and, at their best, they've shown that skepticism is not synonymous with cynicism.

Thanks are also in order to Dr. Jennifer Li, who educated me on the sound transmission properties of Terfenol-D and its use in upcoming personal audio devices. One such device, the Soundbug, is already available from Olympia International.

I also owe much gratitude to:

My wife, Lisa, who keeps the magic and wonder alive.

My agent, Andrea Cirillo, who is the best guide to the publishing world that I could ever hope for.

And finally, my editor, Bill Massey, who became a husband, father, and New York City resident during one of the most traumatic times in the city's history. And through it all, he helped me shape this story with unerring taste, understanding, and intelligence. *That's* a good trick!

ABOUT THE AUTHOR

ROY JOHANSEN'S first screenplay, *Murder 101,* written while he was in college, was produced for cable TV and won an Edgar Award as well as a Focus Award, which is sponsored by Steven Spielberg, Francis Ford Coppola, George Lucas, and Martin Scorsese. He has written for Disney, MGM, United Artists, Universal, and Warner Bros. He lives in southern California with his wife, Lisa.